A COMEDIAN WALKS INTO A FUNERAL HOME

A NOVEL

Dennis Kelly

Dymaxion Press

Comedians perform the same role that philosophers once played, helping us understand and cope with the world. By making us laugh at our own foibles, it makes us reflect on what it is to be a human. This is the reason comedians use self-deprecation—we all have flaws and weakness and it nice to see them in others.

—Chuck Ludwig
Comedian and Writer

CHAPTER 1

DEADBEAT

I stood in the back of Louie's Comedy Lounge and surveyed the well-lubricated crowd. Over the past couple of weeks, I had survived the preliminary rounds in the regional LaughCom competition. Tonight, the best comedic act would advance to the national contest in Atlanta.

I checked my set list. Long gone were the days of the rat-a-tat, non sequitur one-liners and the monologue. Today's comedy acts generated dialogue with the audience and told a story—something that came naturally to me. I had a reliable opener and closer, and some new high-risk jokes slotted for the middle of the set. Hopefully, this would be the night I ignited a creative spark that set the house on fire. Along with advancing to the Nationals, a huge comedic credibility booster, the winner laid claim to the twenty-five-hundred-dollar regional prize, cash I desperately needed at the moment.

Louie, the Comedy Lounge owner, hosted the Midwest Regional LaughCom Contest, held in a converted downtown St. Paul warehouse. In the dimly lit entrance, photos of Louie, posing with the likes of Dangerfield, Pryor, and Carlin, testified to his past comedic success. Now a club owner, Louie worked all the angles. He got himself designated as a regional LaughCom Contest judge, charged the comedic contestants an entry fee, secured a local beer distributor to sponsor the contest and charged a twenty-dollar cover, which included two drink tickets.

To determine the comedy contest winner, Louie concocted something he called the laugh-o-meter. No one knew exactly how it worked. Supposedly, Louie's black box tracked the frequency and decibels of each performer's garnered laughs. The highest score, subject to Louie's oversight, was declared the winner.

My phone chirped—my ex-wife, Jessica. I considered pushing the call to voice mail, but we shared a five-year-old, and I was a nervous father. I clicked her in.

"Is everything all right with Claire?" I kept an eye on the comedic competitor on the stage.

"Fine. We're moving to Wisconsin."

Her declaration landed like a gut punch. "Whoa, what are you talking about? What's in Wisconsin?"

"Financial security for starters. Other than that, it's none of your business."

"You're talking about taking my daughter out of state. It is damn well my business. I'll fight it."

"Even if you had enough money to lawyer up, no judge would side with a deadbeat dad."

"I've got a job."

"Telemarketing, selling crap nobody needs? And comedy? Don't even go there with me."

I had no comeback. I wasn't even good at my lowlife day job. When I took it, I figured I'd be on to something else soon, maybe some legitimate employment. Right now, my position as second to last on the sales leader board did not speak to job security.

"Look, I'm trying to make things work," I said, anxious to wrap up the call. The act onstage was coming to a close. "Give me a chance, I'm on to something here."

"What?"

My booking agent, Toby, a moonfaced, impulsive parasite, circled a hand overhead and pointed at the stage, signaling me to wrap it up. I shot a one-minute finger back at him.

"I'm a finalist in the regional LaughCom Contest. They're offering a cash prize, enough to make things right with you. Please, just stay put."

"Make things right? Hardly."

"I've got a set that's going to blow the competition away. With a win, I'm off to the national contest in Atlanta. This is a huge opportunity!"

"Now, that's funny."

"Come on, work with me. I just need some time."

"Time's up." She ended the call.

I squeezed the phone in a vicarious stranglehold as Louie took the stage. He introduced the only competitor who might stand between the cash prize and me. A single spotlight reflected off her metal face studs. Dressed in a leather bustier, cutoff shorts, fishnet stockings and leather moto boots, she looked Sarah Silverman hot. If Louie gave out contest points for stage presence, she'd nail the category.

The Goth princess missed on her first punchline. Yet Louie, from the edge of the stage, chased her every joke with a huge brayed laugh, and the crowd followed. Something didn't feel right.

Up next, I rechecked my set list. Louie had a formidable presence. He wore a loose-fitting bowling shirt that draped his six-foot-six, three-hundred-pound frame. He schmoozed with the crowd to clear the air between acts and launched a couple of one-liners to let the audience know he was still the big dog in the room. "This next talent is a real comer, so let's give it up for Vince Locker."

I bounded onto the stage, throttled the microphone, and lifted it from the stand. The smell of Goth Sarah's perfume still hung in the air. Maybe it would mask the nervous sweat trickling down my sides. I needed to connect quickly, turn the wheel of life, to tell my story. The spattering of applause faded to the edge of silence. I took a deep breath and launched the opener I'd improvised just a minute ago.

"Wow, that last act was really something, especially the outfit. Fishnet stockings and a face full of tackle. Probably shops in a bait store."

A single hiccup of a laugh.

I cupped a hand to my ear. "Yes, a laugh, I'll take it." Get back on the set list. Too early for impromptu. "Hey, not that I'm a fashionista, but if I could grow a decent beard, you might have figured out I'm a philosophy major, which is code for unemployed. The secret to being a successful philosopher is in asking the right question. So far, it's been, 'You want fries with that order?'"

Groans. A miss.

That usually scored. Reload. Can't let the silence linger… "Philosophers always come off as arrogant, but in reality, we're no smarter than a large pepperoni pizza with anchovies, except the pizza can feed a family of four."

Disinterest, nothing. Keep cool.

"Philosophy majors love to argue, so naturally I got married. Our first argument was whose parents to live with."

Nothing.

"Arguing with one's wife takes special training. I got a nipple piercing, so I'd be familiar with pain and buying jewelry."

Mute.

"The marriage didn't last long, my wife was an existentialist. She always thought about death. Mine."

Why didn't they laugh? Those lines have killed in every joint I've ever gigged in. Stay calm, do not panic. Material was good, so it had to be delivery. Too rushed, timing off. I could fix this.

"Since I've never had a meaningful job, I list dead philosophers as my personal references. My last interviewer said, 'Nietzsche means nothing to me.' I said, 'That's the point.'"

Silence.

Too obscure, bury it. Move on. "The interviewer scrolled a finger down my resume. 'You list your religion as agnostic dyslectic. Why?' 'I don't believe in dog.'"

"Your act's a bitch," someone yelled out to scattered titters.

A taunt. Really? I looked at Louie for support, but there was nothing there, either. My throat felt dry, the lights too hot. Sweat dripped off my face. I had to pull this out, change the tempo, get a riff going. "So I took a job as a mattress salesman at a store in the mall. Hated it, so I went to work in a bathrobe. Everyone called me Howard Johnson."

Blank stares. Was this audience aware of any cultural references?

"I plopped down on a bed in the display window, hoping to get fired and collect unemployment. Shoppers wandered in, saw how comfortable I was and said, 'I'll take what he's on.' Apparently, lounging makes one a better salesman. Who knew?"

Now the audience was mumbling among themselves.

"Turns out I became an unwitting gimmick, a store mascot. Parents dropped off their kids with bedtime books for me to read, then disappeared for two hours. It made me feel Michael Jackson creepy. Adults would lie next to me on the mattress and try out their favorite position. I'm not into spooning, so I quit."

People were out of their seats, heading for the bar on their cell phones.

Oh, my God, they quit on me. I felt my soul escape my body and watched in horror at the floundering idiot in the spotlight, fighting back tears. Reset, reset. Be honest, acknowledge the act's a disaster, get the audience back.

"You know, these jokes usually work. Lucky for you, I'm not a suicide bomber."

No interaction.

The room spun. I searched for the light in the back of the room and hoped it would mercifully flash and end the debacle. The boozed, flushed faces in the crowd wanted blood, not humor. Lecherous Louie had his thumb on the scale in favor of the Goth chick, but I was not dying alone. The morons were going down with me.

No, don't do it. Do not attack the audience. Do not take the bait.

I spotted Toby jerking a thumb over his shoulder and mouthing, "Get off, get off."

"Sorry, the set's not working. Did I say something that made you think? Or is it I didn't do a fart joke? I should have taken more time to explain the punch lines, but I didn't bring the crayons!"

Taunts. Boos. Just offstage, Louie ran a finger under his throat and pointed at me.

"From the sound of it, I'm guessing you all have a hard to pronounce genetic malfunction, so I'll just go with stupidity. Say, with an IQ in the range of room temperature."

Standing. Shouting. I ducked a beer bottle.

"Calm down. This is America! Stupidity's not a crime, so feel free to leave. What are you waiting for? Do I need to throw a stick?"

Louie rushed the stage, poised for murder. I flashed a middle finger at the audience and dropped the mic. He shouted, "loser," and I heard the jeering audience boo as I slipped out under the backdoor EXIT sign in a stupor of self-destruction.

CHAPTER 2

PIECES

So anyway, that's how I ended up with the slippery saddle of a bridge rail between my legs.

I knew the bridge. The Smith Avenue High Bridge spanned a deep gorge across the Mississippi River in Saint Paul. Old Smitty had a deck-to-water dead drop of 171 feet. Not in the same league as the Golden Gate, yet far enough to get the job done.

Tires buzzed as cars crossed the steel bridge deck. The night fog from the river below made the whole tableau a little more unreal. I felt invisible until a passing driver yelled, "Jump!"

"Screw you!" I shouted and lost my precarious balance on the rail. A shoe dislodged as I caught myself. It fell, flashed in and out of the overhead bridge lights and disappeared into the darkness. I didn't hear the splash.

Out of the night, a black and white form with the profile of a killer whale emerged. The strobe of a Cyclops eye painted me red. The vehicle motored past me, then stopped on the narrow shoulder and cut the engine. A figure in a dark rumpled suit stepped out and approached me at a pace of something out of the Cambrian age.

"Whoever called you, it's a waste of time." I tried to focus through heavy-lidded eyes. "Don't need an amboolance." Hmmm. Apparently, I was drunk.

"You're half right," the driver said. "It's a 1973 Cadillac, Miller-

Meteor. They used to make bodies for both ambulances and hearses. This one's a hearse." The man sounded like he was trying to sell it to me. "Get lots of offers from collectors, but just can't part with it. Still runs like a watch. They don't make 'em like that anymore. Got the ambulance V-8 engine under the hood. I walk slowly, but like to drive fast. Not that the dead are ever in a hurry."

"A hearse?" I squinted at the vehicle, trying to bring it into focus. Formal drapes hung in arches on the side window of the coach. The words "Truss Mortuary" were painted in calligraphy script on the back doors.

The old man offered his hand. "Truss, at your service."

"You're just another vulture who wants a piece of me."

"Pieces, I'd say. Take the leap, and you'll hit the water at about seventy-five miles an hour with a force of fifteen thousand pounds per square inch. Most likely your broken ribs will rip through the spleen, lungs, and heart. Your vertebrae will snap and your liver will rupture. It doesn't make you any easier to clean up for a viewing."

"You're a sick bastard."

"But wait, there's more. Try going in feet first, so as to plunge into the water. Tough to pull off in the dark, but at least you'll drown rather than explode. The problem with good form, however, is that the undertow will carry you toward the power plant, where you'll get hung up on the hydraulic equipment and be shredded. Once you surface downstream, what's left will be carp food. You can pretty much forget about an open casket."

"God, I can't believe this. Leave me alone!"

"You scout out this bridge?"

"What?"

"Most jumpers do—kind of have it in the back of their minds for some time."

"No. Yeah. I mean, I know it, but no, I'm not that . . . Why are you screwing with my head? You don't give a damn about me. You're just waiting for my body."

"Actually, I'm all good in that department." The man nodded toward the hearse, then edged closer. "But if you're willing to sign some paperwork, I could claim you downstream sometime tomorrow."

"Stop!" I tried to stiff-arm the old man, but lost my balance on the rail again.

Truss grabbed the front of my shirt, twisted a fist into the fabric and cinched a secure hold. My weight favored the river, my life literally in his hands. Suspended almost two hundred feet above the black water below, I vomited.

"Which way you want to go here?" he asked. "My arthritis is killing me."

"Help me."

Truss yanked me over the bridge guardrail like a rag doll and spilled me onto the sidewalk. Disoriented, I began shaking in uncontrollable sobs.

The old man pulled me up and leaned me against the railing. "Okay, what are you on?"

I could barely hold myself upright. "Booze, drugs, despair."

Truss fished a handful of pills out of my pocket, took note and pitched them over the bridge rail. "You'll live."

He shuffled me toward the hearse and into the front passenger seat. In the back of the hearse, I caught sight of a body in a clear plastic body bag. The feet had red painted toenails.

I rolled down the window and puked again as the hearse sped off.

CHAPTER 3
SUITED

I woke with a monster headache, one that spread to every bone in my body. I peeled my face off a thin vinyl mattress, tried to sit up and almost blacked out. In the eerily silent, dimly lit room, my heavy-lidded eyes couldn't tell if it was night or day. But other senses took over. The air had the dank feel of a subterranean cave. A tangy iron odor tasted like pennies. As my eyes began to focus, my brain resisted. A metal showerhead hung directly overhead. Below, the tile floor tapered to a drain.

I was in a morgue.

I swung my legs over the edge of the wheeled cart. I wanted to run from this nightmare, but my legs felt like jelly and my feet like concrete blocks.

I checked for wounds, abrasions and breaks. Fragmented pieces of the last twenty-four hours dropped out of my head, but I couldn't puzzle them together. I dragged my feet over to the gray, glass-fronted metal cabinets that rimmed the room. I read the labeled shelves: Arterial Fluid, Tissue Filler, Lip Tite, Restorative Wax, Sealant Powder, Dry Wash, Solvents. I paused at a tray and picked up a syringe-shaped instrument with a long, sharp, three-sided tip.

"A trocar."

The voice echoed off the room's hard surfaces. Startled, I turned and saw a woman with raven black hair that fell upon a sleeveless shirt that exposed arms tattooed with curious symbols.

"Excuse me?" I said.

"It's what a wrench is to a mechanic. Can't do without it. Use it to drain a body's fluids before it's embalmed and aspirated with an air pump. It gives the cavities that healthy, rounded look."

I dropped the instrument back into the tray. "Where am I?" My eyes darted like spooked fish in search of an exit.

"Truss Mortuary, at your service. I'm Winona. You had a rough night."

"Mortuary?"

On wobbly legs, I pushed past Winona, ran out the door and down a hallway as if trying to escape a fire, then blasted through the exterior metal door into an alley. The bright of day clamped down on my eyelids. I attempted a step, only to be repelled by the scorching asphalt.

I hopped back into the mortuary. "Where are my shoes?"

"Most likely in the river or on the bridge. Jumpers are notorious for losing their shoes, but shoes we have. No matter how many times we tell people not to bring shoes for their deceased, they always do. I'd say you're about a size 10."

I brushed hot gravel off my feet. "Jumper? No way."

"The Smith Avenue High Bridge, a reliable choice."

A vague picture of the previous night started to form, but I quickly pushed it away, too frightened to look at it. Had I been on that bridge?

I inched back into the mortuary, taking baby steps as though testing thin ice. Winona guided me past a room with double doors marked 'Chapel' and into a library-like setting she called the parlor. A Persian rug with a blurred geometric pattern soothed my feet. The soft glow of wall sconces and ornately framed pastoral landscapes instilled an unexpected sense of calm. A tabby sat on one of the room's two wingback chairs and kept a watchful eye.

"Shoo!" Winona unsuccessfully tried to chase the cat off the furniture. "Thinks he runs the place. Be right back."

I surveyed the room. A high-arched ceiling with heavy timbers supported an elegant gold and crystal chandelier. Ornately detailed, cherry wood cabinets flanked a fireplace with a stone carved mantel. An old photo in a scalloped frame captured a horse-drawn funeral cortege. It could have been the setting for a Masterpiece Theater costume drama.

Then I caught my reflection in an oval wall mirror. A contorted head with sleep creases and bloodshot eyes stared back at me. A more in-depth look revealed a sweaty loser who had been washed up from the rocky shoals of self-destruction. No job, no comedy career, no marriage, no daughter. Nothing.

I dropped into the armchair next to the cat and let out an audible exhale to slow the panic in my chest. The call with Jessica came back to me, followed by the God-awful stage flop that followed. Then… drinking. Then, going to Jessica's apartment to see Claire. But after that, there was a wave of blackness, a void, until I got plucked off the bridge by a mordant mortician.

What had I done?

Winona returned, juggling a tray of coffee with pastry rolls and a pair of wing tips. She set the coffee tray on the desk and held up the shoes. "You like?"

"Looks like they were on their last leg."

"Hey, you're funny."

Where was she last night? I took an inventory of my clothes. The pants had a tear at the knee, and the top three buttons of my shirt were missing. Plus, I reeked of booze and stale sweat. "Not sure the shoes match my outfit."

"We can take care of that, too." Winona handed me a cup of coffee. "Got an entire room of clothes people bring in for a casket viewing. But if the deceased is cremated, we relieve them of their garments and offer them back to the family. They seldom ever want the stuff. So, Truss has the clothes dry-cleaned and donates them to charity."

"Truss?"

"He's the one who pulled you off the bridge."

"Old guy?" Further details of the grainy night started to emerge.

"Old, I guess that pretty much says it all. He's a fourth-generation undertaker. Truss' great-great-grandfather got a start in the business during the Civil War. He plucked the dead off the battlefields, packed them in salt and shipped them north and south, back to their families. He hauled a wagon full of fallen soldiers from Minnesota's First Regiment home from Gettysburg. Once here, he married a widow with six kids and never left. Oldest mortuary in the state."

I flashed back to the foot with the red toenails and hoped I had been hallucinating. "Did Truss have a dead person with him in the hearse when he picked me up?"

"Her name is Riva O'Malley. Know little about her except she came from Angel of Mercy, the county's long-term care center. Apparently, she had suffered a traumatic accident about a year ago and succumbed to some kind of respiratory issue. No relatives or claimants. Arrangements for interment are still being finalized."

Winona's confirmation of a corpse in the hearse made me feel ill. My stomach churned as if I'd swallowed rocks. "How old was she?"

"There's no formal identification on record, but the intake record at the facility guessed her to be somewhere in her early twenties."

It struck me as nearly impossible that someone could navigate life in this age of technology without an ID. "Are you an undertaker?"

"No, just a survivor like you. I'm afraid of heights. So there wasn't a bridge involved, but still..." Winona held out her forearms to reveal old scars and welts from needle marks. She laughed. "Kind of messed with my tats."

"You're an addict?"

"Started shooting drugs to drown out the shame of who I was and where I came from, but my drug-induced dreams always brought me back to the reservation. I finally realized there is no escaping myself."

"So, you ended up on death's doorstep, and Truss saved you?"

"More or less, but I will spare you those details. I'm the Truss Mortuary business manager now. How about you?"

Winona's vulnerability seemed to give me permission to speak to my situation. "I screwed up bad, been screwing up. Got nothing, pretty sure I just burned the last things I cared about. I'm bombing on stage and bombing in life."

"Are you an actor?"

"I attempt comedy. And parenthood." I wanted to say more, but words felt inadequate to describe my plight. I stared at the floor.

The room filled with silence, punctuated by the ticking of the mantle clock. When I finally looked up, I felt Winona's soft smile, a smile intended for someone who had lost his way. I wondered if her kindness would hold if she knew how selfish and lost I'd become.

"Let's look over the wardrobe." Winona rose from her chair. "We even have a shower."

Thirty minutes later, I stood in front of Winona, not quite a GQ advertisement but passable with the downtown business crowd.

"You got someplace to go?" she said.

"Since my divorce, I share a place near West Seventh with my brother. Actually, it's my mother's home, but she spends most of her time in Florida with her boyfriend."

"I've got an errand to run in that neighborhood. If you like, I'll give you a lift. And if you plan on sticking around for a while, you might want this." She handed me my wallet.

I didn't have to inspect its contents. I was flat broke with a debt load that crushed me like a medieval millstone.

Winona stopped her car in front of Keenan's Bar, a windowless joint with a large American flag painted on the one-story building's red brick wall. An old black dog with a gray snout sat outside the bar, its tail pounding the pavement, anxiously awaiting its master. I knew the place as a local West 7th Street dive.

"Could you do me a favor?" Winona turned off the engine and stared at the bar's entry door. A hint of sweat appeared on her upper lip as she watched the patrons, mostly working men, swing in and out. "There's a man in the bar." She reached into the back seat and retrieved a package. "He's waiting for this. Deliver it to him. That's it."

I looked hesitantly at the shoebox size package wrapped in brown paper.

"It's legal if that's what you're thinking." Winona laughed and handed me a twenty. "I'll wait here for you."

"No need, I only live a couple blocks away." I held up the twenty. "And thanks."

And so a failed comedian walked into a bar.

CHAPTER 4

KEENAN'S

The name on the package, wrapped in brown paper, read "Rudy C. Hegler c/o of Bernie Hegler, Keenan's Bar." I knew the place but wasn't a regular. A musty, sour smell of stale beer met me at the door. A huddle of pressmen from a nearby print operation eyeballed my suit but quickly dismissed me. I approached the bar with the package under my arm.

"What can I get ya?" The bartender swiped at the bar surface with a towel.

"I'm good. Looking for a Bernie Hegler."

"On the end." The bartender thumbed toward a heavyset guy sitting alone.

I pushed back from the rail and approached Bernie, huddled tight over a beer. "Bernie Hegler?"

"Who wants to know?"

"Truss Mortuary."

"Is that Uncle Rudy?" Bernie pointed at the package.

Suddenly, I realized what I was carrying, and it creeped me out. I set the small box on the bar so Bernie could read the label.

Bernie picked up the box, shook the contents and listened to it shift and rattle. "Sonofabitch! Thought there would be more to him. What's your name?"

"Vince, but I'm just helping with the delivery."

"Bill, get this guy a beer."

Before I could protest, a sudsy mug slid down the rail. "My condolences."

"Coke killed him," he said. "Goddam tragedy."

"Sorry, I'm not following. Drugs, as in overdose?"

"More like an overload. One-ton Coke machine fell on him." Bernie signaled the barkeep. "Bill, shots for these beers. Damn shame. Uncle Rudy, like most of these guys," Bernie waved a hand in the direction of the bar patrons, "worked hard for his money. Stopped after the late shift at the Amoco, plugged a buck fifty into the outdoor soda machine next to the building and nothing. The station's closed, so he did what any of us would have done. Rocked the piss out of the machine trying to get what was owed him. The thing should have been bolted down. He'd have a good lawsuit if he pursued it. Anyway, the machine tipped over. Pancaked him good, dead of winter, too." Bernie took a long swig of beer. "When the Amoco guys found the Coke machine tipped over, the only thing they could see was a hand curled in a stiff one-finger salute."

"Tough way to go." I was trying for sympathy, but I think some skepticism may have joined the mix.

"Now get this." Bernie leaned into me with a shoulder nudge. "To get the machine off Uncle Rudy, those bolts for brains grease monkeys used a tow truck cable to hoist it upright. Uncle Rudy was stuck to the faceplate, frozen in place. The paramedics had to scrape him off before they could cart him away. You'd think that would be the end of it," Bernie snorted. "But those Amoco guys put the machine back in place and reset the circuit breaker. When the front light panel came on, it revealed an image of Uncle Rudy, like the Shroud of freakin' Turin." Bernie blessed himself. "Drew quite a crowd."

"Good story." I edged off the bar stool. "Thanks for the beer, and sorry for your loss."

"Hey, I am just repeating what Uncle Rudy's drug addled, loser kid told me. The airhead kid is off in some government funded psych ward, and he leaves me with this business." Bernie tapped the box of remains. "The police report did say they found a crowbar under Uncle Rudy, so he may have been trying to get a bit more than his due. Not that it makes any difference, but he had hard times."

"Nice to meet you and good luck." I pushed off from the bar.

"Whoa." Bernie grabbed my forearm. "If you're from the mortuary, you gotta say something. You know, give the deceased a sendoff."

"Hey, I've got nothing to do with the mortuary, plus I've had a couple of awful days."

"Not as bad as Uncle Rudy."

"Point taken."

"It ain't right to let a man die without a proper tribute, some parting words. And even if I had something to say, and I don't, I'd be too nervous to say it. Which is why I let Uncle Rudy sit on the shelf at the mortuary."

I should have bolted for the exit, but Bernie's sincerity gave me pause.

Bernie surveyed my suited attire. "You don't look like no pressman."

"Right now, I'm just bumming jobs, trying to catch on as a philosophy teacher, do some other stuff." I instantly regretted the disclosure.

"Ah, a professor. Deep thinker. Bingo, just the guy."

I opened my mouth to speak, to emphasize my failure on the subject, but let it go.

"Be forever indebted if you could help me out here. Say a couple of words about Uncle Rudy, so I can put this thing behind me."

"I suggest a minister, that's their thing."

"Uncle Rudy wasn't exactly churchgoing. Hey, help me out in my hour of grief. I'd like to get this off my plate."

"Here?"

Bernie seized on the question and called over to the bartender, "Vince here, from the mortuary, is going to say some parting words about my Uncle Rudy." Bernie tapped the box.

The bartender eyed it suspiciously.

"Drinks on the house," Bernie added.

"Coming up." The bartender pounded a heavy stein on the bar, gathering the attention of the patrons. "Drinks on the house, compliments of Bernie on account of his Uncle Rudy's demise."

Bernie shoved the box in front of me.

I put my hands on the package and raised it ever so slightly off the bar. Before I set it down, I gave it a little shake, felt the shifting contents and heard a tumbling sound, like gravel. It seemed improbable that a human being could be reduced to a shoebox. There was just not enough material to account for a life.

The clacking of pool balls and alcohol induced chatter ceased. The bar almost took on the solemnity of a church. The neon signs became stained glass, the beer mugs chalices and the bartender's apron a priestly robe. Everyone held a full glass, but no one drank.

I felt the weight of a room full of expectant attention press down on me. Sweat sprang from my face and soaked my collar, but I had to get back on the horse sometime. I turned away from the bar, stood and faced the patrons with a glass in one hand, and the other hand on the cremated remains of Uncle Rudy.

"I didn't know Rudy, Bernie's uncle. But Bernie has vouched for him, so I guess we can consider he was a standup guy, just hoping to catch a break here and there."

A few heads nodded.

"For most of us, the luckiest day in our lives is having two Snicker bars fall out of a vending machine."

"Got that right," a voice rose from the gathering.

"Uncle Rudy wasn't so fortunate. He plugged a soda vending machine with those Wisconsin cheese-head commemorative quarters, and they got stuck in the coin slot."

Chuckles.

"Rudy did what we all would do, rocked the machine. Apparently, when a Coke machine falls on you, they're not really soft drinks."

Laughs. I'd almost forgotten what they sounded like.

"Kind of like an Orange Crush."

I paused to signal a tempo shift. "I suspect Uncle Rudy, like all of us, was a bit imperfect, doing the best he could with what he had to work with. For that, he deserves some acknowledgment. Perhaps that's what we all want, to be recognized for being a son, a buddy, maybe a husband and father. And to be forgiven for a wrong turn here and there. Uncle Rudy has earned this moment to get his due, a tip of the hat, his name on the lips of brothers before they wet them with a toast." I raised my glass. "So, here's to Uncle Rudy."

"To Uncle Rudy," the patrons shouted in unison and bumped their glasses. Someone dropped coins into the jukebox and fired up the Traveling Wilburys' "End of the Line." Soon the whole joint was hammering the chorus.

Bernie put an arm around me. "God, I can finally sleep. Can't thank ya enough." Then he stuffed a wad of cash into my shirt pocket.

"Hope you're there for me." Another bar patron stepped up with a slap on the back and likewise stuffed some bills into my shirt pocket. Other patrons followed, and suddenly, along with a bulging pocket of cash, I had three unordered drinks in front of me.

CHAPTER 5

OVERBOARD

Two blocks away from Keenan's Bar, I stepped into a coffee shop for a quick caffeine fix, hit the pause button and make sense of the last twenty-four hours. I sat at a counter and pulled out the wad of bills stuffed in my shirt pocket by the bar patrons. Two hundred and fifteen dollars, mostly in crumpled ones and fives, with the odd ten. Plus, the twenty bucks Winona from the mortuary gave me for the errand. Who would have thought you could get cash and a laugh out of a cremation box?

The momentary delight of my modest tribute success quickly faded with the thought of Winona. She would be totally pissed off when she found out about the freelance intrusion. But this wasn't the first time I'd screwed up a task on behalf of the deceased.

I stared into the cup of coffee and saw my twelve-year-old insecure self, lost in the arching maw of St. Stanislaus Church. I fidgeted on the hard oak pew with a pressing urge to pee.

My mother, a toddler on her lap, licked her hand and patted down my colicky tufts of hair, then nudged me into the aisle. "Now say something nice about Daddy."

I hugged the end of the pew. Daddy's flag-draped coffin looked as formidable as a school bus ready to run me over.

My mother waved her hands at me as though chasing blackbirds out of the cornfield. "Tell everyone what a nice man Daddy was."

The priest made eye contact with my widowed mother, nodded, and came down to meet me. With a firm hand, he steered me past the coffin up the three altar steps. The priest wrestled the microphone from the pulpit podium and held it in front of my mouth as if offering a carrot to a horse.

"Go on, son," he whispered.

"I gotta pee!"

The declaration screeched through the sound system. Stifled chuckles erupted from the pews. The priest smiled broadly, letting the parishioners enjoy my awkward moment. I took in the geometry of staring faces. Ovals, triangles, squares and parallelograms, all nodding, coaching, waiting.

Daddy help me, Daddy help me.

Then the words came out. "Come home, Daddy. I know you're not in there." I pointed at the casket. "So this doesn't really count. Momma says we have to move on cause we need the money, but I don't want to go anyplace without you. I . . ."

The priest put a clamp on my shoulder and quickly redirected the microphone. "Kids," he said, with a patronizing smile while firmly guiding me back to my mother. The service concluded with Rod Stewart's, "I Am Sailing", played through the church's screechy PA. The lyrics still haunt me.

That had been almost twenty years ago. Yet to this day, not a smidgen of my old man had turned up in the shipping channels, bewildering chutes, sloughs or backwaters of the Mississippi River. He piloted a barge tow boat that shuttled grain, corn, coal and chemicals to ports between St. Paul and Baton Rouge. Caught in an early winter storm just north of the Quad Cities, his sixteen barge transport stalled out in dense fog and snow. The Coast Guard surmised that during night while waiting for conditions to lift, he went out to inspect the tow lines, slipped on the icy deck, and fell overboard, likely crushed between the tug and the barge. My father's body was never recovered.

I looked up from my lukewarm coffee and watched people line up to place their orders—people in clothes that hadn't been worn by a corpse, with purposeful jobs, with a partner they could trust, happy kids, and a purpose in life. I kept falling into the same hole over and over again. Maybe I should see a shrink. A suicide attempt would warrant the trip, but I'd been through that drill. I've got ADD. I spin too many plates just to watch them fall. So, isn't that the profile of every comedian? Waste of time. Probably just get the Robin Williams pep talk. Hell, I'd kill myself to be as talented.

I tried to fill in the blank spots before I got to the bridge. After the bomb job at the comedy club, I went to a bar. Drank a few beers and then hammered the hard stuff with a Red Bull kicker to jack up the high. At some point, someone handed me pills. The rush of chemicals flooded my bloodstream. I knew better than to drink and dial, at least I did when I was sober. I'd left sober behind a while ago.

My ex-wife didn't pick up. She knew it was me. So what if it was 1:30 in the morning? I wanted to scorch the earth. There was only one thing standing between me and total wasteland—my daughter, Claire. Somehow, she still believed in me.

Although I protested, the bouncer ejected me from the bar. I located my car, not so stoned that I couldn't rationalize my ability to drive. I was on a mission. I should not have driven to my ex's place, but that was exactly what I did.

Then what?

CHAPTER 6

BROTHERHOOD

I pushed open the door to my mother's tired bungalow. Two naked bodies on the living room sofa scampered like cockroaches for cover. The sweet smell of pot hung in the air.

"Jesus, knock or something." Ray, my younger brother, stood behind the sofa and grabbed a throw pillow to cover his lap.

I watched the naked backside of a woman slip into the bathroom. "It's the middle of the day."

"It's called a matinée. It's French, you wouldn't understand." Ray puffed out his chest. "Besides, I live here too, so lay off my case."

"So clean the place up once in a while." I pointed at the food cartons and beer bottles amassed on the coffee table. The place made me feel like a total loser. Here I was with an advanced degree, still living in my mother's house with my brother.

The house was in foreclosure. Our mother had abandoned the place, furnishings included, and moved to Florida with her boyfriend, Jack. Before the housing bust, she had used the place as an ATM—cash flowing freely from second mortgages, refi's, and equity loans. When the value of her home finally came back to reality, the bank moved in to force a sale. To forestall the foreclosure, she sicced a housing rights organization on the bank. Turns out the bank's sloppy paperwork and a class action suit frustrated any near-term eviction. Eviction was inevitable, but Ray seized the opportunity for free rent and never left. I reluctantly returned after my divorce.

"Hey, you're no Mr. Neatnick, so like I said, back off!"

He had a point. Why should any of us contribute to something with no future? The only nod to décor was a print of dogs playing poker hung on the living room wall. My mother's house mirrored the condition of my sad life: nostalgia, resentment and cluttered confusion.

"And what's with the suit, dude, get that at the Goodwill?"

Not in the mood to joust with my brother, I walked into the kitchen to allow space for the copulating couple to collect themselves. I grabbed a half-empty bottle of Gatorade from the refrigerator and held it against my forehead.

"You can be such an asshole," Ray shouted as he pulled on his pants.

I took a deep breath. Ray didn't want to let it go. His bipolar condition seemed to feast on confrontation, and he may not have taken his meds today. Ray had an off the charts IQ. When he worked, he wrote software code, created apps and video games. He had offers to come onboard with major tech companies but conformity and deadlines were deal breakers. He worked mostly from home in an unsupervised environment with irregular hours. I had a suspicion he also engaged in various forms of hacking, but I didn't care to know the details.

I plunked down in a living room chair. "Sorry to bust in," I said in a smooth voice, hoping for a reset. "Who's your friend?"

"Sage, not so new, we've been hanging for a bit. She's a sound engineer at…what's the name of the radio station you work for?"

"Minnesota Public Radio," Sage shouted back from the bathroom.

"Radio's her day gig," Ray said. "She freelances, too. Done some stuff for Prince, Jonny Lang and some gospel groups. Cool, huh?"

"Amen. You brothers talking about me?" Sage exited from the bathroom wearing only Ray's long-tailed shirt and a hint of red lipstick. Her black velvety skin glistened. She made no move to conceal the firm, round breast that had escaped from the shirt. She sat next to Ray. "We're good baby, let it go." She gently stroked Ray's thigh. "Ray said you were a finalist in a comedy contest at Louie's. I bet you tore it up."

"More like shredded."

"Totally slammed," Ray said. "Your contest act at Louie's got posted on YouTube. Not even a pity laugh. Why you would drag out that philosophy crap in front of a house full of drunks is just stupid."

"Leave it alone," I said.

"They got a closeup of Louie popping a bolt as you pissed all over the stage, just after you dropped the mic like you were some big time rapper. You thought this was your ticket to the big time. Where was it? Oh yeah, 'Hotlanta.' Now that's funny." Ray let out a devilish laugh. "Getting tons of comments like, 'Comic's megaton bomb levels Louie's comedy scam.'"

I thought my head would detonate as I thought back to Louie's fury filled, flushed face on my escape from the comedy contest. Louie owned comedy in the five-state area and had an interest in most of the dive bars around. No way would I get another stand-up gig. I'd be lucky now to find work making dog balloons. I just hoped Louie hadn't put a contract out on me.

Ray torched up a Bic lighter, touched it to a pipe and took a long pull. "You?" He extended it my way.

I waved off the pipe and pointed to the new tattoo on Ray's upper forearm. "When did you get that?"

"Last month, week, I don't know, thereabouts." Ray pushed up his tee-shirt sleeve to better expose the colorful river serpent inked on his upper arm. "A tribute to Dad."

Sage put her arm around Ray's neck in a gesture of comfort.

"So, help me out here." I pointed the Gatorade bottle at Ray. "How does Dad going overboard on the river in the middle of an icy storm correlate with a sea monster?"

"The same way as all this crap you've got stashed around here relates. His leather jacket, maps, old cameras, tools, broken down motorcycle in the garage. Look around, this place looks like a pawn shop shrine."

Ray had a valid point, but I didn't want to give it to him. My brother was only three years old when our father disappeared. His memories were fleeting and fragmented, at best a deep assuring voice, the smell of tobacco, a vaguely familiar face. A face Ray inherited from our father. I favored my mother's side. I both pitied and envied my brother. He had been too young to become fully invested in our father, nor did he carry any of the firsthand pain or loss.

"At least I'm not into fairy tales," I said.

"Sure you are," Ray said. "I've heard all your theories. Dad washed up on shore, lost his memory and forgot to call home or he's lying low, got snatched by aliens, avoiding creditors, in a witness protection program or some such shit."

I did the math quickly. Our father would be in his sixties by now, but I never thought of him as any older than on the day he left. And I could still see my mother, at the kitchen table with one hand on her mouth, staring out the window, waiting for the ruggedly handsome tow pilot to appear.

"And on the subject of dead people, your ex-wife stopped by with murder on her mind,"

Ray said tightly as he held in his hit on the pipe.

"What are you talking about?"

"She was on the boil," Sage added. "You must have messed up bad. She dropped off your car keys. Guess you were too tanked to drive, huh?"

I retreated into my bedroom and threw myself on the bed. I thought about my ex-wife, Jessica, so uniquely attractive I couldn't look away. Her sculpted Nordic features worthy of Rodin conveyed a woman of purpose. I'm surprised we lasted as long as we did, adrift on my rudderless boat. I doubt my mother-in-law was; she wished us many happy months together at our wedding.

I held a Master's degree in Philosophy, an area of study I fell into by virtue of availability. It was the only major that did not have a wait list. That, and a class schedule which allowed me to do late night stand-up comedy, grinding away at dive bars for tips, drinks and personal therapy. Somehow, I thought that our having a child together, something we both loved, would bind us in a way that would transcend everything else we disagreed upon.

I closed my eyes and felt the sadness of loss morph into something else, a flashback.

I had gone to Jessica's apartment after the comedic meltdown. There was a car with Wisconsin license plates parked outside her house. I heard laughing, saw Jessica and a guy friend in the window. The rejection of losing both my ex and my child brought tears of anger. I wanted to see Claire. The door was open.

I sat up in bed, lost in the space between nightmare and wakefulness, sweating. The night's memory cycled in and out. I had confronted Jessica about taking Claire from me. She had treated me like a naughty child, shamed me for being drunk. Dismissed me, said she'd talk about it another time. Claire was sleeping. Told me to leave. I broke some stuff, a picture frame, a mirror, maybe other stuff. I called her some names. Her cheese-head friend stepped in, voices were raised. Shoving. Tears. Jessica's face red, wet with running eyeliner. The argument moved outside. Noises. Shouting from nearby apartment windows, a siren. I tried to get into my car, a struggle. A flasher bar approached. Heard her say, "Let him go."

I ran and ran.

And wound up perched on the bridge rail, the black water roiling below. Driven to float on air to relieve all the pressure of rejection and guilt. Shame for being an abandoned child, guilt for wasting my education, a fool's vocation, failing in marriage, losing my daughter.

Then the hearse. The undertaker was right; I had been to that bridge before, scouting out how I'd drift down the river in search of my father.

I got out of bed and thought about calling Jessica and apologizing, but realized I had nothing to say. I was dead to her, gone to myself. I noticed two recent phone messages. One call was from Toby, my manager. I couldn't bear to listen to his rant on how I blew up my comedy career, so I hit delete. The other was from Winona at the mortuary. I felt sick. No doubt she heard about the situation at the bar, the money I collected. Christ, how do the most straightforward things get so screwed up? I hit the Call Back button. Might as well get this over with.

CHAPTER 7

CRAIG'S LIST

Before she even said anything, I apologized to Winona for the impromptu tribute at the bar, while ensuring her it actually came off pretty well. I told her I'd stop by and return the tip money. The right thing to do, but painful. Even more so since I had just been fired from the telemarketing job as a no show, having slept through my shift on a mortuary gurney.

She simply laughed. "Sure, drop in, we might even have another pair of shoes you might like."

"Hey wait, how did you get my phone number?"

"We went through your wallet when Truss brought you in. Checked you out to make sure you hadn't escaped from a psych ward."

"Ouch!"

No way did I want to step foot in a mortuary again. Few people who arrive at a funeral home in a hearse ever walk out. Certainly not Riva O'Malley, my hearse companion. For some reason, I couldn't get her out of my mind. Every time I thought of her, my emotions cycled through anxiety, shame, and a sense of strange luck. I wondered if I had some kind of survivor's guilt for a young lady I never met.

I ventured through St. Paul's West Seventh Street area to meet Winona. The commercial mix of consignment shops, check cashing services, and tattoo operations spoke to the area's decline. A bus bench in front of a health clinic had an ad for a cut-rate personal injury attorney. In an empty lot, kids played pickup soccer, using a broken aluminum lawn chair as a goal. Truss Mortuary, quartered in a hundred-year-old English Tudor, stood alone in its dignity, a reminder of a bygone era.

As I entered the mortuary, a man brushed by me carrying flowers out the door.

"This is theft." Winona followed on the heels of the flower guy. "We've always paid our bills. Okay, a little late sometimes, but you can't do this." The florist bolted for his truck.

"Maybe I should come back another time," I said.

She blew out a lungful of air. "Sorry you had to witness that fiasco." She motioned me to follow her into the parlor.

Truss sat at a desk, his attention turned toward the repair of an old, disassembled pocket watch. A pair of reading glasses hung low on his nose. The old man's gaunt face, stubbly growth of beard and dark bushy eyebrows froze me in place. I hadn't seen Truss since the fuzzy night of the suicide attempt. I wanted to thank him and apologize for the bridge incident, but didn't know where to start.

I didn't get a chance. "They're trying to shut us down," Winona said. "No one will extend us credit. Flowers, chemicals, caskets, everything is cash up front. We're on life support." She sighed. "You know as well as I do that those Reliance franchise bastards are behind this, frigging us over, telling everybody in town we're broke."

Truss frowned at Winona. "You know I find foul language to be a lazy habit without the benefit of persuasion. However, you may be right about the buzzards."

"And speaking of whom," Winona addressed a man who appeared at the parlor door. "Mr. Big-Shot, Ross Dalton of Reliance Funeral Homes, right on cue here to pick over the bones."

"I asked Mr. Dalton to stop by for a visit," Truss said. "I thought we might reach an understanding in regard to our business practices."

"You know he's called our suppliers and pressured them to stop working with us." Winona's angry eyes burned through Dalton like a laser. "You will not push us out of the business even if your mother becomes Governor. Not that I'd vote for her."

"Invoking the name of one's mother isn't very polite." Dalton laughed. "Truss, call off your pit bull." Dalton spoke with the jittery energy of someone overly caffeinated. Instead of conservative funeral attire, he wore a polo shirt, colorful chino pants and thin-soled loafers without socks like he was dressed for a barbecue. His tanned, creamy complexion and bleached white teeth amplified a manufactured smile.

"Winona," Truss said softly, as though soothing a spooked horse.

"Vendors are cautious these days, especially if they get wind of a pending bankruptcy claim." Dalton raised his palms to signal his lack of control. "You know you can't operate without materials. So, let me help you out. You can transfer your in-house clients to one of my funeral homes. And to show you my heart's in the right place, I'll even take your bottom of the barrel county indigent."

"No fricking way are you going to touch our clients," the pit bull said, "and you will not squeeze us out by spreading lies."

"You know I'm the only ticket to preserving Truss Mortuary," Dalton spoke directly to Truss. "Don't make me play hardball."

"Hardball?" Truss seized on the not so veiled threat. "I don't think we play by the same rules."

"Suggest you take my offer and join the Reliance team," Dalton said. "Get out while you can, old man. The days when funeral homes 'waked the dead' are long over. This place is worthless and should be turned into a museum. Look, if you want to keep working, fine. I can always use a back of the house clinician and you're good at that. But, as a practical matter, more people are opting for a fry and a can cremation and the pump and dump corpse work is in decline. All the action is now up front. I've got savvy salespeople making six figures selling celebration of life packages, prepay burial programs, and settling life insurance policies for pennies on the dollar. So, here's how you can fit into that. I acquire Truss Mortuary for its longstanding reputation in the community, which would add some nice credibility to our offerings, and you can walk away with your legacy intact plus retire with a healthy cash nest egg."

"I see it was a mistake to bring you here," Truss said. "Good day, Mr. Dalton."

Dalton looked up at the ceiling. "Before this place is foreclosed on, call me. I'll take the chandelier off your hands."

He walked out with Winona looking at him like she wished she had a Trocar in her hands. When he was gone, she turned to Truss.

"This is harassment," she said. "He's trying to force us to close or sell. Just like all the other privately held funeral homes who've packed it in or caved to the chains."

"I've got some collectors after the hearse," Truss said. "I can probably sell the old gal for a pretty penny. Might help some."

"You love that carriage. No way are we going to give it up."

I wondered how these two could work together; they seemed so opposite. Winona could get into an argument with the weather, while conflict held no purchase with Truss. Yet somehow, they complemented each other.

"Take a breath," Truss said to Winona and turned his attention to me. "Glad you're doing okay."

"I should go." I felt as though I had stepped into the middle of a heated family discussion. I pulled out a wad of bills from my pocket, the tip money from Kennan's bar, and set it on Truss' desk. "Sorry if I caused you any trouble."

Truss looked to Winona for clarification.

"I finally got the Rudy Hegler cremation package delivered. It had been sitting on the shelf for months. Tracked a relative down and he wanted it sent over to Kennan's Bar."

"A bar?" Truss' brow furrowed. "How did that go for you?"

"I had Vince carry in the remains."

Truss nodded.

"I paid Vince for the errand. He seemed trustworthy. I followed up with the client to make sure he got the package. Everything checked out."

"Good."

"Actually, better than good, and I know this will sound crazy, but Vince gave an impromptu tribute to the deceased. The client loved it. Apparently, so did the patrons. They stuffed his pockets full of cash."

"An opportunist?" Truss said, as if I weren't standing right in front of him.

"That's wrong." I made a move to leave.

Winona raised a hand to hold me in place. "Vince apologized about the tribute and offered to drop off the tip money."

Truss glanced at the cash on his desk. "I suggest Vince keep the money, as his intent in the matter was one of good will."

"Yes, I should have offered that. Save you the trip." Winona folded her hands over her heart in an apology. "Sorry, my judgment's a bit clouded lately. We've become the last stop for the impoverished, homeless and county indigents. Clients no other funeral home in town will take in. I know we're providing a community service," she looked at Truss, "and you would do this work for nothing, but it's not paying the bills. I'm just trying my best to manage the business."

Truss gave an appreciative nod. "Couldn't do without you."

"Maybe there's more Rudy Heglers out there." The words escaped my mouth with no forethought. I'd been doing a lot of that lately.

Truss and Winona seemed equally surprised by the assertion and waited for an explanation.

I kept going . . . an idea started to unravel. "Most people would rather be the subject of a eulogy than give one. You might consider offering a eulogy service. Could be a competitive edge. I'd bet Reliance Funeral Homes doesn't do it. It might attract some real paying customers."

I heard a collective gasp from Winona and Truss. Had my self-serving financial desperation crossed some ethical line? I was making this up as I went, but the eulogy gig felt like easy money—tell a few stories to an attentive audience, toss in a little humor, keep it light, say goodbye and pay my child support. Hopefully, a win-win.

"Under what sort of arrangement?" Winona asked with caution in her voice.

"I give the eulogies. Fifty-fifty split on fees and tips."

"Our clients can barely afford the most basic of services."

"Cast a broader net. Hit social media, maybe Craig's List for starters."

"Are you kidding?" Winona gave off a big laugh. "As dumb as that sounds, I like it."

"Truss, you game?"

"Vince, would you be willing to give us some help in other areas, too?" Truss asked.

"Sure."

"Good, I could use a hand about now, my sciatica's acting up."

"Oh, did I tell you?" Winona said. "Vince is a comedian."

"Ha! The profession could use a measure of levity."

CHAPTER 8

INDIGENT

I followed Truss into the postmortem prep room, the same room I had tried desperately to escape from two days ago. It still felt as forbidden and macabre as it did then.

"There's a lab coat behind the door," Truss pointed, "and latex gloves on the counter." Truss entered a walk-in cooler and came out with a corpse on a rolling cart. He positioned the cart next to the stainless-steel table in the center of the room and pointed at the foot end of the zippered bag. "On three."

I had expected the body to be board-stiff from the rigor mortis. Instead, it sagged like a sack of potatoes. The transfer was more of a drag than a lift and ended in a plop on the table.

"You're good to go. Thank you." Truss waved me off.

Just as I pushed open the door to exit, I heard Truss mumble to himself, "Okay, Riva, let's get you some dignity."

Riva O'Malley. I stopped in my tracks as if I had been speeding along the highway and came upon an accident. I knew better than to gawk, but I couldn't help myself. I turned around just as Truss stripped away the plastic bag. I looked at her feet and recalled the red toenails from my ride in the hearse.

Truss seemed to take in the measure of my curiosity, "Suit yourself. Suggest you dip one of those Q-Tips in that jar of Vicks and put a dash on your upper lip."

I stood on the room's perimeter and felt the mentholated topical invade my sinuses. Truss adjusted the overhead light and thumbed through a file folder. "Medical Examiner's report. Riva O'Malley, estimated age 20, no formal identification, resident of Angels of Mercy Long Term Care Center. Transferred from a Crow Wing County hospital eleven months ago. Admitting condition: traumatic head injury/comatose. No known relatives or claimants. Postmortem workup indicates a collapsed lung caused by an air leak into the space between the lungs and the chest wall—pneumothorax. Petechial hemorrhaging present in lip mucosa, interior mouth, nose, and surfaces of eyes. Tear in trachea, occluding beyond normal and mild irritation from plastic tracheostomy tube. Toxicology: Stomach contents and basic screens all negative. Other: toenails were freshly painted red. Cause of Death: Cardiac arrest/hypoxia. Conclusion: Manner of Death, Natural Causes."

Truss shook his head. "This is practically boilerplate. The M.E. wasn't going to waste any time or money on a county client with no advocates." He set the report down and probed O'Malley's suture-scarred head and blue-gray face to review the findings. "In my opinion, the medical assessment is consistent with mechanical asphyxiation, but, curiously, not a word of it in the report."

"Mechanical asphyxiation?"

"She was smothered," Truss said while continuing to probe the corpse. "Bring me the penlight. It's in the top left-hand drawer on the far counter."

I found it and inched toward Truss, who relieved me of the flashlight and bore the beam into O'Malley's open eyes. "Irises non-atrophied, corneas clear." He straightened his back and picked through O'Malley's file folder. "Intake report from Angel of Mercy states, 'O'Malley is lacking in eye movement and motor responses and void of conscious cognition, her condition consistent with a vegetative state.'" He slammed the file down on the table. "A travesty. A proper neurologic brain scan would have revealed her to be completely paralyzed with an active cerebral cortex."

"Are you saying she laid in bed for eleven months, fully conscious, and no one knew it?"

"If my ophthalmologic findings are right, and I'm sure they are, then unfortunately, yes." Truss went back to O'Malley's file, his eyes narrowed. "St. Paul Police Reconstructive Events Report." He held up a sheet of paper and read the account. "Angel of Mercy on-call attendant, Raphael Vieira, reported finding patient, Riva O'Malley, unresponsive at approximately 11:55 a.m. Wednesday, June 2nd. Vieira stated he witnessed a man with an oxygen cart enter and exit O'Malley's room prior to finding her in a compromised state. The on-duty supervisor, Tonette Morelli, called emergency services. Emergency services pronounced O'Malley dead at the scene. They removed a wig from O'Malley to check for head injuries. No new abrasions or trauma were evident. The patient wore a standard hospital shift, with a red dress loosely arrayed on top of her."

Truss turned his attention to O'Malley. "Now why in the world would a comatose patient be wearing a wig? And have freshly painted toenails? As if you were going to a party or perhaps being laid out for a funeral viewing. Yet, there's no indication the police had taken the clothing accessories into evidence."

I was trying to picture the crime scene, and it was a crime scene in my mind. "There will be an investigation, right?"

Truss addressed my question as though it was coming from O'Malley and affectionately patted her arm. "I am sorry, my dear. There's little hope any credible effort will be made to identify your visitor or determine the circumstances of your fateful ending."

"Is fateful ending mortician speak for murder?"

"Even without the benefit of a high-tech CSI, this woman's case should have raised all sorts of red flags. But attention to detail always gets back to money or politics, and the destitute are on the short end of both."

"Isn't there someone to tell about your findings?"

"Unfortunately, I no longer have standing with law enforcement. But I've still got contacts from my days as a coroner. Maybe I can convince one of them to take an investigative interest into her situation. It's a long shot."

"It's sad there's no justice without money. It's not . . ." I sputtered. The Vicks goop under my nose had come in contact with my mouth and infused my taste buds with eucalyptus and camphor.

"No justice and the barest of interment care," Truss said. "Winona would tell you we lose money on every county case we handle. She's certainly told me often enough. But Truss Mortuary has always taken in anyone who required a burial service and at times, we've been overwhelmed. My great grandfather tended to Civil War victims, my grandfather to those who fell in droves to influenza, my father to the impoverished victims of the Great Depression. Today, it's societal indigents. Death does not discriminate, nor does Truss Mortuary. All paths start out the same, get tossed in the winds of circumstance and end up where they started. Rich or poor, death has no favorites."

"Hopefully, a relative or a friend will show up on her behalf."

Truss picked up an instrument from a tray and held it up for me to see. "A needle injector. It's not uncommon for a relative to materialize at the last minute, before burial, and insist on inspecting the deceased. This lack of certainty takes the cremation option off the table. So we do a simple procedure to sew the upper and lower jaw together and get the mouth centered. Keeps the viewing, if there is one, from being a grotesque experience." Truss brought the needle injector up to O'Malley's face and paused. "You may want to take your leave. Things get a little messy from here."

As I left the prep room, an unexpected clutch of sadness caught up with me, and my head the rattled with questions. Who was this woman, so all alone? Would O'Malley be afforded justice for the gross violations she had suffered? Would someone come forward to tell her story?

CHAPTER 9

TEED OFF

George V. Stillman died in a St. Paul hospital of prostate cancer. Retired and separated from his wife, he spent most of his time on the golf course. Lois, his estranged wife from Seattle, had received a call to claim the body. She considered George's death an imposition and let him sit in the hospital morgue for a week. She couldn't say a decent thing about the man, and they hadn't spoken in years. In desperation she came across our ad on Craig's List, 'Funeral with Personalized Eulogy Service'.

Mrs. Stillman purchased an urn and had it forwarded to Truss Mortuary. She also emailed a skimpy bio of George and a directive to have the memorial service at George's country club. "He practically lived there—he might as well end it there." Further, the estranged wife informed Winona she wouldn't be attending. That gave me free rein.

I arrived at the Hillcrest Country Club a half hour before the service to get my bearings. Hillcrest was a second-tier private club and sat on the northeast edge of St. Paul. The members, retired duffers, rejected repeated calls for a dues increase to keep up with the maintenance. Grass sprung from cracks in the tennis court and the once bikini-clad crowd ceded the pool's concrete apron to old ladies doing aerobic workouts with plastic milk jugs filled with water.

I checked the time, 11:50 a.m. George's service was scheduled for noon. I approached the first tee and watched a foursome beat their clubs into the ground and then chase the balls down the fairway. The clang and the pinch of rusty springs caught my attention. A driver in a mini dump truck drove to the tee.

"You the guy going to give Stillman a sendoff?" The ranger eyed my attire. I wore the same suit Winona had provided me at the mortuary, right down to the wingtips. "Generally don't let folks on the course without golf shoes."

"I wasn't aware of the policy…"

"Forget it. George was all right. Got some flowers and a memorial display of some sort, where do you want 'em?"

"How about there?" I pointed to the red tee-off markers.

"Over there, you say? Ha!" The ranger snorted and turned to retrieve a basketball-sized golf ball fixed to a golf tee anchored to an artificial grass base, all in plastic composite. He handed it to me. The name Stillman was stenciled on the ball—George's final resting place. "Always with the gimmicks." The ranger shook his head. "And preacher, make it snappy. We get backed up, everybody gets pissy."

I set George on the stand next to the flowers and checked the time. Where were the guests? The day held a slight breeze under a soft blue sky. I looked down the fairway at the sea of fumigated green grass. Along the golf course's perimeter, oversized houses with large picture windows and wraparound decks sat like dry docked ships.

What was I doing here? A comedian doing a eulogy was like a dog singing—not impossible, maybe entertaining, but weird. I should never have imposed my mercenary self on this sacred event. I thought maybe this was my way back, but perhaps it was a sign of just how far I'd fallen. Sad.

I looked at the notes Winona had given me on George. You'd think there'd be something definitive, something that spoke to his accomplishments, a moment in time uniquely Stillman's. But all I could come up with was ... average schmuck. Never rose above middle management, never took a risk like those above him, never produced anything like those below him. Forced into early retirement at sixty-two. Fretted over his 401K, played the lottery, played golf, went to happy hour, played golf, escaped winter to a trailer park in Arizona, played golf, got up four times a night to piss, diagnosed with cancer and wasted hundreds of thousands of dollars in medical treatments, trying to hang on. Just a guy who played it safe while plodding along the dull path of biologic attrition.

Actually, his life was a pleasant ride compared to my rudderless existence. At least he had golf.

A convoy of golf carts suddenly rolled up to the first tee and parked in a semicircle around the podium. Everyone remained in their carts.

Someone pointed at the golf ball on steroids. "That Stillman?"

"Must be, look he's at the ladies tee," said a tanned, wrinkled face that looked like a dried-up lake bed.

"Noon, just like George to hog the prime tee time."

"Let's get on with it, Preacher."

I adjusted the golf ball urn on the stand. I had always considered that people die in character, and I supposed a eulogy should extend that character for better or worse. "As you know, George ..."

"Louder," came a wheezing voice from underneath a flat hat that looked like a deflated pumpkin.

I took a deep breath and jacked up my voice. "George loved golf and the game's park-like setting, so it's only ..."

"Yeah, we know. He peed on every tree on the course." The laughter rippled through the assembly.

I checked my notes. "George understood golf is a special game. There are not many activities where you win through efficiency.

Where fewer is better, as in his most cherished friends gathered here today."

"Anyone get what he just said?" A golfer swiveled his head around to include his buddies.

"Could be a fable, but that would make us jackrabbits," a golfer leaning on his putter popped off.

"Among his many accomplishments, George is fondly remembered as a member of the club's best-ball foursome. He cherished the camaraderie . . ."

"Didn't use one of his shots." A golfer raised his hand as in an oath. "Fact."

I paused and looked out at the golfers in their little carts and plaid costumes, argyle socks, and floppy-tongued shoes. Maybe there was something to having your sophomoric cronies tee off on you in your last hour—a parting shot. I pocketed the note card. "George's family, from out of town, couldn't be with him today, but . . ."

"You mean his crazy wife? George couldn't stand her. Did she come up with this cockamamie idea?"

From the direction of the clubhouse, the discordant sound of a bagpipe interrupted the tribute. A boulder of a man in a tartan kilt, with bowling pin size calves, approached the gathering.

"Here comes Stillman's girlfriend." A golfer pointed at the bagpiper.

The bagpiper cradled something that resembled an upside-down piglet, being alternately squeezed and inflated through a tube connected to the piper's mouth. With a lot of room for interpretation, I could hear a squeaky Danny Boy.

"Makes no sense, Stillman was Jewish," another crony said. "I didn't know you could play klezmer on a bagpipe."

I saw the ranger's cart rumbling toward the ceremony. The ranger spiraled a finger overhead—a signal to wrap it up.

"You are all invited to a luncheon reception immediately follow-ing," I said, with added enthusiasm. "Remember if you drink, don't drive. Or putt."

"You can bet it's a cash bar—cheap prick." The golf carts peeled off down the cart path.

★   ★   ★

I entered the clubhouse and observed the golfers scarfing Stillman's complementary buffet. No one took notice of me, nor did I feel an obligation to mingle. I ventured into the club bar. At midday, the clubby, dark-paneled room was empty of patrons. A large mirror stood behind the bar. A club-swinging golfer and a flagstick were etched into the glass. My wavy reflection in the silvery scene only added to my confused state. I straddled a padded bar stool edged with brass upholstery nails. "Beer," I called out to the bartender.

"You know what they say, party like a mortician. Grab a cold one." Truss seemed to appear out of nowhere. "Make mine a bourbon—put 'em on my tab."

Had Truss witnessed the botched tribute? "Oh my God, I'm sor-ry," I said. "The entire thing fell off the rails. I won't take any money for it."

"No, you did good out there, tough bunch of old farts."

I took a big gulp of beer and let out a resigned exhale. "I bombed, been doing a lot of that lately."

"You gave those clowns what they wanted." Truss levered his thumb over his shoulder in the buffet's direction. "A chance to let off a little steam. Guys don't take much to public emotion, getting intimate. So, they revert to the next best thing—wise cracking, feeling cocky for outliving their crony. Stillman would have joined in if he weren't the one in the urn."

I tried to process Truss' take on the Stillman fiasco, but I couldn't get my mind around it. I stared at the muted TV locked on the golf channel.

Truss picked up a handful of bar peanuts and rattled them in his hand. "I apologize for bringing you in on the O'Malley work up, as unprepared as you were."

"I can't stop thinking about her." I rubbed the back of my neck. "The isolation, the injuries, being trapped in her body, unable to move."

"She deserved better."

"Has anyone else been looking into her death?"

"No traction on the investigation, but I'm still pressing my contacts. Got an investigator, works for the state, I'm hoping he'll pick up her case. For now, all we can do is bring some dignity and respect to her passing."

The conversation trailed off. I felt a quiet reverence for O'Malley set in.

Truss held up two fingers to the barkeep. "Winona seems to think you have a gift for connecting with people."

"What makes her an expert?" The words landed like a challenge, not what I intended. I wished I could take them back.

"She reads people from instinct and she's usually spot on." Truss' deep-set eyes took on a distant focus as he spoke about her. "She's an old soul, you know, the granddaughter of a revered shaman, and she understands from personal experience the fragility of life."

"I didn't mean to offend."

"She's also a hell of a lot smarter business person than I'll ever be. Trying her best to keep us afloat." Truss took a long pull of his drink.

"My problem is, I never really thought of my trade as a business. But that's what it's become. Taken over by the McMortuary locusts. Run by accountants, actuaries, merchandisers and slick marketers."

"Like Dalton?"

"Sorry, you had to witness the seamy underside of the trade."

I propped my elbows on the bar. "I know this was my idea, but I don't think it will work out. I feel like a vulture picking over carrion. I'm . . ."

"Helping people in their hour of need."

"Feels more like bullshit," I said.

"Perhaps, but it can be comforting hogwash. Like much of what I do."

I looked into the bar mirror, more confused than ever. "This is all beyond me. How can I legitimately speak about the deceased, especially when I don't even know them?"

"If you were dead, lying in a casket, what would you want people to say about you?"

"That's easy. 'He's still moving.'"

"Good one." Truss smiled, let things settle. "The living and even the dead don't want to face death. We all understand life ends, but somewhere in the back of our minds, we think we'll beat it. We want to be insulated from our own mortality. So we pump up the deceased with preservatives, plaster their face with makeup, and dress them as if they're going to a party. Then we all sit around and tell fairy tales about going to Neverland. Or trump up rituals like tossing ashes out of an airplane, only to have them blown back into the cockpit and swept out onto the tarmac. As I say, that kind of comforting stuff is part of my profession."

"So if I don't want to tell fairy tales, then what?"

"Speak the truth."

"Need a little help here."

"Practice death. It binds us all."

"Practice how, like role playing?"

"Make believe you're on your deathbed. Take account of all the things you've strived for—education, job, family, home, friends, recognition, bank accounts, stuff, pathetic experiences and your egocentric identity."

"That won't take long. I got nothing."

"Now blow it away, like the dust you will soon become." Truss waved his hands as to brush away an imaginary fly. "Only then, the truth of who you are, who everyone is, will reveal itself."

"This is all a little too heavy for me. Why don't you just do the eulogies? You seem to have the playbook and are quick with the one-liners. You don't need me."

"I'm the hard-bitten, dour undertaker. Winona thinks you're on to something, comedy guy." Truss pulled an envelope from his coat pocket and set it on the bar. "From Winona, your fee for today."

"Kind of feel like I am being pimped."

Truss snorted. "Then I think you'll find Winona has an assignment that should hit the mark."

CHAPTER 10

CAT-NAP

I sat slumped in my car in front of Truss Mortuary, trying to gather the strength for another eulogy. Exhausted, I felt totally victimized by the past several days: a train wreck set off by my ex-wife's relocation gambit, the comedic debacle, and the ongoing cash pressure that tethered me to Truss Mortuary. The hijacking of my daughter hurt the most. Yes, I overreacted by trying to visit Claire drunk in the middle of the night. But somewhere in my twisted logic, I considered it a justifiable fatherly intrusion.

I had not talked to Jessica since the altercation, but it was not for lack of trying. I had called her repeatedly over the last few days. She never picked up, so I left the same tired plea for forgiveness. While I was pulling myself together, I dialed her number again.

To my surprise, she answered. "What?"

"Jessica, we really need to talk."

"Vince, quit pestering me with your whiney calls. It's over. If you keep calling, I swear I'll get a restraining order. After you threatened my friend and smashed stuff in the apartment, I'm pretty sure I'll get one."

"Your friend? How healthy is it for our daughter to have your friend hang out there in the middle of the night?"

"Claire and I are moving on with our lives. Suggest you do the same."

"Look, I know it's all about the money. I'll come up with whatever it takes to keep you from going out of state. Claire needs a proper dad, not Mommy's special friend."

"Too late. You had your chance. I'm serious, I've got a lawyer on speed dial." She clicked me off.

I got out of my car and kicked the door shut. "Not fair!" I yelled to the sky and walked into the mortuary.

Winona met me at the entry. "You look like you're ready to detonate."

"Something like that."

She guided me into the tranquil parlor. "Make way for the Eulogist," she said to the cat, sprawled out on the wingback chair.

"Eulogist? I'm more like a carnival barker and a poor one at that."

"Step right up!" She swept an arm into the air, "the clients are dying to hear you."

"Yeah, yeah, got it." I really didn't want to be cheered up. I had become comfortable with self-loathing. "So the dead business is your life's calling?"

"Thank Truss for that. He showed me my purpose."

"I'm detecting a theme here. The old man pulls people back from the edge and they become indentured servants?"

The question seemed to trigger a sudden mood change in Winona. The light dimmed in her eyes and her gaze slipped away to some place else.

"Winona," I said, "I didn't mean to pry. You don't have to . . ."

"After living on the streets of St. Paul for a year, I arrived at Truss Mortuary in the middle of a winter night, four years ago." She shook her head. "No idea how or why I arrived at his door, but I was pretty messed up. With Truss' help, I went into a treatment program. Thirty-two months later, just as unexpectedly as our first meeting, I again showed up at his door. Surprise!" She let out a hearty laugh. "Clear of drugs and alcohol and sporting an associate business degree."

Her honesty and straightforwardness about her struggles made me feel small. Here I was, whining about my life, when she had it far worse off and had pulled herself together.

Winona gave me a soft, knowing smile, and reached over to arrange a floral bouquet on the desk. She was saving me from feeling awkward.

"Truss seems to appreciate your skills," I said.

"I had to give up on anger or be devoured by it. And now, I'm trying my best."

Anger had become my full-time job. I wanted to commiserate on the subject with Winona, but I hadn't come to terms with an exit strategy from my personal failures, so I let it go.

"I'm worried about the mortuary's future," Winona said. "Truss has never turned anyone down for lack of money. We're everyone's last resource for funeral services. But, if we don't become a proper business, we will be out of business."

"I get this Jedi Master Yoda vibe from Truss, like he's not from here."

"Does that make me Princess Leia and you Luke Skywalker?" She bit on the easy setup and the mood lightened. "Truss is old school for sure, but he'll grow on you."

"I don't plan on making this a career. I'm just trying to get through a cash bind."

"Of course. You're a comedian."

"Comedy was for therapy. Technically, I'm a Philosophy Teaching Assistant."

"So you have an advanced degree, impressive."

"Right," I said dismissively, not wanting to go down that road.

Winona picked up a stack of note cards from the desk. "We're getting lots of interest for your services." She plucked a card from the file. "Josie Tschida, mistress of the deceased Frank Hammerschmidt, is in a tiff with the deceased's wife. She wants you to tell her side of the story."

"Tell her to call Jerry Springer. Next."

Winona selected another note card. "Timothy Norton, age fifty-seven. I had a nice chat with the executor of his estate. Mr. Norton died from zoonotic disease, an infectious disease transmitted between cats and people. The condition is rare, but not out of the realm of possibility since Mr. Norton kept company with over fifty cats. He was single and, by the executor's account, friendless. Mr. Norton left his entire estate to his cats. He also had requested a funeral service with his cats in attendance. The executor is looking for someone to address their loss."

"I don't do cat whispers. Have the executor call a veterinarian."

"There'll be catnip afterwards."

"No."

Winona thumbed through the note cards.

"Barring a life-threatening situation from attendees or animals," I said, "who pays the most?"

"I've got just the client." She extracted a card. "A big party, cele-bration of life sort of thing."

"So if this is such a fancy gathering, why are they tapping a stranger to do the eulogy?"

"A close friend of the deceased who was scheduled to offer the tribute called and said he was too distraught to go through with it. Needed someone to bail him out. He sounded desperate. Which usually means ready to pay."

"When's the tribute?"

"Tomorrow. Do you own a tuxedo?"

I rolled my eyes.

"Yeah, I know, silly question, but we have one if you don't and you'll need it for this assignment."

"More dead people's clothes?"

"Yes, but it will need some alteration."

I took in Winona's easy, carefree nature. What was it Truss said about her? She's an old soul, a good judge of people? But she must have missed the mark with me. I picked up the eulogy assignment card, shoved it in my pocket and stood to leave. "Look, I really appreciate all your help. I feel like I am getting back on my feet. Just hope I'm not messing things up too bad."

"Not at all, I think we'll make a great team," Winona hooked my arm and walked me toward the exit. We passed a room with open double doors and a grouping of caskets. I stopped to look. Winona picked up on my curiosity, stepped into the room and turned on the overhead lights. The walls were painted a soft yellow. An oriental rug sat on a polished wood floor.

Winona's cell phone chirped. "Sorry, I need to answer this. Take your time, you know the way out." She disappeared before I could register a response.

I wandered over to a cabinet that held a library of music. There were stacks of CDs and cassettes that featured light pop and rock classics, plus religious standards in multiple languages. Must be Winona's doing. I picked through the collection and considered what song I'd choose for my funeral. I settled on "Unsung Psalm" by Tracy Chapman. On top of the cabinet sat an old boom box and headset. I inserted the disc, slipped on the headset and listened to Chapman deliver her disarming lyrics on repentance in a subtle, bluesy voice. Next on my burial shopping list, a casket.

I thumped the side of a metal casket with a dull finish. It sounded cheap. Next to it sat a wood coffin that could have been high-end furniture. I ran my hand along the smooth finish and traced the finely crafted tongue-and-groove finger joints. A pillowy satin lined the inside bed. It practically called to me, as exhausted as I was. Hadn't Truss said that if you want to understand death, reflect on it from your deathbed? I put a hand inside the coffin. I guess it didn't get any more real than this. I leaned in with an elbow, kicked a leg up into the casket, and rotated into the bed. With my weight settled, I adjusted the pillow. I folded my arms in repose, took a deep breath, and tried to imagine my death.

Fewer friends than I anticipated attended the visitation. My mother paid more attention to my brother than the service, and the overwhelming scent of flowers made me nauseous. Who would speak of me, pay me tribute? Jack? No please not Jack, my mother's boyfriend, who I hated, addressed the gathering.

A clicking sound caught my attention. The house cat had deftly perched itself on top of the casket's lid.

"Scat!"

The cat sprung off the lid with more force than I thought possible. The lid slammed shut.

Surprised, I instinctively tried to sit up and hit my head on the inside of the latched casket. In the darkness, disoriented, I twisted and thrashed in panic. With my hands pinned to my chest, I continued to bang my head on the lid. I tried short choppy kicks with my feet. I screamed for help in the dead air. Sweat soaked my clothes. I tried rocking from side to side to knock the casket off the display pedestal, hoping to crack it open. The heavy wood vault didn't even wobble.

I started to hyperventilate with fear.

"Breathe, breathe," I said. "Please, Winona, come find me. Please, someone, help."

The cell phone was in my front pocket. If only I could reach it. Through a series of deep inhales, I inched an arm down my torso. I felt the rectangular outline of the phone through my trousers. I fingered the phone. A hint of illumination escaped from my pocket and momentarily calmed my panic. To my surprise, I heard the phone make an outbound call.

"You must be out of your mind. Stop harassing me."

The phone had automatically redialed my last call. Jessica's voice was surprisingly clear inside the coffin. "Jessica, please, please, please don't hang up, I'm in trouble."

"Yes, with me. Apparently, a restraining order is the only thing that will keep you away."

"No, real trouble. I need help, call 911. I'm locked in a coffin."

"If only it were true."

"I swear, I'm not kidding. I'm at Truss Mortuary on West Seventh Street. Call 911 or Winona at the mortuary. Get me out of here!"

"Who's Winona?"

"I'm sorry about our relationship, it was all me, I ruined it for us."

"Are you crying?"

"Please, I'm suffocating."

Jessica hung up. I had no idea whether she would follow through. I tapped the phone again, and it went dark. I felt like vomiting, but held off to keep from choking on my puke.

The coffin began rocking gently, almost like a cradle floating down river. The current sped up, the water rising. Along the bank, faceless people watched as I drifted past. A storm.

Wind-whipped waves. The drum of rain. A ship's horn. Pitching. Flooding. Coffin sinking.

Can't breathe. Bubbles rising, a foamy swirl.

A man in a yellow slicker. *Dad, I'm here, help me!*

Suddenly the lid opened. I sprung up like a jack-in-the-box.

"You really are in here," Winona said.

Jessica stood next to her and shook her head. "Idiot," she said, and disappeared.

CHAPTER 11

POSTCARD

I bolted out of the mortuary, shaking off the oxygen-starved hallucination. I dropped to my knees and inhaled in a fast bellows breath to the point of hyperventilating, then staggered to my car and headed home.

I almost died. I needed to be a better person, give thanks to all the people who supported me, be grateful for the gift of my wonderful daughter. I felt like crying.

On the way into the house, I snatched the mail from the box, dropped it on the coffee table, and collapsed onto the sofa. Little brother Ray had taken his dysfunction elsewhere, and I had the place to myself. I should have been pleased, but I hated silence. As a child, the loss of my father showed up in missing sounds: the jangle of pocket change, the clank of beer bottles, the whine of a saw, heavy footfalls, dinner table chatter, an infectious laugh. To keep the silence from hollowing me out, I filled the void with laughter. I created it, sought it, needed it. The comedic rush of laughter amplified the buzz in my head. I liked taking risks because when I was scared, the noise never stopped.

A flash of color on a postcard in the middle of the mail pile caught my attention. Addressed to Vince and Ray Locker, a colorful illustration depicted a palm-treed island and a fanciful pirate with his boot on a treasure chest. The caption read, Día de Sol. Sunny Day. I turned the card over. In neat cursive handwriting were the words Happy Birthday. My birthday was last week, Ray's was the following week. As usual, the sender left no message or indication of identity. I went to my room and brought out the stack of postcards from previous years and checked the handwriting for a match. Same, same, same.

I picked up the phone and dialed my mother, who lived in Florida with her boyfriend Jack. She escaped the wintry Minnesota scene a little over two years ago with no thoughts of returning. The only connection with us now was her precarious ownership in the dilapidated bungalow and the underachieving sons who clung to it like barnacles.

Jack answered the phone. "Well, if it isn't the professor," he said, in a two-packs a day voice.

Jack had bad knees, emphysema and a small pension and knew how to push my buttons. He had worked on a barge tow crew with dad. My mother somehow seemed to tolerate him, so I let the digs wash over.

"Good here, Jack. Put my mother on."

A moment later . . . "Vince dear, how's my baby Ray? Is he taking his meds? I do so worry about him."

"Hi, Mom."

"Do you have a cold? You sound stuffy."

"Just a little oxygen deprivation."

"Well, I guess it is allergy season there. You and your brother should come for a visit. Florida gets a bad reputation for being too hot in the summer, but Jack installed a new solar-powered air conditioner in our trailer home, practically feels like a refrigerator in here."

"Glad you're comfortable."

"We've also raised the trailer up four feet on cinder blocks just in case this global warming nonsense causes a flood. If nothing else, it's really improved our view."

View? They lived in a five-hundred-unit trailer park next to a highway.

But I was letting myself get distracted. "Got another postcard." I turned the card over. As in prior years, they were postmarked from various islands in the Caribbean.

"Junk mail, probably a vacation offer, toss it."

"Mom, don't play dumb. I've been receiving these cards ever since dad's disappearance. You know something."

"We have been through this. After your father drowned, we would get all sorts of letters and cards. Maybe it's from some crazy, automatic pen pal, or you're on a mailing list with a thousand other people. I don't know, but let it go."

I heard a muffled sound, and Jack was back. "You're upsetting your mother. If you've got a problem with your mail, call the postal inspector or get professional help. We don't want to hear any more of your Robinson Crusoe adventure theories about your old man." Jack hung up.

I tossed the postcard on the coffee table. The place suddenly seemed to swallow me up with the memories of my father and the dysfunction of my mother. I needed a nap.

A knock on the door woke me. I had fallen asleep on the sofa. Winona stood on the stoop holding a garment. "What, didn't get enough sleep in the casket?"

"Not funny."

"Tuxedos R Us." She handed me a garment bag and walked past me into the disastrous den of a home.

I tried to hurry ahead of her in a mad dash to do emergency house cleaning.

"Don't worry," she said, "I'm good as long as there's nothing here that will bite me,"

"So you talked to my ex?"

"Jessica. She's not much for chit chat on your account."

"I'm surprised she showed up so fast. But then again, she was probably more curious about you than rescuing me."

"Keep me out of it."

"I've tried calling and texting to thank her, but we're back to radio silence. I'm sure she's done bailing me out."

She nodded at the garment bag. "Try on the tux."

After a quick change, I came back to find Winona at the kitchen table thumbing through the postcards. "Quite a collection. I didn't know people sent postcards anymore. Total old school snail mail."

"Mystery cards, get one every year, addressed to my brother and me. No message, just 'Happy Birthday'." I arrayed several cards out on the coffee table for Winona to inspect. "I've been at a loss to make sense of it. My mother thinks someone's pranking me."

"Wish someone would prank me on my birthday. Closest I get to a greeting is a driver's license renewal notice."

"Maybe this is a clue to buried treasure." Winona tapped the photo of the pirate.

"Buried as in maybe something to do with my dad. I've been getting them ever since he disappeared from his barge tow boat on the Mississippi twenty years ago."

"Sorry." Winona touched the back of my hand and turned her attention to my outfit. "Hey, you look studly in that tux."

"I'd like to say you hemmed the crotch a little too tight, but that joke is beyond tired, like me," I said and flopped down on the couch next to her.

"Truss wanted me to let you know he's working his contact at the Bureau of Criminal Apprehension about O'Malley. His early impression is that she comes from a messy situation, something about an abusive boyfriend, drug related activity and other stuff. He's pushing to get some investigative traction into her situation. Said he'd keep you in the loop."

"It's strange how connected I feel toward O'Malley," I said. "A person I've never met, at least not alive. That ever happen to you?"

"With every client that comes in the door," Winona said, and gave my hand an affectionate squeeze.

CHAPTER 12

BROCK

I left the house, all tuxedoed-up for the eulogy assignment, and jumped into my rusted Corolla. I checked my phone and saw a text from Jessica. *Rather than wasting time on childish coffin pranks, start taking some responsibility. Your daughter wants to go to horse camp and she'll need cowboy boots, so pony up.*

I thought about texting her back, telling her to quit being a smartass. I was doing everything in my power to provide for Claire, including horse camp, so she should lay the hell off. But for once, I practiced some self-control and let it go. Besides, Jessica did come to my rescue at the mortuary. I owed her more than money now.

It started to rain. Since the wiper blades had long outlived their shelf life, they scraped across the windshield, scoring the glass in a broad eyebrow arch. I cautiously pulled into traffic, aware of the compromised visibility. I fiddled with the radio, only to be blasted with recycled old-school rock, and switched it off. The raindrops pinging off the car's roof like pebbles on tin were more in sync with my mood. I was in no hurry and had time to kill before the memorial assignment.

I parked in front of Shamrocks, my local pub haunt. Wearing a tux into a workingman's bar was a ready-made invitation to catch a ration of crap, but I had developed a high tolerance to insults.

The bartender took the opening shot as I straddled a barstool.

"Whoa, Jesus, look at you. Somebody's wedding? Or have you dipped into the prom pool?"

"Shut up, Rory." I rapped a knuckled fist on the bar. "Jack and a beer. Double Jack."

"Testy, are we?" Rory set the drinks down and backed away.

I slammed the double shot of Jack Daniels and chased it with the beer. I could feel the booze scorch my empty stomach. "Reload," I barked, and took a deep breath, allowing my shoulders to soften.

While Rory set me up again, I bowed my head and caught a grainy reflection of myself in the lacquered bar top. A distorted face, fresh off the road from chasing souls to hell and back, stared back at me. From my breast pocket, I dug out the business card Winona had given me for the eulogy assignment. *Come Midnight Productions, Wilson Brock, Producer.*

I set it on the bar. "Sorry, Ror. Just under a lot of pressure."

"Aren't we all?" Rory worked the draft handles like they were upside down cow udders delivering mother's milk. He slid the drinks down the bar rail and spotted the business card. "Hey, you know this guy?"

"No, never met him."

"Used to be one of the biggest names in the porn business. Won a bunch of awards. Not that I know much about that sort of stuff. Hey, is that what this get-up is about? You making a move from philosophy professor to porn stud?"

"Which one pays better?"

"Dunno, but porn sounds like more fun."

"Yeah, I am definitely getting screwed, but no, I'm delivering a eulogy for this Brock guy. Never met him, got no clue what to say."

"Brock used to stop in here once in a while with a few of his associates." Rory tapped the business card. "Word had it he got out of the business."

I left the bar and sat in my car. What the hell was I doing? I knew nothing of the deceased and in no way wanted anything to do with the porn industry. Sure, I had watched porn in college, everybody did. Sexual voyeurism could be indulged by category, preference, or at the lowest depths of sexual depravity. I now equated porn with losers, guys who either couldn't make it with chicks or were total jerk-offs in need of ever more perverse acts to get off. I thought about passing on the assignment.

Then I thought about horse camp.

"Damn, damn, damn!" I pounded the steering wheel.

Come Midnight Productions was located in St. Paul's Lower Town. The burnt-red brick building with neoclassical stone corbels was a former mercantile building that had been converted into artist quarters. A security system-controlled entry. I scrolled an electronic menu, found a CMP and hit the call button.

"Mr. Fleur?" I read out loud the name on the back of the card Winona had provided me.

"I see you."

I looked toward the overhead video camera. "I'm Vince, Mr. Truss from the…" I heard a click.

"It's open, ninth floor."

CHAPTER 13

WOODY

The freight elevator stuttered to a stop and dumped me into an unattended reception area. I had half expected to hear breathy, high-pitched staccato moans. The only sound came from the buzz of an overhead fluorescent light. It could have been any corporate office, except for the framed original art on the wall. Nudes, yes, but not the naughty girl next door, airbrushed works of Alberto Vargas. Rather, the women were rendered with an emphasis on reality in non-idealized proportions, and reflected a strong emotional charge reminiscent of some Matisse paintings I had seen in a museum. The name Wilson Brock and a date underscored each piece of art.

"In here."

I followed the voice through a door off the reception area, down a hallway into a galley kitchen. A slight man, no bigger than a jockey, bounced from foot to foot with a glass of wine in his hand.

"Look at you, handsome," Fleur said. "Just yummy in that tux." Fleur revealed a wide grin that stretched lips the color of a pencil eraser over tiny teeth. Then, as if he suddenly remembered the purpose of the occasion, he touched the back of his hand to his forehead. "I don't know if I can bear it, it's so hard," he said. "But this is about Brock." He regained his composure as if he'd flipped a switch and handed me a glass of wine. "To Brock."

"Mr. Fleur, considering Brock's profession, I'm really struggling with delivering an appropriate tribute."

"I know, I know, so last minute, you're a godsend. Let's get some air."

Fleur motioned me to follow along a hallway. He stopped at a double set of doors with an overhead sign marked, *Studio.* "Brock's in there." Fleur tapped the door with a pointer finger. "But I'm not ready." We continued down the hall to a large window which led to a fire escape. Fleur handed me his glass of wine, opened the bottom half of the double-hung window, stepped over the sash and out onto the black ironwork. I relayed the wine glasses over to Fleur and followed.

The rain had stopped. I leaned over the fire escape rail and surveyed the flat, tarred and gravel rooftops of the adjoining buildings— conical water tanks, ventilation housing, a rooftop garden and a homing pigeon loft. Somewhere in the distance, a chain clanged against a flagpole. I sniffed at the air and watched the dark clouds move out to the west, trapping the sunset turning the sky red and orange. The sepia tones made me think of old photos and lost souls.

"The man was a giant, an innovator, a true visual artist. Won three Woody Awards, the Oscars of Porn." Fleur spread both arms out wide as if to convey the recognition to the world at large. Then looked reflectively into his wineglass. "Brock hired me twenty years ago. I was homeless, couldn't find a job, considered ending my tortured life. I was the fluffer before the day of chemically induced hard-ons, back when you had to be a real stud to work this trade. Sometimes shoots would go six to eight hours, but I kept our horses in the race. Now, I'm . . . I was Brock's bookkeeper."

"Sorry for your loss."

"He cared too much. He collected broken people and outcasts and tried to find a place for them in a line of work most people find disgusting. But with Brock, you were family, and he always had you laughing. Before getting into the business, he was a starving artist. The only job he could get was swamping out bars and toilets. One of the joints was in a strip club. He started sketching the girls on his break. Sold a few pieces of his art to the customers, and word got around about his talent. He picked up some freelance magazine work, saved enough to buy a movie camera, and made it big."

"Sounds like Brock had some noble qualities, although it's a little tough for me to get past his smut peddling."

"The people who judged Brock ultimately ended up hanging him."

"I don't understand."

"Figuratively and with the help of a ten-foot rope and an eleven-story drop." Fleur patted the fire escape railing.

"Right here?" I looked over the rail to the alley below, lined with trash cans and dumpsters.

"He hung like a piñata for over an hour before anyone saw him."

"Geez." I shuddered. "But are you suggesting that because I'm not a fan of porn I contributed to Brock's death? Look, I never met him."

"Exactly." Fleur slipped through the fire escape window, scampered down the hall and pushed through the studio's double doors. I followed and felt immediately off balance on the studio's rolling, polished wood floor. Overhead, track lighting canisters hung at odd angles from large, rough cut wood beams. Camera heads and light umbrellas stood around lazily on tripods as though on break. Along a far wall hung an unfurled roll of silver background paper. In front of it sat a small stand with flowers on each side. On top of the stand, a crystal shaft, a not-so-veiled phallic symbol. The four-sided tapered form resembled a miniature replica of the Washington Monument. The set of ornamental peaches at the base of the shaft anchored the intention of the form.

Fleur stood in front of the glass urn and shuffled flowers in an already perfect arrangement. He picked a flower and magically produced a safety pin, stuck the boutonniere onto my lapel, and stepped back to admire his work.

A woman who had been preparing food in the galley kitchen stuck her head through the door. "The guests are arriving."

I felt my head about to detonate as I watched a swarm of young people enter the studio. Most of the men, twenty-something stud muffins who bore the overly relaxed look of male models, were casually dressed wearing skinny blue jeans, tight tee shirts, sport coats, and a three-day growth of facial hair. The women, scary vixens, arrived in compulsory little black dresses, stiletto heels, and carried little clutch purses. The moussed-up blown out hair, heavy eyeliner, caked-on makeup and glossy lips could not conceal the weathering of a life of hard knocks.

"Hey, look, there's Doctor Kim." Fleur waved his hand as if signaling for a life ring. He quickly introduced me and darted off to join the other guests. The doctor, wearing a conventional suit, had a round face and large dark button eyes which gave him the look of a plush toy.

"A bit frenetic, our Fleur," Dr. Kim laughed. "I'm Doctor Kim, head urologist at University Hospital, and you're the eulogist." Kim shook my hand to formalize the introduction.

"Seems pretty dedicated to Brock," I said, trying to keep an eye on Fleur.

"Yeah, he's been running interference for Brock for a long time. He's got a good heart and so did Brock. Quality resources are hard to come by."

"Sorry, I'm not tracking."

"We often use erotica in our fertility and sexual therapy clinic."

"Therapy?"

"We treat for erectile dysfunction, low libido, sexual addiction, fetishes, victimization and any number of other areas where people experience sexual problems. Our research and clinical work are funded by a significant government grant that includes custom sexual therapy videos produced by Brock's studio. Unfortunate." Doctor Kim glanced over at Brock's urn.

"Don't you feel a little out of sync dealing with someone who promotes sexual perversion while you repair it?"

"Brock made a clean break from the commercial porn business eight years ago. Put it behind him."

"Seems like a lot of bad karma to overcome."

"He did a good job of it. He became one of our biggest benefactors."

A host with a tray of finger food stopped and offered toothpick skewered shrimp. We passed.

"Fleur said Brock killed himself."

"Brock dealt with depression. He often talked about being branded by his early days in porn. It was a box from which there was no escape. He devoted his life to other people with blemished histories, offered them grace and forgiveness, but somehow he couldn't extend it to himself."

I fell silent and thought about what Fleur had suggested, about judging Brock based on a public chapter in his life without even knowing him. I supposed with my own bombed out comedic performance at Louie's club on YouTube, I was also being branded as a loser. Not that I disagreed.

Fleur clinked a wine glass with a spoon to quiet the gathering. He stood in front of Brock's memorial table and waved for me to come forward. I felt off balance, as if being pitched on the high seas as I weaved my way through the guests. Someone had cut the lights in the back of the room so that the overhead spots focused on the memorial table and me. The only sound I could hear was the blood pounding in my ears. The guests looked on expectantly.

What did these people want to hear? That Brock was a saintly figure that plucked miscreants from aimless destitution and gave them a bright future in the promising pornography business? Or a list of his accomplishments, industry awards, and AIDS donations? Or a testimonial from a twisted, sick soul who found sexual healing through his erotic work for Dr. Kim? Anything except that Brock, like everyone else, was a hapless scamp, spinning through the life cycle, born of dirt, rolled in muck and returned to dust.

What did Truss say? Insulate them from death, give them what they want to hear.

An energetic overhead arm waved from the back of the room and caught my attention. Toby? God, no. My comedy agent. What the hell was he doing here?

I brought my attention to the crystalized shaft and heard myself speak. I was looking forward to hearing what I had to say.

"I didn't know Brock, but from the looks of this thoughtful memorial tribute, I'd say he led a life well *urned*."

A restrained chuckle or two escaped from the gathering. That gave me my tone.

"Met some of Brock's friends tonight. Doc Kim told me Brock attended one of his sex therapy counseling sessions. The doc drew two circles and said, 'Brock, what do you see?' Brock said, 'Sex.' So, the doc draws telephone poles. 'Brock, what do you see?' 'Sex.' The doctor drew a star. 'Sex.' Doc says to Brock. 'You're obsessed with sex!' Brock replied, 'Me? You're the one drawing all the dirty pictures!'"

"Heard that one before," a voice shot out from the back of the room.

"Hey, if you're going to kill the clown, go for the juggler." I pointed playfully at Fleur. "He hired me."

Fleur picked up on the impromptu casting, and in a dramatic gesture, ran his finger under his throat.

"Done." I smiled to keep the reins on the gathering and then paused for a tempo change. "We all know Brock's passion in life was his art and filmmaking, and he had a difficult time in his final days. Wouldn't it be great if we could live the movie of our life in reverse? The opening scene has Brock swaying from a fire escape. He comes to life and experiences the good work he's done helping people cope with their sexual issues, yet feels the ever-present shadow of those who won't release him from his earlier days, a time when he did what he had to do to survive and helped ease the burden of friends on hard times. As he gets younger, he discovers his intuitive, artistic talents, he basks in the thrill of possibilities and lives pain-free days, playing. He runs into the comfort of a mother's arms, floats in the warmth and heartbeat of the womb, and finally on his last day he's snuffed out by an orgasm."

The gathering erupted in a mix of horselaughs and cheers.

"Yeah, I think Brock would have liked that." Fleur stepped forward, beaming from ear to ear, and handed me a glass of wine.

I raised my glass. "To Brock."

Fleur raised his. "And orgasms."

I walked to the back of the room in the wake of appreciative applause. In my tux, I stood like a brideless groom in a reception line while guests bestowed upon me good-natured slaps on the arm and stuffed my pockets with cash. Fleur had fired up AC/DC's "Highway To Hell" so loud the floors vibrated.

At the first opportunity, I bolted out of the studio. The raging chorus followed me down the elevator. I stripped off the tie and pushed out of the building into the heavy night air.

CHAPTER 14

LOST BOYS

A block away from Brock's event, I heard my name, "Vince."

I stopped and looked at a chubby little guy, running after me with sweat dripping from his red flush face—Toby.

Toby worked for the Pioneer Press, both print and online editions. He tracked the local entertainment scene under the banner heading, 'What's Hot'. The content featured insightful artist profiles, performance reviews, and off beat happenings. On the side, he booked talent. In my case, it meant local comedy clubs and one-night gigs at fundraisers, corporate events, private parties, bowling alleys, pizza parlors, dive bars, senior homes and restaurants—basically any venue he could squeeze for a hundred and fifty bucks from within a five-state area.

"What the hell were you doing crashing Brock's tribute? Stalking me because I'm not returning your calls? Come to see how far I've fallen since bombing out of the LaughCom Contest? Maybe looking for a little porn action?"

"Two out of three. Not bad."

"Get out of my face." I kept walking but couldn't shake Toby.

"Nice eulogy, you killed it." Toby panted and leaned on me. "Give me ten minutes, please, plus I'll buy you a drink."

I reluctantly let him steer me down the street to the nearest bar. A neon sign that read 'Lost Boys' twitched above the entry. In Toby, I found someone who liked to pound back the drinks as much as I did. We ordered doubles.

"Almost missed it," Toby said. "Saw your name listed in the Brock obit notice."

"So you troll death notices?"

"Before I worked for the newspaper's entertainment section, I posted obituaries. Now I'm in the habit of checking them out, on the lookout for quirky listings. One of my favorites was a braggart who claimed he attracted more women than a Macy's shoe sale. Then there's the 'o-bitch-uary' category submitted by disgruntled relatives. I've posted a few of the more creative notices on my blog."

"And now you're going to post me on your site—'Busted comedian now bottom feeding off the dead.'"

"Hey, lighten up on both of us. I think you're onto something with the comedic eulogy. Baby boomers are posed to drop at a rate of one every thirty-five seconds, which is a huge, ready-made market. They'll die for a humorous tribute."

"The only thing I'm on is Ritalin."

"Funny." Toby jiggled the ice in his glass as if it were a maraca.

"Life is funny—loss, joy, sickness, broken relationships, failure, success, all the stuff that makes us relatable, but most people are relegated to having their lives reduced to a list."

"Lists are efficient."

"Hanging around Truss Mortuary I hear people itemizing their deceased—Carleton grad, nurse, garden clubber, avid reader, cat lover, knitter, bowler. If the deceased is lucky, someone might throw in an anecdote. 'No one could spot a bargain like Joan, a hell of a bridge player, her rhubarb pie was to die for.' Then the hyperbole will follow. 'She's in a better place', nonsense, not unless someone's been there. 'She's looking down on us.' What, Joan stands in judgment? But at least you won't be waked, visited or viewed, as in days of old. The new-age lexicon is a 'celebration of life'."

Toby signaled for refills. "Or how about the party of a lifetime?"

"Yep, but unless Uncle Harold left enough for everyone to party in Cancun, skip the pretense. On the other hand, if everyone's thrilled Uncle Harold's dead, party on. Some relative or friend will insist on a 'send off'. A useless euphemism, as no one's going anywhere unless their ashes are loaded into a shotgun shell or floated down a river on a burning Viking ship. No one will ever say she's dead, it's she 'passed', as if we all got together and scored her life a C plus, not great but good enough. Or 'passed' as in he just blew by me on the highway in a chariot. Or he's 'past,' as in gone, perhaps more appropriate."

"And your surprised people avoid death?" Toby held his drink mid-air. "When the time comes, they don't know how to address the great mystery."

"Neither do I. I'm just making it up as I go."

"Guess what? So is everyone else," Toby sprayed his words at me. "If one's predisposed to leaving the sum of his or her life up to 'come what may,' and most people are, be careful what you wish for. You can count on the death service being cobbled together by a nervous, grief-stricken, out of their element amateur. Or perhaps they'll do some planning and cede the capstone of their lives to a boilerplate proselytizing rant from some clergy whose mission is to recruit souls rather than reveal yours."

The pulsating beat of dance music suddenly erupted and two men moved off the bar and hit the dance floor. One stripped off his shirt as the pair contorted and mirrored each other's movements.

Toby looked at me. "Hey, not the way I roll."

"Toby, what do you want?"

"You've got a gift for capsulizing people's lives and everyone has a story. Even everyday folks whose lives have been lost in the stampede to nowhere and have fallen over the edge of time."

"I don't do fiction."

"All eulogies are fiction to some degree. Every time we try to recall something about someone else, we're rewriting the story, warping the replay and details to fit our own perceptions. Family members seldom can agree on the details of past events. The revisions never stop so there are no final versions."

"I can't make stuff up about people and be credible."

"You don't have to. Let's say Uncle Harold's a back-stabbing, pussy chasing drunk. He's radioactive. No one will touch him. But I bet you could find fifteen minutes of humor and possibly redemption in everyone's life."

"You give me way more credit than I deserve. You saw how I stunk up the place at the LaughCom Contest. Not only did I bring the house down, figuratively, but I'm scared out of my mind Louie's going to retaliate by burning my house down, literally."

"Your meltdown was actually kind of funny in a Rodney Dangerfield, self-pitying sort of way, and besides, Louie's a pig who operated a rigged game. His heart attack was as close to poetic justice as it gets."

"Wait, what? Heart attack? When? Where? Is he alive?"

"Thought you knew. The night you bombed out at his club, he chased after you and blew a gasket. Someone found him on the sidewalk and hauled him to the hospital. He's still alive, but he's got more pressing issues at the moment than retaliation."

I felt a strange sense of guilt mixed in with relief. I wondered if I should send Louie a get-well card, or would that be working against my self-interest? I did what I often did when I was confused and ordered another round of drinks.

A thirty-something man with a shaved head, a neck tattoo, and side-zippered, silver ankle boots, approached our table and touched my shoulder, "Hey, dimples, let's dance."

"No thanks, we're kinda in the middle of something here."

He looked at Toby, then back to me. "When you're done with this Quasimodo cock-blocker, I'll be waiting."

After he left, Toby shrugged. "I've been called worse."

"Yeah, you should put it on your business cards." I waved off the intrusion. "It's late, I'm exhausted. If there's a point to be had in any of this, get to it."

"The point is..." Toby leaned in and lowered his voice as if to convey confidentiality. "One-off eulogies are a slow train to nowhere, but there's a way we can monetize this thing—scale it up, make some real dough."

"What's with the 'we'? You trying to cut in on my gold mine eulogy action?"

"Tell me more about this Truss Mortuary you work for."

I woke up the next morning to a crushing headache. For a little guy, Toby could really pound the drinks. From the sick anise and licorice taste in my mouth, I must have been doing Jager-bombs.

I checked my phone and saw a message from my little brother Ray. He had sent a link to a newspaper article written by Toby. Through blurred vision I read, 'Dead end comedian finds life in death tributes... Vince Locker sent off the deceased porn king, Wilson Brock, in a hilarious *riff*...'

"Nooooooo! I'm going to kill him!"

I was so absorbed in my rage that I flinched when my phone buzzed.

"They're tearing the Mortuary apart," Winona said, in a panic. "Can you please come over? I need somebody to keep me from killing Dalton."

CHAPTER 15

INSPECTION

As I approached the mortuary, there appeared to be a utility project underway. Pickup trucks and plumbing and electrical vans with the Capitol City logo on the side door panels lined the street. Inside the building, men in hard hats and tool belts milled about. A skinny guy topped in a camouflage ball cap fumbled with a flashlight in an open electrical panel. Another worker, with an unlit cigar stuck in the corner of his mouth, ran a cable down a drainpipe. I caught sight of Winona in panic mode.

"Thank you for coming, I just needed someone sane to lean on." She turned her attention to a passing worker. "You have no right to be here. Who's in charge?"

The worker stuck out a thumb in the direction of the basement. "Murph, the Senior Code Inspector."

Winona headed down the stairs and I followed at a safe distance. Musty, humid air rose to meet me. Low hanging pipes wrapped in asbestos bandages ran at twisted angles along the ceiling. The basement had a series of wooden stalls, each with a table and a corded, bare light bulb overhead. I recalled many decades ago, during the winter months, mortuaries kept bodies in these corrals until the soil thawed. The thick stone foundation walls provided natural refrigeration and a measure of preservation until burial.

"Inspector, you down here?" Winona shouted into the recesses of the basement's dark chambers.

"Be right there." The inspector appeared with a clipboard; head bowed under the low ceiling. "Don't see many of those monsters anymore." He pointed toward a large furnace. "Converted from coal to oil, and now natural gas. Practically the entire history of mechanical heat contained in that iron maiden."

"What are you doing here? Did you clear this with Truss?"

"One question at a time, lady. I don't multitask well, messes with my blood pressure. Got a complaint about a code violation and we were told to send in the troops. Mr. Truss let us in."

"So there's a problem?"

"Here's what I got so far." The inspector scanned a clipboard. "The plumbing needs updated waste interceptor traps, the electrical service needs to be replaced with a 220-circuit breaker panel, and the asbestos pipe insulation has got to go. But, like I said, I don't have the entire work up."

"Holy shit! Who put you up to this, that scumbag Dalton from Reliance?"

"I have no idea who that is. I just go where I'm told."

Winona retreated into the parlor. I followed. Her face tightened as if she had a toothache. "That buzzard Dalton's won."

"What? How?"

"Asbestos, plumbing traps, electrical, we're talking tens of thousands of dollars we don't have."

"You mean you can't process your clients because of the danger they'll be exposed to from asbestos? Do they know what you do here?"

"O'Malley is the only client in the house. But no pressure there. The only person who seems to have an interest in her is that scavenger Dalton."

O'Malley, what was it with her? She was like a song stuck in my head. "Where's Truss?"

"He went to visit the mayor. Truss Mortuary has buried everyone in his family since they came over from Ireland. Hopefully, he can get him to cut us some slack with these trumped up code violations."

The cat appeared and brushed its tail against my leg. I pointed to the feline, recalling its role in the casket lockdown. "So the doctor says to the cat, 'Bad news, it's curiosity.'"

She snickered, then tilted her head toward me. "You make me laugh, even when I want to cry."

"Mental stability is not exactly my strong suit. I tried to make a living as a comedian."

"You're stronger than you give yourself credit for. I'm just sorry for involving you in all this. I was hopeful our business relationship would work out."

I patted Winona on the hand.

"I'm going to pay Dalton a visit, show him two can play this game," Winona asserted. "It would be great if you can come with me."

Whatever she had in mind, it sounded like trouble. "Think I'll sit this one out."

Winona let my declaration hang in the air as a small smile played on her face. "So the Lone Ranger and Tonto are riding into town when they come across the local bar. The Lone Ranger suggests they pop in for a beer. The bartender says, 'Sorry, but we don't allow Apaches in here.' Tonto, being a good friend, agrees to wait outside with their horses.

"The Lone Ranger has a beer, chats away, gets bought another beer, then another. Outside, Tonto is feeling the cold and starts jogging around in circles to keep warm. By this time, the Lone Ranger is on his fourth beer when a cowboy walks in and shouts, 'Is there someone in here called the Lone Ranger?' The Lone Ranger raises his hand. And the cowboy says, 'You've left your injun running.'"

I let out a courtesy laugh. "You realize I could never tell that joke? It's racist when I do it."

"What can I say, I just love Lone Ranger jokes." Her face held the mischief of a nine-year-old. "So, you coming with me, Kemosabe?"

Loyalty aside, I made a quick assessment and realized I had a vested interest in supporting Truss Mortuary and stopping Dalton. An enemy of my cash flow was an enemy of mine. "Hi-yo Silver, away."

CHAPTER 16

RELIANCE

We waited in the Reliance Funeral Home headquarters parking lot for Dalton to show up. His car wouldn't be hard to spot—a yellow Porsche with *Mortuss* on the license plate.

Winona wanted to catch him by surprise. "I want Dalton unprepared and off-balance for the smack down I intend to give him. Just like he did to us."

I had no idea what Winona had in mind, but it didn't sound like she was on a goodwill mission. I didn't know much about Reliance other than their bullying takeover tactics aimed at Truss Mortuary and their TV ads. Reliance hammered the airwaves with past prime celebrities, pitching pre-paid burial plans and some kind of life insurance offer. But now that I'd had a chance to think about it, getting arrested didn't sound like a reasonable business plan. "You're sure this is a good idea?"

"Our building may not be up to code, but they're outright crooked."

Smarmy I could buy, but crooked? "How so?"

"Reliance's pre-pay funeral commercials are a bait and switch scam at best," Winona said. "The pre-paid funeral service is supposed to allow people to set their affairs in order and offer peace of mind. In reality, Reliance hopes most of their clients lose their minds and forget about the pre-paid funeral voucher that fell behind the dresser or that the survivors are just unaware of the transaction."

"So Reliance just keeps the money?"

"Yep. But even if they have to perform, the Reliance pre-pay plan only provides for the barest of services, a ripe opportunity to upsell grieving survivors. 'You know, Aunt Shirley always put the needs of others before her own. That's why the pre-paid service is so frugal. Wouldn't it be nice to see Aunt Shirley afforded something special? A fitting tribute for all she's done for everyone around her. May I suggest a modest upgrade to the solid rosewood casket?'"

I couldn't help but laugh.

"Once a schemer, always a schemer. If it wasn't for his mother, Governor Wannabe, he'd be in jail."

"For what?"

"Madelyn Dalton runs a sleazy scrap metal business that's been in her family forever. She wanted something more respectable for her precious son, specifically a law degree. After law school, mommy found her dimwit son a job at a firm that did estate planning, wills and stuff. Hardly a year into it, he was charged with siphoning funds from inheritance trust accounts. Should have gone to jail, but mommy came to the rescue. He agreed to disbarment and mom covered the restitution."

"The mortuary business sure seems like a strange choice for someone who has violated the public trust."

"Taking advantage of vulnerable people in the shadow of death? It's his wheelhouse."

"How do you know all this?"

"From Truss. Nothing related to death gets by him in this town."

I scanned the parking lot and looked at my watch. "Doesn't look like Dalton's going to show up. Suggest we visit another time."

"Screw it." Winona opened the car door. "Let's check out Dalton's house of scams."

We went in. The soothing colors and natural wood accents gave Reliance's headquarters the feel of a new age spa. The traditional parlor and chapel had been rebranded as a memorial showroom and event center. Despite its attempt to project dignity, the place still gave off a used car showroom vibe.

The receptionist asked if we needed assistance.

"We're looking for Ross Dalton," Winona said.

"Do you have an appointment?"

"No, we'll wait."

Winona sat in a visitor's chair and scrolled through her phone messages. I drifted into the memorial showroom and wandered around the video displays. It seemed technology had penetrated the world of the dead. A headstone with a QR code connected visitors to an internet site with a perpetual video recording of the deceased. A pyrotechnic display featured Roman candles, fountains and rocket flares, all with the ability to launch granular remains into the starry night. Biodegradable floatation devices in the shape of fish provided an opportunity for a watery send off. Decorator urns molded in the shape of a baby shoe, heart, pistol, extended middle finger and a giant pepper mill lined the display shelves. I spun the little crank on a device that reminded me of a fertilizer spreader used to broadcast cremation remains neatly and evenly. In an adjoining room, caskets were aligned like beached whales. I thought I'd never want to see another one after the narrow escape at Truss'. However, a casket with a flat gray metal finish and a skull and crossbones graphic caught my attention. It sat on a trailer frame with two wheels on one end and hitch tongue on the other. Perfect for hauling a dead buddy out to Sturgis.

I stepped back into the reception area where Winona pressed the receptionist to see if there was an update on Dalton's arrival.

"Sorry, nothing. Would you like to leave a message for Mr. Dalton?"

"You can tell Dalton that Truss Mortuary will not surrender to his harassment and we plan to make public his scam death insurance operation."

"I have no idea what you're referring to," the receptionist said a little too quickly, "but if you'll excuse me for a moment." She turned on her heels and disappeared into an office.

"She's probably calling the police to arrest us for trespassing," I said, just to brighten things up.

"Nah. That would be bad press, and that's the last thing the Dalton name needs right now."

The receptionist returned and handed Winona a card. "Mr. Dalton is with his mother. As you probably know, she's running for Governor and is very sensitive to any issues that involve the family name, legal matters or the press. They're at a political event and have requested that you join them there immediately."

CHAPTER 17

DEAD POOL

I had never been to a political fundraiser before, especially one held at a gun range.

The directions put us on a path parallel to the meandering Minnesota River, southwest of the Twin Cities near Shakopee. On the way, I asked Winona to stop at a convenience store to pick up some Maalox. The thought of meeting Madelyn Dalton was doing things to my stomach. I washed the chalky tablets down with a gulp of scorched coffee and gently suggested we skip the visit with Dalton's mother. Winona pushed on.

I held up a brochure I picked up from our visit to Reliance Funeral Homes. "What's a Viatical Settlement? I missed the Latin class."

"It's a life insurance rip-off. Reliance buys existing life insurance policies from cash-needy folks and pays them off at a lowball rate in relation to the policy's full benefit. They then pick up the ongoing premiums and wait for the insured to die so they can rake in the total payout value."

"So . . . a Viatical Settlement occurs when Reliance bets on someone dying sooner rather than later so they get the policy benefit without having to make a lot of premium payments?"

"Yep, they're running a death casino."

"I'm still a little fuzzy on the concept."

"Kind of like the Dead Pool Contest. You familiar with it?"

"Not really."

"The fastest growing pastime in America," Winona laughed. "It's like one of those fantasy sports games. You pay a contest entry fee and predict individuals whom you think will die in the next twelve months. The person with the highest score at the end of the contest period is declared the winner. I'm a regular player. Pretty good at it."

I shuddered and leaned into the passenger door. "Keep me off your list."

"No offense." She shot me a wink. "But you have to be a celebrity to qualify."

"So you load your list up with ninety-year-old movie stars and death row inmates. Doesn't seem to be much of a challenge."

"You get twenty picks and earn points for each person on your list who dies during the contest period. Points are calculated by subtracting the deceased's age from one hundred. So loading up with all old-timers is not going to put you in the lead. You've got to take some risk. Twenty-seven-year-old rock stars are a sweet spot—think Joplin, Morrison, Hendrix, Cobain and Winehouse. Oh, and you can't include people who are condemned to die twelve months before the start of the game. There are lots of other rules, too, like conjoined twins only count as one death. Suicides are awarded bonus points, Anthony Bourdain scored big. Dead Pool Contest members are also prohibited from harming, murdering, or in any manner affecting the general health or well-being of any celebrity on their list."

"It does sound like what Dalton is up to. My guess, Dalton doesn't play by the rules."

"He's ruthless," Winona tightened her grip on the steering wheel. "It's not just old people he preys upon. Reliance also encourages young people with life insurance to cash in. They position the settlement as a pawnshop loan. Should the insured want to reclaim the policy, they have to pay back the premiums, plus loan shark interest. But very few can afford to buy the policy back so Dalton's left betting on an early death."

"Seems like a long shot."

"Nothing I can prove but..." Winona cocked her head. "I wouldn't put it past Dalton to accelerate the death of those poor suckers who sold Reliance their life insurance policies."

"That's a scary thought."

"We're here." Winona handed me a tissue and pointed at the chalk on the corners of my mouth.

CHAPTER 18

TANKED

The political event, held on a private, hundred-acre estate with the feel of a country club, sounded like a war zone. Prominent *Dalton for Governor* signs with the tag line, *Stomp on Crime,* were posted about. I thought about Madelyn Dalton's son Ross, not exactly a family values poster child. But then most politicians had someone in their family they found to be a political liability. President Obama had his uncle, Onyango Obama. Picked up for drunk driving and barely able to walk, he told the cops to call the White House, because he had presidential privilege.

An event security person checked the guest list and directed us to the hospitality tent. Potbellied white guys in shoulder padded shooting vests, swilled cocktails, and gathered ammo. Madelyn Dalton seemed to have left no stone unturned in her run for governor. What better way to grease the skids with bigwig conservative contributors than to appeal to their second amendment privilege with a campaign shooting event? A server told me the price of admission was a ten thousand dollar contribution.

Guests selected a weapon of choice—muzzle-loader, fully automatic AK 47, or grenade launcher and toted it off to the downfield range to fire away. Much like a county fair shooting gallery, a conveyor featured an array of familiar targets—Michael Moore, Sylvester Stallone, and Nancy Pelosi.

An air of excitement gripped the gathering as an earth shaking 68-

ton, M1 Abrams Tank rumbled onto the scene. Its 105 mm gun swiveled like a magic wand and cast a spell over the gathering. Attendees immediately queued up to jump inside the armored cabin. The guests yelped like frat boys as they fired the big tank gun and the roof mounted 7.62-mm MGs machine gun at a group of junker cars parked down range. Gunpowder and dust turned the sunlight into a yellow-green haze, more like dusk than late morning. If there was ever a doubt as to whether the hefty campaign contribution was worth it, the tank put the question to rest.

"Come with me." A big athletic guy tapped me on the shoulder. He wore a Navy SEAL hog's tooth necklace on a green cord. I knew this because my dad had once rescued a SEAL at sea, who thanked him with the necklace. I surmised this guy's duties went beyond escorting guests.

He directed us away from the tent, a safe distance from the contributors, to where Madelyn and Ross Dalton stood.

"I'll take it from here, Tommy." Madelyn waved him away and turned her attention to us. "What's this about going to the press?"

I had an immediate appreciation for Madelyn's beauty. At fifty-two, she looked thirty-nine and remained fearlessly attractive. She wore a V-neck cotton sweater under a form-fitting Beretta shooting vest with ammo pockets, tight cropped white jeans, and a gold ankle bracelet above platform shoes. Sunglasses sat pillowed in her hair of blended shades of blond. Gold bangles hung from her wrist above elegant hands, long fingers and manicured clear nails.

Winona stepped up to Madelyn. "I just thought the public would like to know that mommy's boy is up to no good again."

Dalton made an aggressive move toward Winona. I stepped in between them, despite my conspicuous lack of firearms. "Back off!"

"Son," Madelyn said, "I'll handle this."

Dalton dutifully stepped back.

"Whatever the beef is between you all," Madelyn said, "I want it stopped right here and now."

"Your son has been harassing Truss Mortuary," Winona said, "trying to shut us down, disrupting our business."

Madelyn flicked her bangled wrist to dismiss the claim. "He's strong-armed every funeral home in town. That's just business."

"And are insurance schemes just part of the business? Suggest you check the Better Business Bureau complaints, mostly from seniors, who, as you know, are reliable voters."

"That's a defaming lie," Dalton said. "I'll sue you and Truss Mortuary for . . . for . . ."

"What the hell's going on?" Momma had turned on her darling boy with the look I imagine tigers gave before they ate their young.

"It is all legal." Dalton looked nervously down range. "Trust me on this one,"

"Don't even go there with me, Ross. You better start making good on whatever you're selling or the Better Business Bureau will be the least of your worries. And lay off Truss Mortuary. Old man Truss has buried every major politician since forever. Believe me, he literally knows where all the bodies are buried."

"Yeah, yeah," Dalton shrugged, like a little boy who had been scolded in front of the class.

Madelyn turned her attention toward us. "I suggest you listen carefully to what's really going on here. You've got a beef with my son over his aggressive business practices. So to save your ass, you are now attempting to extort me with a story that will harm my political campaign." She waved an arm toward the firing range. "If you get in the way of my election, the only life insurance policy you'll need to be concerned about is your own. Now get out of here and pick up a yard sign on your way out."

We retreated to the hammering sound of big guns.

CHAPTER 19

PRANK

On the silent drive back from the ass-kicking Madelyn Dalton gave us, Winona spotted a funeral procession. The hearse displayed a Reliance Funeral Home logo.

"They're going to Resurrection Cemetery," Winona said, and sped ahead.

I knew we should leave well enough alone. Why poke a hornet's nest? But Winona was on a mission.

We arrived ahead of the procession and spotted a Reliance burial crew scurrying about in preparation for an interment ceremony.

"Where's the catering wagon? Looks like they're running a damn picnic up there." Winona opened the car door and yanked on my sleeve. "Come on, let's see how the rich get buried."

The cemetery's imposing polished granite stones carved into crosses, tablets and angels reminded me of the hoodoos, tall tapered rock spires in Bryce Canyon. But unlike hoodoos that are a wonder of nature and impermanence, these machine shaped rock memorials represented a last ditch, frivolous effort at immortality. A pursuit of the legacy crowd—get your name on something, a building, a sponsorship, a plaque, or a park bench, to extend your perceived importance.

The self-talk rant felt intellectually right. But emotionally I wished there were a touchstone for my father. Something other than an empty grave and a flat, grass covered metal marker.

To my surprise, the Reliance attendants scarcely noticed us as they busied themselves with the setup. Workers covered the freshly disturbed soil with turf carpet and neatly arrayed flowers, and set white folding chairs in a semi-circle in front of the burial platform. A trio of string musicians arrived and tuned their instruments.

I hung back at a safe distance and watched Winona approach the burial platform. As she bent down to admire the flowers, it appeared as though she dropped something into the burial vault. Then in a voice that drew everyone's attention, she emitted a chattering—tsik, tsik tsik, chrrrrrrr, siew siew siew.

"Allergies" she said to a passing attendant and forced a sneeze as she retreated from the platform.

"What was that all about?" I asked.

"Patience, Grasshopper," Winona said, her attention drawn to the Reliance funeral procession winding its way through the cemetery. A white hearse, followed by three white town cars with their headlights on, led a convoy of mourners. "The show is about to start," she said, and motioned me to the outer edge of the service.

I watched as six pallbearers rolled the casket onto the burial platform. Winona's focus seemed drawn to the surrounding oak trees and their luscious canopy that arched over the gravesite. Music gently played as mourners took their seats.

A clergyman in a colorful cassock raised his hand. "Dearly beloved friends and family gathered here today." He turned his attention to the widow in the front row. "And to Doris, Hubert's beloved wife, we are gathered to pay a final tribute . . ." The clergyman stopped, turned an ear toward the casket for a moment, then continued. "As you know, Hubert . . ." The clergyman again halted, listened. "Hubert . . ."

"Stop, I heard it, listen, scratching!" The widow shouted. "It's coming from inside." She jumped up from her chair and tried to pry the casket open. "He's alive! Get him out!"

The gathering gasped.

A Reliance attendant put a bear hug around the widow and pulled her away from the platform.

"This is murder," she cried. "Someone, help!"

Another attendant removed several pots of flowers at the base of the burial platform and peered into the vault. Out of the dark cavern, a screech erupted, followed by a flying fur ball. The attendant screamed, fell over backwards and attempted to swat the squirrel away. The startled squirrel ran through the legs of the visitors, up onto a chair, and launched itself on to a nearby oak tree. It scampered to an overhead branch and squawked at the gathering below.

The widow collapsed.

"Call an ambulance," A Reliance attendant shouted as he tended to her.

The widow sat up and pushed the attendant away. "I'm all right, leave me alone."

Winona grabbed my arm and led me a safe distance away from the service. We sat on the lawn and laughed to the point of hyperventilation.

"Somehow, I think you had something to do with that fiasco," I said.

"Old Indian trick. Snickers bar and squirrel mating call."

"You realize you're going to hell."

"It's worth it."

The hijacking of the Reliance funeral had the markings of a juvenile prank, but I understood where Winona was coming from. I also felt sorry for the widow and knew without a doubt, as a co-conspirator, this stunt would come back to bite me in the ass. I was the kid who always got caught.

CHAPTER 20

GLITCH

As Winona and I drove back to Truss Mortuary, I toyed with an idea. Group eulogies. Actually, it was mostly Toby's idea. It was the kind of harebrained scheme hatched after a couple of drinks, the plan no one takes seriously or even remembers the next day. I laughed it off when I first heard the concept.

Toby had persisted. He claimed, from his obit experience at the newspaper, that there were troves of people who, for one reason or another, never found closure over a deceased relative or friend. Never gave them a proper life tribute. The survivors were too emotionally crushed or in the middle of a family dispute over estate issues. But more often than not, it was just too much effort to pull a service together. And the survivors were often left with a sense of guilt. Without a memorial service, the remains, held in urns, often became household fixtures—bookends or doorstops. A group event would be both a productive and uplifting activity among like-minded people. As in, a local radio station marrying a hundred couples in one shot at a shopping center or two thousand people running naked through a public park. Toby had also pointed out it's not like people were knocking down my door for onstage comedy gigs.

Now sober, I realized that to pull such an event off, it would need credibility and the backing of an entity such as Truss Mortuary. I felt certain Truss would consider a group eulogy a huckster play operating without regard to respectable norms. But it was worth a shot. I thought about hitting Winona with it first, but I wasn't sure I'd get her on my side, either.

"Come in." Truss waved us into the parlor. "I've got good news. Agent Kirchner from the BCA has agreed to take on the O'Malley case. I suspected a muddied ME report related to an indigent wouldn't get any serious attention, but the old coroner in me wouldn't let it go. It went to the sacred bond that exists between homicide victims and the coroners who speak for them."

Thankfully, some justice. "When do you think we'll hear something from Agent Kirchner?"

"He's doing some background digging. Hopefully, before we bury the poor woman. Now, what was it you wanted to see me about?"

"I've got my own good news." Winona took a seat in a floral-patterned wingback chair. "I think I've got Dalton to back off."

"How'd you do that?"

"I told his Mommy on him."

Truss dropped back in his seat. "If anybody can reel him in, it's Madelyn Dalton. She's one tough woman. Now, if we can just get the building code citations fixed."

I saw an opening. "I've got an idea." I pitched the group eulogy concept. Winona picked right up on it, and to my surprise, Truss gave it his approval.

"Just one thing, though," he said. "The service should be open to all and free of charge. We can't be seen to profit directly from it."

I remembered people stuffing cash into my pockets. "How about donations?"

"I would be comfortable with contributions. Exercising gratitude and generosity in the presence of grief helps with closure."

I considered Truss' terms a potential deal killer. The cost to procure and publicize the event was beyond chump change. But if I could deliver an entertaining performance, the donation angle held upside potential.

I just hoped that Toby, the financial backer, was willing to take the gamble.

CHAPTER 21

URNED

Toby, Winona and I noodled over Truss' constraint of free admittance and the donation angle. Toby considered it risky play, especially if we got a low turnout. We needed a gambit to amp up the attendance. After a lot of brainstorming, Winona suggested we offer each attendee a complementary mini memorial Bundt cake, glazed and floral frosted, while supplies lasted. She said she could call in a favor from a bakery client to whom Truss Mortuary had been referring funeral reception business for years.

"Who doesn't like a Bundt cake?" Toby licked his lips. "I'd walk over cut glass barefoot for a free Bundt cake. Let's do it."

One week later, with Winona by my side, we stood outside the Palace Theater and looked up at the marque in total disbelief. Toby billed the event as 'The *Very* Last Laugh, A Comedic Tribute to the Dead.' He even posted the event on Facebook with a cameo video of me doing a comedic riff at a bar mitzvah.

The old Palace Theater had first seen life in the late 1930s as an art deco movie house. Over the years it had served as a bar, restaurant, homeless shelter and adult bookstore and finally had a date for demolition. The arc of the wrecking ball failed to connect, however, as civic-minded historic preservationists came to the rescue with taxpayer funds and converted it into an exhibition venue.

And today I was the exhibitionist, or the exhibit, one or the other.

Toby took on the role of promoter, contracted with the Palace for the event and came up with the rental money. Truss Mortuary lent its name to the event, and Winona handled the logistics—reservations, flowers, refreshments and Bundt cakes. Survivors were encouraged to bring friends, relatives and photos or remains of the deceased—urns only, please. Toby hammered the event on social media and billed it as a free event that included a free Bundt cake. The local press picked it up. To everyone's surprise, the event booked two hundred guests within thirty-six hours. A local television station truck, antenna extended, camped outside the entrance.

I watched as the attendees entered the Palace Theater in solemn procession. They carried the remains of their deceased in all manner of containers—Folger's Coffee cans, Mason jars, ornately carved boxes, and something that looked to be a Ming Dynasty vase. One woman brought a vacuum cleaner bag, said there had been an accident. As they dispersed the urns among the tables set up through-out the theater, the collection of odd pieces looked as though they belonged at a flea market stand.

Winona had the artist Enya's music piped into the venue. The New Age singer from Ireland slathered her pieces in reverb and overdubbed it into an angelic choir. It gave off the effect of gliding through a misty fog. Perfect for the occasion.

The cash bar, another revenue stream, was set up in the back of the room and was quick to see action. Two bartenders worked feverishly to keep up. As I walked past the guests, I could sense the booze kicking in. It was as though the attendees had taken a collective breath and exhaled an audible *ahhhh*. The conversation started to flow freely. Winona played hostess and chatted up the guests.

I checked out the front of the room. A low stage platform with a single microphone looked out onto round tables with white tablecloths and fresh flower arrangements. Unlike my comedic stand-up gigs, I had little prepared in the way of a routine, and it frightened the hell out of me. I had some experience with improv and hoped I could make it work tonight.

Oh, hell. It couldn't be any worse than the bomb job at Louie's.

Except that the stakes were much higher. Along with scrambling to meet my child support obligations, Jessica's latest text message said she needed new tires for her trip to Wisconsin! Truss Mortuary's survival was also on the line.

And then, looking out at the crowd, I realized something else was at stake. When I'd bombed at Louie's, the crowd had enjoyed heckling me. I was the only one hurt by it. Now this crowd was looking to me to provide them a service—emotional support, closure, comfort, whatever. If I bombed, they were the ones who would suffer.

"Ready, Vince?" Toby shot me a big smile and slapped me on the back. "I'll hang off to the side and bookend your intro and exit. Got it?" Toby tapped the mic for a quick sound check. The thump set off a last-minute rush to the bar.

I felt sick to my stomach as I approached the microphone. "Welcome to this . . . unusual event. You're all amazing people, gathered here in the company of others who, like you, have suffered a loss and grieve for a loved one. Hopefully, we can all take a breath and have a laugh." I lifted the mic from the stand to signal an end to the formality.

"What a fantastic display of urns." I waved to the remains table. "Wish my family was so considerate. If you've ever been a pallbearer, you know how heavy caskets are. And without fail, there are going to be slackers who don't carry their share of the weight. When my grandfather passed, we didn't have enough muscle to carry him into the cemetery, so we set the coffin on the grass and pushed it to the gravesite like a car with a dead battery. No pun intended."

A couple of chuckles, an icebreaker.

I moved off the stage and strolled among the attendees. If the venue had been a nightclub, I'd be stirring the lounge lizards. But I was feeling my way into this crowd. "Good evening, ma'am." I held the mic out to a woman with a full head of platinum colored hair and fire engine red lipstick. "And your name is?"

"Evelyn."

"Evelyn, thank you for coming tonight." I pointed at the two urns planted in front of her. "Who are the loved ones you have with you today?"

"Loved ones? Well, we can debate that, ha!" She tapped an urn with a long, polished fingernail. "This one's Charles, married that fool for love, before he ran off with a woman half his age. I wanted to kill him, but turns out he couldn't keep up with the little bitch, had a stroke, dead in the bed." She paused, picked up her cocktail glass and pointed at the second urn. "I would have liked to have killed this one, too. Eddie, married him for money. Turns out number two thought paying taxes was for idiots. Every damn possession we owned got confiscated and sold off. He didn't like doctors, either. When the cancer in him finally bubbled to the surface, he was dead within six weeks."

I knew she was the right pick when I saw her. "You're not the only one looking to expedite matters, Evelyn." I turned to the gathering. "A woman walks into a pharmacy and asks the pharmacist for some arsenic. The pharmacist says, 'What for?' She says, 'I want to kill my husband'. He says, 'Sorry, I can't do that.' She then reaches into her handbag and pulls out a photo of her husband in bed with the pharmacist's wife and hands it to him. He says, 'You didn't tell me you had a prescription.'"

A smattering of laughs.

I withdrew from Evelyn's table, building the act. "Watch your step guys, cause you never see it coming. One day my ex-wife, out of the blue, asked me, 'If you could know how and when you were going to die, would you want to know?' I said, 'No.' She said, 'Okay, forget it.'"

Some good-natured groans. I strolled among the tables and pointed at a Buddha urn. "Old Deepa believed so strongly in reincarnation he wrote a will leaving everything to himself."

A fragile middle-aged woman with a heavy perfume scent sat with a heart-shaped, red enameled urn. It reminded me of a Valentine candy box, and she looked like the kind who could take a joke. "I wondered what happened to Forrest Gump. As momma says, I guess you never know what you're going to get."

She laughed good-naturedly, and that gave the audience permission to laugh with her.

"A man goes for his yearly check-up and is told he only has one day to live. He rushes home, explains his condition to his wife and says, 'I want us to spend my last night having wild, crazy sex.' His wife says, 'Well, that's easy for you to say. You don't have to get up in the morning!'"

Some laugh eruptions.

The energy in the room still seemed lukewarm. I needed to find my voice, heat things up. No more set jokes. What I needed was real comedy, the kind that expressed weird experiences not spoken.

I stopped at a young couple's table, with a playful looking urn set between them. "Who have you brought tonight?"

"This is Mathew," the woman said, tight-lipped. "He left us at four years old." The woman started to cry, turned and buried her head in her husband's shoulder.

"I'm so sorry—this was a terrible idea," the husband said to his wife and attempted to comfort her. Then to me, "Not so funny is it, comedy guy, with your re-tread jokes." He took his wife's hand, "Let's get out of here. This is so wrong."

He helped his distraught wife to her feet. She grabbed her purse, and they headed up the aisle.

All eyes followed them out, then back to me. The room deflated. I felt crushed and culpable at a deep cellular level for something. The irreverent eulogist hustle? That I had failed as a husband, a father? The shame of a suicide attempt? Yes, all of these things, but something else. A grip, like an enormous claw, clutched my heart.

And suddenly, there it was. I was grieving. Tears began to flow, and I felt the sorrow of my own loss and of a hundred thousand others suffering a loss at the same moment.

"Please give me a moment," I said, and then wished I hadn't. I had nothing to offer, no capacity to console this couple. The room stirred. But I'd already decided there was no giving up on this gathering or storming out. *Please help,* I prayed, into the cosmos, *this is not about me.*

Words unexpectedly came out of my mouth and my ears picked up on the sound as though I was in the audience. "I am genuinely touched and saddened by your loss. I don't know if this event is a good idea or not, if it will provide a sense of closure, community or any other restorative benefits. Comedy for remembrance. Maybe it's totally absurd. But one thing I know is that children are all about laughter and playfulness. It's in their nature."

The couple paused near the exit and turned to look at me.

"Laughter lives in all of us, naturally, easily, until we let the weight of things crush our joy. I had my laughter snuffed out as a child. When I was ten years old, my father left for work and never came home. We held a funeral for him, but the empty coffin and his absence left me feeling incomplete and alone. Other kids saw me as weak, fatherless, an easy target. I latched on to laughter to outwit and sidetrack the bullies. Then it became a sort of personal therapy to exit my dark place, and then a way to observe the quirkiness and the mystery of life. I suspect everyone is at a different point on his or her journey of grief. But for me, laughter was a gift that came to me in a most unexpected way. Maybe you have the same unwrapped gift waiting for you."

I dropped the microphone to my side in total resignation, then brought it back to my face. "Like many of you, I really don't know what I'm doing here tonight. I guess looking for something. I sincerely hope we find it."

The wife looked at her husband and slowly walked back down the aisle toward me. I braced, not sure what was coming.

She extended her arms and gave me a hug. The husband followed and circled his arms around us both. Together, along with the gathering of attendees, we cried until we laughed.

The rest of the evening was a blur. I stopped to chat at every table, found humor in unexpected places, led the audience to experience it more and more, and worked myself into exhaustion. A couple of people left their urns behind. Friends were made and Evelyn found another widower to torment.

CHAPTER 22

FEMA

On her way to work the next morning, Jessica unexpectedly dropped off Claire, just as I was about to leave the house. Claire's school had been canceled because of a gas leak.

"I'm hungry," Claire said.

"How about we go to a restaurant?"

I had planned to meet Winona for coffee at the Day by Day Café, a short walk from the mortuary. I texted her to see if it was okay to bring Claire. The cafe's name was in recognition of their usual clientele—recovering alcohol and drug abusers. In the entry, with Claire in hand, I glanced at a rack of self-help brochures: Dry Harder, Boozer Loser, and Yesterday, You Said Tomorrow.

"Someday," I mumbled and led Claire through the restaurant to an outdoor patio where I found Winona sitting near the koi fishpond.

"Claire, this is Winona, daddy's friend from work I told you about."

"Are you a real Indian?"

"Sure am, and I hear you like horses."

"I'm going to horse camp."

"Yippee-yi-o-ki-yay," Winona circled a hand overhead. "You'll have great fun, cowgirl."

The waitress dropped a kid's coloring menu and a box of crayons in front of Claire.

Winona ordered a mocha latte and a caramel roll. I was good with black coffee.

"I want Mickey Mouse pancakes with chocolate chips and chocolate milk," Claire said without looking up from her coloring.

"I like a gal who knows what she wants," the waitress said and retreated. Claire dug into the coloring.

I hadn't slept, I couldn't shake off the weirdness of the eulogy event. I arrived at the theater thinking it was just a cash grab comedy gig for people who wanted to check off the memorial ceremony box for their dead. But the event cracked me open, and I was still trying to get my head around what I found.

"I'm still buzzed from last night."

"Oh, my god, group eulogy, how crazy was that?" Winona said. "A total roller coaster ride. My heart is still racing."

"We did it. The donation angle was a huge success." I extended a fist bump to Winona. Claire held out a fist to get in on the action. We all laughed and Claire returned to her coloring.

"Toby made good on his investment. Truss Mortuary should be able to fix some of the code issues and hopefully, I can get caught up on my back payments." I nodded discreetly at Claire.

"The publicity has been great, too. Getting lots of calls, people asking about the comedic group tribute service." Winona paused as the waitress set our order on the table.

"Those pancakes look amazing," Winona said.

"These are Mickey's ears and this is a chocolate chip smile." Claire pointed.

"Let daddy cut that up for you."

"I can do it. I'm five."

"Do you think there'll be more group events?"

"Toby says it's probably an annual sort of thing, so I've got to keep the wheel turning with other stuff."

"What do you have in mind?" Winona asked, trying to keep from laughing at Claire's chocolate milk mustache.

"Toby said that since Louie owned the Midwest comedy market, I'm locked out of local gigs, but he could get me a stand-up job on a cruise ship for seniors."

"Exciting! Maybe we can be a team." Winona held her mocha latte in mid-air. "You knock 'em dead, and we'll take it from there."

"I get seasick, but I like the way you're thinking."

"Bummer."

"Daddy, can I go look at the fish?"

"Sure, let's clean up first."

"I can do it." She dabbed at her face with a napkin and ran off.

"She's beautiful," Winona said. "She's got her mother's brilliant blue eyes and your wide-open smile."

"More importantly, she's a lot smarter than me."

"Oh right, mister college philosophy professor."

I waved the subject away. "Toby's other comedic salvage opportunity is for me to do a laugh therapy CD for disaster survivors. He's got a college buddy who works for FEMA, and they have a mental health allocation in their budget. Says he might be able to get FEMA to sponsor me."

"That sounds promising."

"Yeah, brilliant concept. 'Kids, we've just lost everything in a hurricane, but hey, let's listen to Vince and forget about the dog blowing away and our lack of insurance and that we're in a FEMA trailer home, breathing formaldehyde.'"

Winona pinched off a piece of her sticky pastry. "So, maybe not?"

"I'm thinking podcasts are where it's at."

"Lay it on me,"

"The idea is a little loose at the moment."

She winked. "No surprise there."

"Yeah, yeah, but I think there's a niche for presenting a more in-depth account of someone's life versus the standard five-minute eulogy. More space to talk about the quirks, the foibles, the wrong turns, dead ends and the successes that make our unscripted journey humorously unique. Plus, a podcast will give family, friends and the curious, near and far, access to the farewell tribute."

"Admirable, but do you know anything about podcasting?"

I suddenly became fascinated watching Winona lick the caramel off her fingers. I shook it off. "I've been working on the technical aspects with my brother's girlfriend, Sage, who works for a radio station. If you can generate a podcast following, it's possible to make some real money from sponsors."

"Any clients lined up?"

"The podcasts thing is a downstream idea. I'm good with doing eulogies for Truss Mortuary." The acknowledgement left me feeling desperately insecure about my future.

"Daddy, that person says I can feed the fish if it's okay with you?"

I looked over at the waitress who waved back at me. "Sure honey, be careful."

"Craig's List continues to be productive. Who would have thought?" Winona laughed. "Plus, you're starting to get referrals, so hopefully it works out."

"Next, you'll be telling me I'm in demand."

A slash of sunlight cut through the patio latticework and shadowed the table in a diagonal pattern. The sun highlighted Winona's black hair, revealing silver strands, a scar on her chin and the little gap between her teeth.

"Earth to Vince," Winona said.

"Sorry, I'm a little spacey today," I said. Knowing she could see right through me, my sensual thoughts so easily read, I signaled for more coffee, "You?" I pointed at her cup.

"All good." Her soft smile let me off the hook, and I realized how quickly I'd grown accustomed to certain things about her, as if I'd known her for years.

"Oh, and before I forget," Winona reached out and touched my hand, "I wanted to let you know we're preparing to bury Riva O'Malley. Perhaps you could say a few words on her behalf."

I knew very little about O'Malley. She'd spent nearly a year alert but unable to move. Then someone had killed her, none of which told me anything about who she was. What could I possibly say about her? Yet every time I stepped into the mortuary, I felt a strange connection to her, a fragile confluence of life and death bumping down the road together in Truss' corpse wagon.

I had no idea what to say, but I had to say something. Someone had to speak for her, and it may as well be me.

"Daddy, I want a goldfish. Can I get one please?"

I dropped Claire off at home with a goldfish in a glass bowl and a packet of fish food. Let's just say it didn't play out well with Jessica.

CHAPTER 23

CELESTIAL

I knocked on Truss' partially opened parlor door, eager to get the details on Riva O'Malley's interment service. "Sorry to interrupt."

Truss' eyebrows arched over a file he was reading. "Vince, come in."

"Maybe this isn't a good time?"

"Sit." He set the paperwork aside. "Winona said you put on quite a memorial tribute at the Palace Theater."

"It was a crazy idea." I squeezed the back of my neck. "I just hope my performance doesn't blow back on Truss Mortuary."

"Reputation doesn't matter much to the welfare clients the county offloads on us. The truth of it is, Truss Mortuary is no stranger to group bereavement."

"Probably not a comedy act, though."

"Never that clever." Truss gave off a hint of a smile. "Before your time, in the day when the frozen ground resisted a shovel, we kept corpses until the spring thaw. At the first eruption of flowering crocus, we dug the graves and lined up the coffins to be claimed. Sometimes there would be twenty to thirty deceased, especially during the time of pestilence. Before the families carried off their loved ones to be interred, we'd hold a group service. I've often thought we should revisit that practice. I'm of the mind folks find support, and maybe clarity, by coming together in their grief. Perhaps they become aware of death not as an isolated tragedy, but a natural part of life that they simply need to accept."

"Do I detect Determinism?"

"Ah, yes, you're the philosopher." Truss leaned back in his chair. "Didn't mean to impose on your territory."

"Oh, no, we're all good. It just caught me by surprise—philosophically."

"I don't subscribe to labeled thinking. But I've studied some and like what Siddhartha and Einstein had to say about cause and effect. Those fellows, the mystic and the physicist, seemed to have a fair amount of insight into how things work. Something about all events, occurrences and actions follow the laws of nature."

"No slouches there, but not exactly comedians."

"Did I mention Jerry Seinfeld?"

"Damn, you're quick and hip."

Truss smiled. "I'm just a babbling old man who should keep his thoughts about such things to himself. There's not much comfort in explaining the laws of thermodynamics to a heartbroken daughter—pointing out that mother now survives as a constellation of repurposed, electronically charged atoms and manifested as light and heat particles amid the vibrations of the universe."

"Maybe we should get Winona to package your physicist eulogy with a celestial map and a star named after the deceased. She's always looking for an angle to keep Truss Mortuary afloat."

Truss waived the scheme away. "You didn't come in here to listen to me. What can I do for you?"

"Just wondering if you had any more information on Riva O'Malley. Winona said you're about to bury her and asked if I could say a few words on her behalf."

"She's been here for ten days, poor woman." Truss taped his desk calendar. "Without claimants, I've taken the liberty to delay her interment in hopes someone would take an interest in finding some forensic clues to her demise. But it's time."

"It's a shame there's no justice for her."

"Well, it won't be for lack of trying." Truss held up a file folder marked BCA CONFIDENTIAL: Case File No: 37662.

"Did I hear my name?" Winona popped her head into the parlor.

"Come in," Truss said. "Just about to share a BCA investigative report I received from Agent Kirchner on O'Malley."

"So the BCA has agreed to take on the case?" Winona sat down next to me and gripped my hand.

"Sadly, no." Truss rested his elbows on the edge of the desk, his hands poised over the BCA folder. "Unfortunately, Agent Kirchner could not persuade the BCA to open an investigation into O'Malley's death. Apparently, the county morgue's medical examiner's incompetent report holds more weight than the observation of an old coroner."

Winona pointed. "But the BCA report?"

"It was written before O'Malley was admitted to Angels of Mercy Care Center. Agent Kirchner thought it would give me a more complete picture of her background and injuries. Most likely, he's throwing me a bone to keep me at bay as he knows I won't let the matter rest, if I can help it."

"So he thinks we're running a kennel here?"

I leaned away from her. "Well, you probably bite."

"Ruff." Winona snapped at me and turned her attention back to Truss. "So we're on our own here, trying to find out what happened to O'Malley?"

"It appears so."

Winona waved at the report. "Is having that going to get either you or Agent Kirchner in trouble?"

"Only that Kirchner reminded me I no longer have standing in law enforcement. The file on O'Malley is for my eyes only and in no way is to be acted upon. Something about my days as a wild west inquisitor being long over."

Winona laughed. "Just let 'em try to take your spurs away, cowboy." The phone rang, and she stood up. "I'll take it in the other room. Be right back."

"Need a little help here," I said. "What exactly does the BCA do?"

"Minnesota Bureau of Criminal Apprehension. They're an umbrella law enforcement agency with a mandate to provide investigative services, crime lab resources, and criminal database records to local police and sheriff departments throughout the state. They also coordinate with federal agencies. I buried Agent Kirchner's father, a St. Paul police officer killed in the line of duty, twenty-two years ago. We've been friends ever since."

Winona bounced back into the parlor. "Major crash on 35E last night. A teenage driver collided with a car full of women on the way to a bridge party. Six DOA. Morgue is full so they're looking to off-load pronto. Paying clients—oh yeah!" She shot a fist in the air, then caught herself. "Hey, better us than those Reliance schmucks."

Truss winced. "Schmucks?"

"Ancient native American insult."

He shook his head and let it go. "Vince and I will handle the morgue call." He picked up the BCA file and held it in the air. "I'll debrief you on this when I get back."

CHAPTER 24

MORGUE

Truss tossed me the keys to the Cadillac Miller-Meteor Hearse. I had only a fuzzy recollection of the vehicle from the night on the bridge. Now, in the early morning light of day, I could see that the black and white, two-tone body truly resembled a beast. Truss had informed me the hearse was the same vintage as the one featured in the movie Ghost Busters. The details were perfect, from the brightly polished chrome to the spotless red velour interior. Not a squeak as we rumbled over St. Paul's potholed roads. I turned on the overhead flasher and ran a stop sign.

"That would be illegal," Truss said.

"So, what did the BCA report have to say about O'Malley?"

Truss cocked his head toward me. "O'Malley's condition resulted from a blunt force injury, sustained on a farmstead near Baxter in central Minnesota. The Crow Wing County Attorney, Carl Schwabel, attributed O'Malley's near-fatal condition to foul play. He initially tried to pin the assault on Jacob Zenk, her live-in boyfriend. Zenk said someone tried to kill O'Malley to cash in on her life insurance policy."

"Life insurance? How does an indigent person have life insurance?"

Truss held up a palm. "Neither Zenk, nor the investigative team, could produce an insurance policy in Riva O'Malley's name to substantiate the story. The county attorney found the account far-fetched, and as a practical matter, O'Malley had not died, which made the death benefit claim a moot point. The county attorney also had a weak hand in pursuing Zenk on an assault and battery charge—no witnesses, no 911 call, no history of domestic abuse. Zenk also delivered her to the local hospital for medical attention. In the scheme of things, the county attorney considered O'Malley's assault a nuisance event. There were bigger prizes to be had, with more downstream career opportunities than domestic crime."

"Is this Zenk still around?"

"Take a left at the light." Truss pointed. "Local law enforcement, in a follow-up to O'Malley's injuries, discovered an underground bunker on Zenk's farm. It had been torched, but the remains indicated an illegal drug operation. Zenk pleaded guilty to the production and distribution of highly concentrated cannabis, a Schedule 1 drug offense, and was sentenced to three years in Stillwater Prison. The county attorney, however, would not let the matter rest and made it known he wanted Zenk squeezed until he gave up information on the neighbors who abetted his illegal growing operation."

Truss rapped a knuckle on the window to call my attention to a 'Dalton for Governor' billboard ahead with a photo of Madelyn Dalton. Her eyes followed us as we passed. "Our friends," Truss said wryly.

I shook my head. "One scary family."

"Back to Zenk," Truss said. "In prison, he shared a cell with a violent sex offender and a member of the Aryan Brotherhood. After a month of abuse, prison officials offered Zenk a new, kinder, gentler cellmate if he gave up the names of his pot-growing neighbors. He resisted and returned to the torment of his former cellmate. Over the Crow Wing County Attorney's stern objection, Zenk was released after serving just one year. As a first-time offender with severe health issues, the political winds were in Zenk's favor. Although, in the bigger picture, Zenk's finite days are numbered. According to the prison medical reports, he suffers from pulmonary edema, acquired from an acute smoke inhalation injury related to a fire in the underground drug lab. He now requires supplemental oxygen. His condition has been classified as terminal."

"Is he still alive?"

Truss closed the file. "I couldn't tell you."

I had a sudden recollection of being with Truss in the mortuary prep room as he attended to O'Malley. "Didn't the police report from Angels of Mercy say that O'Malley had a visitor the morning of her death, someone with an oxygen cart? Everyone knows that most crimes are committed by people with a close personal relationship to the victim."

"Pull into the driveway on your left. We're here." Truss stuck a hand out the window and waved at the security camera. The door to an underground garage opened.

I guided the hearse down a ramp way as the garage door closed behind us. The garage was filled with hearses. It looked like an undertaker's convention—sleek new coaches, with franchise names stenciled on the windows in about every showroom color available. The Miller-Meteor moved among them like a dowager at a teen rave.

A gaggle of casually dressed men, with Ross Dalton from Reliance Funeral Homes in their midst, turned their attention toward us. Dalton pointed at Truss. "Boys, give witness to this man who has paved the way for our thriving enterprise. I give you Truss, the embodiment of mortuary history, a dinosaur, for whom profit holds no motive. A man content to leave prosperous bygone souls to our care, while he picks up the cast-offs and remnants of the trade. Sir, we thank you." Dalton bowed as his colleagues laughed.

Truss' face remained neutral.

Mine didn't. "Idiot jerk off!" I shouted at Dalton, as Truss steered me into the morgue office.

A large window looked out onto the morgue's processing area. In the brightly lit tile room, attendants in plastic gowns and rubber gloves shuttled gurneys, depositing or withdrawing bodies from a bank of stainless-steel roll-out cabinets along the wall.

"Hey, Doc, long time no see," Truss said to an older, stooped-shouldered man in a lab coat. "Doc Harrington, this is Vince. He works with me at the mortuary."

Harrington and I shook hands.

"Doc and I go way back, top-notch ME," Truss said. "Thought they retired you?"

"Sort of—I spend my winters in Naples, hang out in Minnesota over the summer to be with the grandkids. The coroner's office asked me to fill in, part-time, when things are on overload."

"Got a call about a bad one out on I35E," Truss said. "What do you have for us?"

Harrington looked puzzled. "I didn't call you. Maybe one of the other MEs did? Let me check. Be right back."

"Something's off here," Truss said.

Harrington returned. "No one claims to have called you in. We've notified the next of kin, Reliance Funeral Homes has obtained releases and divided the 35E crash victims among themselves."

Damn, they set us up. I wanted to throw punches but held tight. This was Truss' business.

"I'm sorry," Harrington said. "Truss, you know this impropriety would not have happened on my watch. There's so much money being tossed around by the mortuary chains and by death sensational-ists we don't know whose pockets are getting lined these days. Over in

Minneapolis, they fired a morgue technician for taking pictures of Prince and selling them to the National Inquirer for big bucks."

"So, is that how the ME work-up went down on Riva O'Malley? Someone's pocket got lined?"

"Don't know the name," Harrington said. "Not one of mine."

"She's a deceased indigent of the county. When they released her to me, it was obvious from my exam she was a victim of foul play but not a word of it in the ME's report."

Harrington shook his head.

"I'm of the same mind. Ms. O'Malley deserves better. We are duty bound to do better." Truss said.

"You know . . ." Harrington removed his glasses. "I'm often asked what's the worst death I've seen, and after fifty years, I've seen a lot of them. Everyone expects a gory tale, but the worst death, I believe, is a person who dies alone, without anyone who cares about them." Harrington straightened his back and put his glasses back on. "You're a good man, Truss. Let me know if there is anything I can do to help."

We left the morgue office, and Harrington followed us out. Dalton and his posse had vacated the premise.

"Still driving this old beast?" Harrington smiled and patted the fender of the hearse. "One other thing, there's a note in your service vendor file—says Truss Mortuary's license to operate a mortuary is under review by the Minnesota Department of Health, related to code violations. Someone's got it in for you. Be careful."

CHAPTER 25
ANGEL OF MERCY

On the way back from the morgue, Truss seemed undaunted by the harassment. "Turn here." He pointed, interrupting my route back to the mortuary.

"Where are we going?"

"I spoke to a supervisor at Angels of Mercy the other day regarding O'Malley. Now I'd like to have a look."

I parked the hearse in front of the Angel of Mercy Long Term Care Center and recognized the building as the former Visitation Convent. It sat quietly in an old historic neighborhood, dotted with turn-of-the-century Victorian homes in St. Paul. The Sisters of Visitation had been a cloistered order. A brick wall around the property had secured their privacy. The nuns kept the grounds impeccably landscaped, with gardens, pathways and benches. The current property owner, Ramsey County, had little regard for the spiritual ambiance of the place. Sections of the graffiti-splattered brick wall had fallen away. Rusty air conditioners dripped as they perched precariously on window ledges of the three-story brick French Colonial. Dead trees, long-ago victims of Dutch elm and emerald ash bore, stood bare and added to a sense of foreboding.

We carefully approached the main entrance. Gnarled roots had buckled the sidewalk and pushed concrete slabs up into tented ramps, perfect for skateboarders. A woman with her back against the building puffed on a cigarette as she waved us toward her.

"You're the guy from Truss Mortuary?" The woman pointed her cigarette at Truss.

"Yes, ma'am."

"I'm Tonette." She took a deep drag off her cigarette and exhaled with relish. "We talked on the phone. Figured it was you. You look like you sound."

Tonette, short and broad in stature, reminded me of a Russian-nesting doll. She had a full-moon face, with a mole on her cheek and weirdly bulging eyes. Her rounded shoulders dissolved into her arms.

"You look familiar." She studied my face. "YouTube or maybe a dating service? Good-looking guy like you, bet you're on Tinder. I don't forget faces. It'll come to me."

"Just a helper at the mortuary." Chances were, she'd seen my co-medic disaster at Louie's club. I was hoping her recall wasn't as good as she thought.

Tonette mercifully turned her attention back to Truss. "Like I already told you on the phone, not much to O'Malley, but come on in." She flicked the butt away and ambled back into the building to her manager's station.

"Do you keep a log of visitors?" Truss said.

"Sure, but we don't get many visitors, given the condition of these patients." Tonette shoved the log toward Truss.

Truss reviewed the registered names and dates of entry. Most weeks, there were only one or two visitors. There were no visitors assigned to Riva O'Malley.

"Do you have surveillance cameras?"

"Aren't you getting a little out of your territory here, Mr. Mortuary?"

"Perhaps, but Ms. O'Malley has no other advocates. If there's the slightest chance she had a visitor, friend or family, we feel duty-bound to notify them of her demise."

"We only have one exterior camera. Have at it." Tonette motioned us around the reception counter to the security monitor. The lone exterior security camera proved to be a bust. Although active in real time, they'd never bothered to hook it to a recorder.

"The police report," Truss pulled it out of his jacket pocket, "stated that one of your employees, a Raphael Vieira, claimed Ms. O'Malley had a visitor the morning of her demise."

A trace of guilt ran across her face, but she quickly reined it in. "I don't see how they could have gotten past me. Maybe I was in the bathroom or something."

"Could we speak with Mr. Vieira?"

"Raphael quit. With what the county pays, nobody hangs around very long. Fact is, immigrants, legal or otherwise, are the only people we can get to do these jobs. Don't take much skill to empty waste bags and turn the residents over. The county is always claiming they're broke. I ain't had a raise in two years."

Truss asked to see O'Malley's room, and Tonette led us down a dimly lit hallway past open doors. The once cloistered Visitation nuns, now long gone, had taken a vow of poverty, a vow now imposed upon the Angel of Mercy patients. We passed a room with a man in bed, his head as shrunken as a dried-out potato, toothless and gape-mouthed. He fixed a milky-eyed gaze on a TV mounted on the wall. In another room, a baby lay motionless in a crib.

Tonette opened a door and flicked on the overhead light. "O'Malley's room," she said, and hung back. I stepped into the room and absorbed its dreariness. An industrial strength disinfectant permeated the air and stung my eyes. A single incandescent light bulb hung from a cord. The old cracked, plastered walls, painted a dull yellow, sprinkled chalk dust on the floor. Electrical conduit snaked along the baseboards. A slow drip pinged from the rusted metal sink bolted to the wall. A single bed and a small three-drawer dresser crowded the space. The bed, stripped of its sheets, exposed the soiled ticking. The sagging mattress still held the outline of Riva O'Malley and everyone else who had died in that bed.

I imagined that upon her death, she had inflated to the ceiling like a helium balloon and looked down at her dead self—happy to be free.

Truss turned to Tonette. "I'd like to see her personal belongings. The police report said they found her wearing a wig and a red dress bunched around her."

"That sure is strange." Tonette instinctively touched her head. "Most anybody has around here are odds and ends, nothing of value. We generally wait a couple of days, and if no one claims the stuff, we pitch it." She gave a shoulderless shrug. "Guess you'll have to talk to Raphael about that. He cleaned out the room."

"Besides your staff, do residents get visits from outside volunteers, say clergy and the like?"

"Only if you include ghosts."

"Sorry, I don't understand," Truss said.

"Those Visitation nuns never left. I hear all sorts of racket throughout the night and they leave things behind, too." Tonette shivered as if coming in from the cold. "One night I found an old glass baby milk bottle next to a chair that was rocking with nobody in it."

As I drove away from Angels of Mercy, I carried the weight of the care center's deplorable conditions. "How did O'Malley end up in that rat hole?"

"She had no money, advocates or self-care help." Truss looked back at the facility. "You could say Angels of Mercy is the last resort."

"So, who do you think did it—Zenk, the guy with the oxygen tank?

How about the attendant Vieira? Strange how he suddenly quit after finding O'Malley dead. Or maybe the place really is haunted and we should become ghost-busters." I patted the dashboard. "We've got the right rig for it."

Truss shook his head, not amused by my speculation.

"I'm obviously grasping here."

"Try grasping the steering wheel."

CHAPTER 26

MOWED

Upon my return from Angels of Mercy, I dropped into the parlor desk chair at a loss as to what I could offer on Riva's behalf other than a weak tribute filled with random platitudes. I felt she deserved more from me. Perhaps I assigned more meaning to our intersection on the bridge than common sense would dictate, but the sudden twist of being involved with a mortuary put me beyond rationale thinking. Like a bat shit crazy person wearing a foil antenna receiving a transmission from the outer world, I heard a woman's voice inside my head say, "Tell my story."

But what story? As an observational comic, I practiced finding the most mundane, albeit peculiar, details of peoples' lives. Plus, I had a philosophy degree that inferred a discipline of problem solving, reasoning, and research. Like a time traveler, I knew how to discern people from the past—connect the dots. But all I knew about Riva was that she'd survived as a conscious vegetable for a year and had been visited by someone who painted her nails and outfitted her in a red dress and wig. And then murdered her. That wasn't enough to work on.

But I had the internet.

I dug into the usual sources—birth and school records, census data, marriage certificates, employment history, criminal records, social media, ancestral sites. All came up empty for O'Malley. I even visited the Reliance Funeral Homes website. By Winona's account and intuition, she felt a strange association between the unscrupulous competitor, Reliance Funeral Homes, and O'Malley. But I was at a loss to find a connection.

In the end, I found myself in the mortuary's records room. Wood filing cabinets with brass nameplates and bookshelves filled every inch of the place. I extracted the O'Malley file and read the reports Truss had paraphrased for me the day I unwittingly watched him unzip her from the plastic bag.

"Hey, stay in your lane, buddy." Winona spotted me. "Paperwork is my world, what are you after?"

"Trying to get a handle on O'Malley's story."

"So what did you find, super sleuth?"

I spread O'Malley's file out on the top of a file cabinet and tapped the 'St. Paul Police Reconstructive Events Report' that Truss had previously paraphrased for me. I pointed out that the Angel of Mercy, on-call attendant Raphael Vieira, reported he witnessed a man with an oxygen cart enter O'Malley's room, prior to finding her unresponsive. "The next day he quit his job. This guy knows something."

"Something that's been nagging at me," Winona picked up the BCA Case File, "is the life insurance policy she supposedly had in play. If there is a policy, there must be a record of it someplace. You're not the only Snoop Dog in the kennel. I'll do some digging."

I groaned at the Snoop Dog reference and let it go. "Vieira's phone contact is in the police report."

"Be careful," Winona said.

From the parlor, I called Vieira.

"Lawn servicio."

The greeting threw me for a moment. "Is this the number for Raphael Vieira?"

"Si, Raphael, you want grass cut?"

I hesitated.

"I come today, give you buen servicio, you give address."

I gave him my home address, feeling a twinge of guilt for facilitating a set-up. Not that the dandelion-ridden patch of lawn surrounding my mother's house didn't need attention.

I rushed home. Ray was at the kitchen table, bent over the mystery birthday postcards that had been lying around for a week. "Trolling bastards," he said, without looking up.

I did a quick mental review of where we were at on the calendar. "Happy birthday."

"Yeah, yeah, thanks. Who keeps screwing with us?" Ray picked up one of the birthday postcards and tossed it like a frisbee toward the wastebasket.

"Mom's bone-headed boyfriend tried to tell me they're a vacation solicitation from the Caribbean Tourist Board or something."

"I just talked to mom. She was crying. Said Jack was being stubborn about this and that. You know how they always want us to come to Florida? They better be careful what they wish for because I'm this close to showing up at their door and putting that Jack ass down."

From the kitchen window, I saw a Chevy sedan pull up to the curb with a lawn mower secured by a bungee cord sticking out of the trunk.

Ray spotted the car, too. "Who's that?"

"Lawn mowing service. Happy Birthday."

"Christ, I don't need that noise." Ray got up from the table. "I've got a headache to start with." He retreated down into the basement and yelled back, "Why don't you hire a maid while you're at it?"

A whip thin man limped toward the house. I met him on the steps. "Raphael?"

"Si." He glanced around the tiny weed patch. "First, I cut grass and then you pay fifteen dollars, si?"

Thirty minutes later, he knocked on the door. "Lawn good, no?" He wiped a shirtsleeve across his brow.

Well, the lawn was at least cut, and it looked better. "I need to get my wallet. Come in. You must be thirsty. Water, soda, cerveza?" I pointed him to a chair at a kitchen table.

"Agua."

I set a twenty-dollar bill on the table along with a glass of water. "Keep the change."

"Gracias." Vieira made a move to leave.

"How come you quit your job at Angels of Mercy?" I said evenly.

Vieira jerked as if being hit by a cattle prod. "I go now."

"Please wait, I'm not the police or immigration, and as you saw, my grass really needed cutting. But right now, I just want to talk to you about Riva O'Malley. I work for the funeral home and I'm just trying to learn more about her." I paused. "She suffered terribly."

Vieira seemed to settle but avoided eye contact. "I no get in trouble. I do nothing to O'Malley."

"No trouble. Can you tell me about the man with the oxygen cart you saw enter the room?"

"I only do what Tonette say about O'Malley," Vieira said in a gloomy voice. "Tell her when O'Malley get visitor. Then tell her when I see man with oxygen tank leave. He very sad, cry."

"Was O'Malley alive when the visitor left?"

"Si, she wear . . ." He gestured to his head. "No real hair, and have dress on her."

"Did you tell Tonette about the wig and dress?"

"Si, wig, si. She say leave, take break, go to Walgreens, get her cigarettes. When I come back, I check on O'Malley, she dead." Raphael traced a cross along his chest. "Then I tell Tonette. Police come, I tell them everything."

"Why did you quit your job?"

"Tonette say O'Malley die is very bad for me. Tell me to quit or big problem with immigration. I go now, please."

I walked Vieira out to his car, watched him leave, and retreated to the front steps. I needed to let things settle. My mental motor had been running hot, and I felt on the verge of a burnout. I sniffed at the air, took in the watermelon scent of the freshly cut lawn and began to relax. Then my ever-sabotaging brain took a deep dive and recalled that the scent of cut grass is the smell of trauma. The butchered grass and the slashed dandelions release a first-aid chemical. The lawn was screaming, trying to repair itself.

My chest tightened. Jesus, why can't I ever just leave well enough alone?

My phone chirped. It was Winona. "We have an exceptional client and need your help. We'll pick you up."

An exceptional client, as in what, a rock star?

CHAPTER 27

Boom

A fourteen-foot U-Haul truck with a power liftgate pulled up in front of my house. I thought it might be someone looking for directions until I spotted Winona.

"You ready?" she shouted. I could see Truss at the wheel.

I opened the truck's door and squeezed in. We took off with Winona in the middle, balancing the weight of our bodies.

"Afternoon, Vince," Truss said.

"What's with the truck and the exceptional client mission?"

"Jonathan Downey is the deceased's name, but I'll explain that soon enough. Winona informed me you've been following up on the police report related to O'Malley and any life insurance connection. I'm very concerned about your safety."

"Doesn't seem like anyone else is taking an interest in her murder."

Truss turned the corner, and I heard rattling in the truck bay. "So, you met with the Angels of Mercy attendant, Vieira?"

"Nothing much came of it. Probably spooked him. Wouldn't be surprised if he's left town." I omitted the grass cutting ploy. "I can't see him having anything to do with O'Malley's death, but he said the supervisor, Tonette, was aware of O'Malley's visitor, contrary to what she told us. I think we should follow up with her."

"Stand down on Tonette, at least for now. Let me keep pushing the

BCA. If this Tonette's involved, they'll bring it to light."

"Light? You mean from people who meet for quiet drinks in darkened bars, weighing up cases that offer the most career advantage? Good luck with that."

I spotted a parked fire truck and a rescue squad ahead, Truss pulled up alongside of the emergency vehicles. "Truss Mortuary," he said to an EMT.

"Got a boom lift coming."

"So the exceptional client is in there?" I pointed to where firefighters on the second floor had ripped out a window and rows of bricks on either side of it.

"We use the term 'exceptional' to define clients who don't fit typical mortuary standards. Mr. Downey was morbidly obese, poor fellow."

"As in close to six-hundred pounds," Winona said.

I was at a loss for words, trying to picture someone of that magnitude. Neither Truss nor Winona seemed interested in sharing with me the logistics ahead.

"I got nowhere on the O'Malley insurance angle," Winona said. "Unfortunately, there's no central database to track the owners of life insurance policies so there still may be a policy out there somewhere, as her boyfriend Zenk claimed."

"Here's a consideration," Truss said. "As a licensed mortuary, it is our responsibility to file O'Malley's death certificate with the state. The death certificate includes cause of death, and since I'm not happy with the county ME's assignment of 'natural causes', I've been sitting on her death certificate. If there is a life insurance policy in O'Malley's name, a certified death certificate is required to collect."

"Which means someone who wants to cash in on the policy will have to come knocking on our door," Winona said.

"A beneficiary that knows something about her." I offered and watched the approach of a large truck with a telescoping boom draped over a flat bed.

"And if I can prevail in casting doubt about O'Malley's cause of death," Truss said, "the insurance company will bring in their claims professionals to check things out, investigative resources we're not getting from law enforcement."

A firefighter appeared in the enlarged window opening on the second floor and guided the boom arm into the apartment.

"Won't we get in trouble for delaying the death certificate?" Winona asked.

Truss shrugged. "Documents get lost in the mail or misfiled. But the whole insurance thing is speculative so let's not get our hopes up." He dropped to the pavement and went over to talk to the EMT.

It felt like Truss took away the spiked punch bowl just as the party was getting started.

Truss signaled for us to join him at the back of the U-Haul. He threw open the cargo door and with a spryness I didn't think he possessed, pulled himself up into the bay. He handed off a roll of thick mil plastic, a box cutter, and a roll of duct tape. "Stand aside."

I stepped back as the power lift gate unfolded and he pushed two gurneys, latched together, out onto the lift platform.

Truss brought the jerry-rigged gurneys to the ground. "They're rated to transport four hundred pounds each. The question is, will they be wide enough?"

I held up the plastic. "What do I do with this?"

"They don't make body bags to handle this situation, so we'll have to improvise. Roll out and clip off a couple of fifteen-foot sheets."

A gathering of gawkers lined the sidewalks.

An EMT came over and pulled Truss aside. "We have the deceased harnessed and covered in a shroud. He died in an oversized recliner, like he'd grown into it. We had to break up the chair to get him out."

"Clear, coming out," A firefighter yelled from above.

We stood off to the side as the EMT guided the boom with the harnessed deceased toward the U-Haul and landed it with a rattled thump on the gurneys. With the harness removed, I stood dumbfounded, unable to comprehend the body mass that enveloped this person. Winona nudged me and we went to work wrapping strips of plastic around the deceased, securing it with duct tape.

As we pulled away from the apartment building, Winona seemed to anticipate my questions.

"We're going to drop the deceased at a cold storage locker since we don't have the facilities to handle this situation."

"You sound like you've done this before?"

"Sadly, yes," Truss said. "It's not without complications."

"What are the arrangements—cremation or burial?"

"According to his sister, Mr. Downey wanted to be cremated," Winona said. "But the crematoriums aren't built for this size client, either."

"Too much chance of a grease fire," Truss said, dead serious.

I flashed on the time my barbecue grill caught on fire from dripping fat off a pork roast. "So, what? Burial?"

"We've ordered a custom coffin," Winona said. "Should take about a week, then into the grave, or more specifically, graves,"

"Not following?"

"The deceased is wider that than the width of a standard burial vault, and therefore it takes two graves to accommodate a respectful interment," Truss said.

I wish that same dimensional rule was in place for airplane seats.

No, I needed to be more respectful. "I guess being exceptional and dead comes with a price tag."

Winona looked at Truss, who kept his eyes on the road.

"What?" I said.

"Mr. Downey is without resources. He was on welfare," Winona said. "Truss Mortuary is picking up the difference beyond the county's allowance."

"Aren't there other mortuaries that can take this on?"

"You mean like Reliance?" Winona groaned. "They'd just wrap him in a sheet, squeeze him down to size, and pop him in an unmarked grave."

"It's part of our mission," Truss said, "to provide the deceased a respectful interment regardless of condition or resources."

"A suicide mission, from the looks of it." My assessment landed harder than I intended, "Sorry, I'm just concerned."

"No worries," Winona patted my thigh. "Something always turns up to help us get by."

"Like what?"

"Podcasts. I've got your first client."

CHAPTER 28

TESTING

I packed up my laptop computer loaded with a podcast hosting app, along with a broadcast-grade microphone, Sage had loaned me, and headed over to the mortuary. I was technically ready to set up a podcast, but had zero experience in delivering one.

I caught Winona just as she walked out of the prep room. "So who's the client?"

"Joaquin Vasquez." She grabbed my hand and pulled me into the parlor, then released her grasp in a flourish that launched me into a chair. She plopped down behind Truss' desk. "Just got off the phone with the deceased's mother. Joaquin, age nineteen, died in a drive-by shooting. The mother told me her son got caught up in gang retaliatory violence. She's afraid a public funeral and personal tribute for Joaquin could erupt into an open battle."

"So why doesn't she hire security and issue everyone a bulletproof vest?"

"She wants a lasting eulogy for Joaquin, one that will let the entire world know her son was a kind person, not some random gangbanger."

"Entire world?" I gulped. "I've never done a podcast, not sure I want to start with one where the expectations are so high, especially with a family that's no stranger to firearms."

"You'll be fine. Plus, I'm sure I can buy you some time to prepare.

Suggest you do a practice session."

"So you want me to eulogize you in a podcast?" I wiped an imaginary tear from my eye.

"I was thinking O'Malley. Her burial is tomorrow. Might give you a chance to connect with her, think about what you'll say at the gravesite."

I hated the thought of venturing into Truss' eerie prep room of finality. I slowly opened the door. O'Malley was laid out on the center table. Winona had respectfully dressed her, likely from the same stash of dead peoples garments she had dressed me in. Truss had done a magnificent job in restoring O'Malley's face to a youthful plumpness. Even her patchy hair looked stylish. A far different presentation than the one I witnessed when Truss released her from the plastic body bag.

I set up my podcast gear on a rolling cart and wheeled it over to O'Malley. "Hi, I'm Vince," I said to her. "We met the night Truss picked you up from the morgue and had that unscheduled stop on the bridge to pick me up. Hope you don't mind, I'd like to do a practice podcast."

The acoustics were awful. My voice bounced off the room's hard surfaces. But I had to start somewhere. I accessed the podcast hosting app, set up the mic, and proceeded.

"Hello." I adjusted the microphone. "I'm Vince Locker, and this is a pilot episode of 'The Very Last Laugh', coming to you from the prep room at Truss Mortuary. The prep room, sometimes called the wet room by folks in the funeral business, is starkly lit, tiled and has a drain in the center of the floor. They keep the deceased in an adjoining walk-in cooler before getting them ready for cremation or burial.

"Let me further introduce myself. I have an advanced degree in philosophy, which means it was either stand-up comedy or flipping burgers. My comedy act was so bad, clubs posted bomb-sniffing dogs at the door to keep me out. So now I give eulogies and tell stories about the dead. Weird, I know.

"Death creeps a lot of people out, I get it, and I'm no fan myself. But if we're willing to look at death with eyes wide open, we see it's one of the few places you can experience life in the raw. We're talking ground zero, the present moment, where nothing stands between you and the joy of life, just as it is. I first met death hanging onto a bridge rail, a hundred and twenty feet above the water, ready to jump without a bungee cord. But you're not crazy and probably afraid of heights, so you don't have to go there. Just come along for my podcast ride, where we'll demystify and unpack death through the stories of those who have died. Like archeologists, we'll dig through their closets and go beyond the accompanying fear, loss, and grief to find humor. The treasure that makes us human.

"Oh, for the record, I don't channel the dead, nor can I tap into the spirit world. But I've met a few mortuary psychics working on behalf of survivors left with the unexpected death of someone whose affairs were in disarray. As in, where's the password to the bank account? Or who's this Karen who keeps texting with heart and kisses emojis?

"Everyone has secrets they take to their graves. My guest today is one big secret. Let me introduce you to Riva O'Malley, recently deceased, estimated age, early twenties. She's laid out in front of me right now on a stainless-steel table. Dressed in a fluffy white gown, Riva looks like Snow White awaiting a visit from Prince Charming. No shoes, but she's sporting red painted toenails the color of maraschino cherries. Although she's dressed for a party, there will be no guests to entertain. She is an indigent without the benefit of friends or family. Tomorrow she'll be buried in a pauper's grave at Oakland

Cemetery in St. Paul.

"Before coming here, Riva suffered physical trauma at the hands of a person or persons unknown. They left her for dead, but she survived in what was diagnosed as a vegetative state. Her care defaulted to a dreadfully run county care facility, where the treatment consisted of regular watering and turning. Upon Riva's death, a medical exam revealed that, although she was paralyzed, she had maintained cognitive brain function. Imagine the horror of being trapped in your body, aware of the surroundings, the sounds and sensations, and yet not able to cry out. That was Riva's life for her last year. It's enough to make you want to kill yourself. But she couldn't even do that.

"But someone murdered her. Who? We don't know, and no one seems to care enough to find out. Thus, it always is with societal castoffs."

I turned to Riva. "Riva, my dear, now that you're dead, most people assume you're beyond sense perception. But what if they're wrong now, as they were before, and you actually can hear me? Please give us a sign, send us a message. Let us know who you are and allow us to bring those who harmed you to justice. If not, no worries. I and hopefully some listeners will commit you to our hearts and you will know you're not alone."

Behind me, I heard the service door to the prep room open. I turned and saw Truss enter the room and collect a gurney. He saw me next to O'Malley, unaware of what I was up to. "Vince, can you give me a hand?"

I hit the mute button on the podcast. "Sure, just give me a minute."

Even without the pressure of an audience, I had broken into a nervous sweat. The podcast felt rudderless. Note to self, work off a script. Thankfully, no one would ever hear the practice session, so a little comedic riff couldn't hurt. I clicked the sound back on and spoke into the microphone.

"Thanks for listening to this podcast. I hope you will join me again. Full disclosure, Truss Mortuary, the oldest and most respected funeral home in Minnesota, is a sponsor of 'The Very Last Laugh' podcast. Stop in and visit with Truss and Winona. Their day begins when yours ends. Can't afford a proper burial? Truss Mortuary will put you in the ground, no money down. For you smokers, take advantage of the early bird special on a coffin for your coughin'. If you're listening to this podcast while you're driving, text 666 and you'll get 50% off your funeral. See you soon."

CHAPTER 29

MPR

Truss, Winona and I arrived at the cemetery just past noon. My shirt had begun to stick to me. I had hoped we could get O'Malley buried before the mid-August humidity became even more unbearable and the gnats swarmed. As Truss stood next to O'Malley's pressboard casket mounted on a platform above the grave, he cast a glance toward the road in search of any unlikely visitors. Finally, he flipped open his pocket watch. "Let's give it another ten minutes."

Winona and I wandered off through the sun-bleached headstones and the conical arborvitae standing guard. We were drawn to the dates and calculated the age of the deceased, birth to death. I could find no fault with the math but often found the days, months and years too few to add up to an entire life. Occasionally, we'd come across something familiar, a shared birthdate or a family name. Winona seemed particularly moved by a child's marker and stopped to trace her fingertip on the gravestone's inscription.

Truss, who had been chatting with the shovel men, dismissed them as we arrived back at O'Malley's burial site.

"This poor woman is the fourth unclaimed county interment this month," Winona said as she stood next to the coffin. "I don't know how long we can keep doing this. We're now just a host for public welfare ticks to feed on. And speaking of parasites . . ."

I followed her eyes toward a man with a purpose in his stride, picking his way around the headstones. He walked straight toward the O'Malley gravesite. Ross Dalton.

"If it isn't the last of the morticians," Dalton said. "Oh, and the comic eulogist. Not much of an audience here. You bring a recorded laugh track?" He turned his attention toward Winona, "Mother sends her regards. Need any more yard signs?"

Winona shot him a middle finger.

"Aren't you a little out of your territory, Mr. Dalton?" Truss said.

"Not as out of bounds as these knuckleheads." Dalton swung a finger back and forth between Winona and me. "Did you know about their little prank that hijacked one of my funerals? By the look on your face, I'd guess not. Well, in your soon to be retired state, you'll have plenty of time to reflect on the nail in the coffin."

"I'd suggest you take your leave, Mr. Dalton," Truss said.

"Who do we have here?" Dalton ignored Truss' directive and pointed at the flat metal marker. "Riva O'Malley." He then turned to the casket and rapped knuckles on the hood. "The things they can do with cardboard."

That snapped something in me. I gave Dalton a shove. "Back off!"

The jolt knocked him on his ass. He sat on the grass, folded at the waist, and gasped for air.

"You'll all regret this." Dalton pointed at me with hateful revenge.

We stood in silence and watched Dalton stumble off to his bright yellow sports car and motor away. Truss stepped forward to conclude the interment of Riva O'Malley.

Winona placed a single rose on the casket and produced a cell phone. She clicked on her music app and played Sarah McLachlan's "In the Arms of An Angel". The music emanating from the phone's tinny speaker couldn't compete with the buffeting wind. The ubiquitous funeral song, and now the musical backdrop to a pet charity solicitation, sounded sadly small and distorted.

The beep-beep of a car horn coming from a vehicle parked next to Truss' hearse caught our attention. A man stepped out and waved at us. "Is this Riva O'Malley's burial?"

"Yes," Winona shouted back.

"Hold on, we've been trying to find you." The man looked off into the distance and talked into his phone. Soon a parade of cars came rolling down the lane. The occupants scrambled out carrying signs and started for the burial platform.

"Who are these people?" As they got closer, I could make out the homemade signs, *Jesus Wants You Dead or Alive, O'Malley Died For Our Sins Who's Next? Shit Happens Roll With It.* I felt my stomach knot. "I hope they're not the Waterboro Baptist crazies crashing our funeral."

"Well, crazies, but not the Baptist variety." Winona pointed at a couple costumed in Druid ceremonial horned hoods with animal skins draped over their cloth tunics. "Must have taken a wrong turn on the way to the Renaissance Festival."

"Hey, Vince." I felt a tap on my shoulder. It was my brother Ray's girlfriend.

"Sage, what are you doing here? Who are these people? Is this some prank Ray's in on? If so, I'll kill him."

"Slow down, hound dog, you're barking up the wrong tree. I was picking through the podcast directory and I saw you posted. I listened, liked it, and brought it to the attention of the MPR Program Director. We grabbed some interesting sound bites, slotted it into our 'Daily Dose of Strange' broadcast segment and suddenly, the phone lines are lighting up by people concerned about O'Malley. Some want to make a donation on her behalf, others want to show up at the service. Yeah, there are some weirdos." She swept a hand toward the ballooning gathering. "But we've got some regular folks, too."

O'Malley's unexpected mourners, proselytizers, gawkers and do-gooders milled around the burial platform. I shooed away a woman taking selfies with the coffin.

Truss looked over at me and nodded. He was right. A graveside eulogy was called for. I stepped forward and felt the same grip of inadequacy I had experienced as a twelve-year-old boy in front of my father's coffin. As with my father, long passages of O'Malley's life were not accessible.

Overhead, gravel gray clouds formed. The temperature dropped.

"Thank you all for coming to support Riva O'Malley." I raised my voice to keep my words from being swept away in the intensifying wind, "Riva's life is a mystery…" I felt a raindrop, then another and quickened my pace. "Hopefully we can find out more about her life . . ." Blat-blat-blat, the rain's tempo accelerated and drummed on the coffin.

The wet, hand-drawn posters now resembled Rorschach inkblots. I could feel the commitment of the guests unravel. "But everyone's life is a mystery to some extent. I know mine is . . ."

Boom! A clap of thunder shook the ground. A wall of water swept across the cemetery, bowing trees in its path. Instantly the guerrilla rainstorm was upon us and chased the guests away, leaving Truss, Winona and me to attend to O'Malley.

CHAPTER 30

BURRITOS

The day after O'Malley's burial, I navigated my way around a long line of people queued up outside the Dorothy Day Homeless Shelter. People on crutches and using walkers, women with children, young backpackers and weathered elderly—all held their ground waiting for the soup kitchen's doors to open. At the entry, I dispatched a cluster of pigeons fighting over the greasy contents of a White Castle carton.

Truss and Winona were regular volunteers. Burritos were the fare of the day. In the close quarter kitchen, Winona worked the tortilla press. Truss cooked up the meat, beans and rice and I prepared the cheese, tomato and salsa toppings. My presence held an ulterior motive—volunteers got to eat for free if there were leftovers.

"Wasn't it strange," I asked, as I cut up tomatoes, "that with all those people showing up at O'Malley's funeral, no one claimed to know her?"

"I think Dalton's in on this somewhere." Winona paused and looked at Truss. "You know when you said that if someone had an insurance policy on O'Malley, they would come knocking on our door looking for the death certificate? I think I heard that knock when Dalton showed up at O'Malley's gravesite."

Truss sprinkled chili powder over the meat and shook the frying pan. "I won't be able to withhold the death certificate much longer if there's no formal investigation, and the BCA hasn't authorized one, despite Agent Kirchner's recommendation."

"That Dalton creep makes me so mad I could scream."

"You're not the only one screaming." Truss held up a spatula. "I got a call from Madelyn Dalton. Said her son had contacted the law firm of Frisch and Morgan, human pit bulls. They're preparing a civil suit on behalf of Reliance Funeral Homes for the willful and malicious disruption of a funeral service and a criminal complaint against Truss Mortuary contractor Vince Locker for the aggravated assault on Ross Dalton."

"Total bullshit!" Winona's eruption sent flour into the air.

"Language, please. I believe this is a Christian charity."

"Yeah, yeah."

"Seriously, that was not your finest hour, either of you." Truss turned off the stove burner and made sure he had our full attention. "Madelyn confided that she normally wouldn't interfere in her son's business, but she doesn't want any blowback on her gubernatorial campaign. She'll get Ross to drop the suit on the funeral prank, based on Truss Mortuary making a significant donation to her campaign."

"No freaking way!" Winona turned in a circle. "That's extortion."

"You could also view it as settling a legitimate court case," Truss said, evenly. "Although I understand the motivation to get back at Dalton, I cannot abide by the tactics."

"You're right. I'm so sorry." Winona's face bunched in on itself, releasing a flood of tears.

Truss held out his arms, drawing Winona in against his chest, "It's all right, my dear, we'll get through this." He looked at me. "On the matter of aggravated assault, Madelyn said the only possibility of forgoing the charges against you, as frivolous as they are, is for you to offer Ross Dalton a direct apology."

I felt like I'd been hit by a stun gun. I tried to say something but could only emit an anger entangled stutter, "I-I-I . . ."

"First group coming in!" A volunteer working the dining hall shouted into the kitchen.

I took up a position at the serving station and spotted a guy I knew from the comedy scene. He held out a plate in front of me. I avoided eye contact and slipped him an extra burrito.

Winona gave me a lift home. We both felt frustrated by Dalton's legal threats and attempt at humiliation, but neither of us had the energy to discuss it. I needed a break from the world of the dead.

I needed to see my daughter.

CHAPTER 31

DADDY

Except for the one desperate occasion when Jessica had dropped Claire off at my house, she'd been withholding her from me. She pointed out I was unstable, I drank too much, had attempted suicide, and had some weird, morbid fixation with coffins. But when I promised to drop off two months' worth of child support, she agreed to a brief visit.

As I stepped onto the front porch of my ex-wife's rental duplex, Claire blasted through the screen door. "Daddy, daddy!" She jumped up to meet me. Jessica followed her out.

"Have her back by six and no more gold fish, I'm not running a pet store."

I never tired of looking at Jessica. Conversation was another matter, as it always led to the subject of money and deteriorated from there. At one point, before the divorce, Jessica suggested our marriage might be salvageable if I'd become a stay-at-home dad. I briefly considered it but the arrangement would only have amplified my sense of failure.

"Don't even think about bringing her to that creepy mortuary."

"What's a morthury?"

"Just some place daddy works," I said. "Not so fun for kids."

"Let's color," Claire said. "Mommy, I need my crayons." She wiggled out of my arms and grabbed Jessica's hand.

Jessica and Claire retreated into the house to get the art supplies. I followed, only to be gut punched by the sight of stacked cardboard boxes.

Jessica handed me Claire's backpack.

"Hey . . ." I cleared my throat. "Hey, it looks like you're moving."

"What, are you dense? I told you we're moving."

"Yeah, to Wisconsin, with your cheese-head friend."

"You're on thin ice with me already. Don't push it."

"What's the rush? You've got six months left on your lease."

"Are you paying the rent?"

"Give me some time. I'm working, trying to catch up on the payments. You don't have to move."

Claire came and stood between us. "I don't like it when you fight."

The front door opened, and in walked Pete, Jessica's twin brother. "Hey, Vinney." He moved in and gave me a hug.

He reeked of stale booze and body odor. I pried myself loose. "What's up, Pete?"

Jessica stepped in. "None of your business."

Pete hadn't worked in almost two years. He'd been a contract worker, rigging stage lighting, and had suffered an on the job back injury without the benefit of health insurance. He turned to street drugs to ease his pain, got hooked and had been arrested multiple times for theft and public disturbance. Jessica, to her credit and Claire's detriment, never abandoned him.

"Uncle Pete's been sleeping on the couch," Claire said.

I felt my fuse ignite—Claire didn't need to be exposed to anymore dysfunction. I grabbed her hand and left before I detonated.

The visit with my daughter proved to be a wonderful, restorative oasis. We went to the library and played the day away, drawing animals, real and imagined. I marveled at Claire's resilience. She'd been tossed around in the wake of her parents' storm, yet she engaged me with unconditional love. I thought about the rogue wave my father unleashed on me and all that went with it. Over time, my love for and the loss of my father fueled the neurotic son I had become.

When I took Claire home, I left Jessica two months of overdue child support along with Horse Camp tuition, money I had earned from eulogy work.

Eulogy work. Wow, never saw that coming. But I guess if eulogizing had taught me anything, it was that most folks lived by the seat of their pants. For some, life was mostly about avoidance of pain, emotional or physical. Others lived their lives for someone else, with regret for the missed opportunities they let slip away. All of the above applied to me.

CHAPTER 32

ICU

Toby had left me a voice message. He most likely wanted me to do a pro bono fundraising gig or needed an emergency stand-in for some comic who bailed on him at the last minute.

I hit the play button.

Hey, Vince, Toby here, this is important, don't blow me off. I'm sitting with your favorite comedy club guy, Louie. We're in the ICU. He's recovering from a triple bypass. I wanted to put you two together. Although at the moment, he's confused and has short-term memory loss. Maybe that's for the better.

I just got the news that Louie's Goth chic, the regional winner in the LaughCom Contest, bailed on the Nationals. Word has it she's living on a yacht in Australia with some tech dude who made a zillion on a meditation app.

So Vince, that moves you up to the top spot. Them's the rules. I brought the contest paperwork with me for Louie to sign, to officially bump you up to the Nationals.

All good, Louie? How about a thumbs-up for Vince?

I might be here a while. Louie's hitting the pain button like it's a Pez dispenser. But when he settles, I'll get him on the dotted line.

I need you to sign the contest release forms too, so call me—ASAP.

Wow, the Nationals. Everything I'd worked for. But this felt like sloppy seconds or some kind of weird setup.

My phone buzzed. I slapped it to my ear. "Toby, I don't appreciate you effing with my head like this."

"This Vince, the eulogy guy from Truss Mortuary?"

Oh, damn. "Sorry. Just Vince. Who's calling?"

"Jacob Zenk, a friend of Riva O'Malley. We need to talk."

CHAPTER 33

SARTRE

Zenk? The oxygen tank guy, Riva's significant other. On the short list of people who might have killed her.

"You there?" the gruff voice asked.

"Did someone from the mortuary tell you to call me?"

"No. I wanted to skip the middleman, save time, which I'm mighty short of. Got a health problem going to put me down soon, so appreciate if we could get to it."

Get to what? "Mr. Zenk, I'm sorry to inform you Ms. O'Malley was buried two days ago."

"Yeah, I know. Just need to get her story straight."

Her story? Riva still left me feeling incomplete. In fewer than two weeks, I had built a relationship with someone I had never known. I felt as though she spoke to me, but I didn't feel insane. It's more like I'd been called—called to put aside my shiftless wondering and salvage the secrets of the dead. To tell their story.

"Are you planning another ceremony for Riva?"

"We'll get to that."

"Look, let me clear this with Truss Mortuary."

"Do whatever you like, but we gotta meet today. I'll pay you what you need. Meet me downtown in Mears Park, in an hour." He hung up.

I considered Zenk could be dangerous, despite his disclosure of a terminal condition. However, a meeting in the open, with plenty of people around, seemed like a safe place to listen to what he had to say. As I walked through the park, past the topiary, dog walkers, homeless, tai chi dancers and helmeted Segway tourists, I spotted a man who met the description Zenk had provided. The slouched figure, topped in a Pioneer Seed cap, sat on the base of a patinated bronze statue. Clear plastic tubes stuck in his nose were tethered to an oxygen tank by his side. Birds chased breadcrumbs sprinkled about his feet.

"Mr. Zenk?" I took in the man's face and the rosy capillary blooms spread across his nose and cheeks.

"Yeah, grab some concrete." Zenk patted the ledge. As I sat down, Zenk secured a cigarette from his pocket and scratched a farmer's match against the oxygen tank. "I hear you're good at getting pigs to fly."

I edged away, nervous about the combination of fire and oxygen. "Excuse me?"

Zenk connected the match to the cigarette with a deep inhale. "I heard you sent Wilson Brock, the porn guy, out on a good note." He coughed on the words.

Zenk's mention of the porn producer caught me off guard. The association made me uncomfortable, as if I were part of something sleazy. "I knew nothing about Brock until I arrived at the service."

"I had a cellmate in the joint, sexual predator who prided himself on knowing all the big names in the porn business. Talked up this Brock guy like he was Scorsese until his mush for brains splattered the floor." Zenk waved his hands as to brush away the subject of Brock as if it were a fly. "But you weren't so clever in spinning a tale for my Riva at that carnival event you put on for her burial."

"You were there? Why didn't you come forward and tell her story yourself?"

"Need to lie low. I've been accused of battering Riva, a blow that sent her to that rat hole Angels of Mercy. Now, I'm an easy mark to be blamed for her death. But the fact of it is, there's more to Riva's story than I know."

How did I get myself into this mess? I had called the mortuary to tell them about Zenk's urgent request to meet. Truss had picked up the phone in the middle of the ancient answering machine's outgoing message and shouted hello, hello, while the instruction for me to leave my name and number played in the background. I left a message but wasn't sure if it got recorded. I dropped my hands to the steps, ready to boost my exit.

"Relax, I don't bite." He took a deep drag. "I've been hanging around bad actors so long I forgot my manners. Civil conversation is a weakness in prison." He held quiet for a long moment and turned his head to the sky. "I appreciate there are people like Truss who take on all comers regardless of their station."

Despite the caution signs blinking in my head, my curiosity about Riva propelled me forward. I pulled a small notebook from my pocket, eager to get the assignment on track.

Zenk stubbed his cigarette out against the oxygen tank and fixed his eyes on me. "Why would someone want to get in the middle of other people's grief?"

It's a question I had asked myself but still hadn't come up with an answer. No rationale for how the corkscrew path of my life had brought me to this place. "Just a gig I stumbled into, trying to catch on to something else full time."

"Done a lot of different jobs. Most of them went nowhere. Fact of it is, never knew what I was supposed to do in this life. Just kept walking through one door after another. Then one day I found myself in a place where all the doors were made of iron."

Maybe I was being played, a con's con, but I let my guard drop for the first time since I arrived at the park. "I'd hoped to be a teacher, but philosophy, my graduate degree, has fallen out of favor. It's all about hard skills now. Thought I might have a shot as a comedian, but that didn't work out either."

"Comedian, ha!" Zenk snorted. "Never met a real one before, just jokers."

Once again, I opened my notebook. "Sorry about your loss. How long did you know Riva?"

"Loss?" Zenk put emphasis on the word. "With every sunrise, Riva provided me with the potential to experience life as it is. To work, to laugh at myself, to care about someone." He shook his head as though deciding whether he should revisit the experience. "But I was care-less."

Zenk's eyes misted over. We sat in silence for a solid five minutes. I watched a police officer on a horse clip-clop along the street.

"Tell me about your loss," Zenk said, lighting another cigarette. "No one takes to accounting for another person's life by accident or otherwise, unless they've experienced something of it."

"Everyone experiences a loss sometime or another."

"Sure, but it takes people to different places. This intersection is one of them."

What was it about older men who made themselves sages of wisdom and insight? What was it the undertaker Truss said? That I was drawn to the bridge, scouted it out, before the interrupted suicide attempt. Now this broken down criminal wanted me to believe this meeting, based on mutual loss, was preordained. No, these human fossils were not wizards of sixth sense perception. It's just they'd recognized my childish attraction to be fathered and how vulnerable I was to their premonitions and baseless parapsychology.

I would not take the bait. I'd throw Zenk a bone so I could get on with the interview and leave. "Lost my dad when I was twelve. He got caught in a storm and never came home."

Zenk raised his hand to his lips, drew on his cigarette, and let the matter dissipate along with the exhaled lazy smoke plume. "That your car?" He pointed a yellow stained finger down the street. "Tell me it's not that piece of junk Toyota with the Al Gore sticker?"

I shrugged.

"I knew it." He shook his head. "Give me a hand off this slab and grab the land anchor."

As I extended an arm to assist Zenk, I read the inscription at the base of the bronze statue of the French philosopher Jean-Paul Sartre. *Man is the sum of his acts.*

Zenk also took notice of the philosopher's quotation. "Missing a few acts in Riva's life, so things don't add up, but we'll get to that," he said, and we ambled toward the Toyota.

I followed Zenk to the car. He opened the car door, motioned me to dump the oxygen cart in the back, and slumped into the passenger seat.

"Where to?"

"Home, with a stop in Nisswa."

"That's over two hours from here."

"You got a booking you need to get to? Besides, that's where the money is for your eulogy assignment. Thousand dollars good with you?"

I nodded. He had me off balance and totally at a loss as to where this junket might lead. But in truth, I got excited about road trips. It meant leaving my aimless life behind, an adventure for better or worse.

As I pulled away from the park, my phone buzzed. It was Toby.

"Excuse me," I said to Zenk. "It's my comedy agent. I better take this—he keeps calling."

"Not on my time."

I pushed Toby to voicemail.

"Let me see that phone," Zenk said, as though he wanted to make a call.

To my surprise, he turned it off and tossed it into the glove compartment. "Don't need any distractions."

I gripped the steering wheel. What have I gotten myself into?

CHAPTER 34

ROAD TRIP

I navigated through the city's morning rush hour traffic and out onto the open highway with the wheezing Zenk in the passenger seat. Feeling tense under Zenk's control, I opened my window. The morning air felt crisp and streaky cumulus clouds brushed the baby blue sky. I took a deep breath. Dew glistened on the knee-high cornstalks and bushy soybeans. I passed a Dalton for Governor sign, her omnipresence creeped me out.

Zenk seemed content to let the miles tick by and watch the same identical stretch of ground roll past. Suddenly, he rapped his knuckles on the side window.

"Hey, pull over."

I turned off the highway onto an isolated county road near Little Falls and parked on the shoulder. A parade of wild turkeys emerged from the drainage ditch and bobbled across the asphalt. Zenk got out and relieved himself, came back to the car, leaned on the front fender and fired up a cigarette.

"Soil's fickle in these parts." Zenk stared off into the distance. "We're sitting just south of the Laurentian Divide. Everything in this territory is mixed up. Rich farm patches and hardscrabble ground side by side. Rivers twist and turn—some flow north, others south. With my luck, I fell on the barren side of things. Pretty much the story of me."

Zenk nodded his head toward the robotic white stanchions, tilting their arms in hypnotic cadence. "Wind turbines. Know some of those boys who planted that iron. The only thing they're harvesting is dead birds."

"So, you're from this area?" I turned my face to the sky, taking in the warmth of the morning sun and the smell of sage, milkweed, freshly cut hay and manure. Air I would have missed if we'd kept rolling along the highway.

"Born in North Dakota." Zenk lit his next cigarette off of the last one and related his early days. His mother took off when he was four and his father drove him to central Minnesota and dropped him on a farm with relatives. "Said he'd be back but never returned. Guess we have that in common."

"Is your father still alive?"

"Wouldn't know, but imagine time would have won out this late in the game." Zenk turned and studied my profile. "Appears you have some inclination your father is still on this earth."

"I get a postcard, once a year, from different places in the Caribbean. Could be from my dad. A long shot, but it's something."

"Maybe so. Lot of guys in the joint use mailing services to hide their incarceration from family, friends and creditors. Sometimes those cards keep on coming long after they're out or dead."

Zenk erupted in a deep rattled cough and rushed a tissue to his mouth. He sat a good spell to let the subject of fathers settle. I counted four cigarettes Zenk had inhaled and now he was coughing up blood.

"Need me a piece of pie," Zenk said, as he got back into the car and secured the oxygen tubes in his nose. He pointed the way to Nisswa, a resort gateway for the Gull Lake chain. On the way into town, we passed the Paul Bunyan Land Theme Park featuring the twenty-six-foot-tall, animated lumberjack and Babe the Blue Ox.

Zenk directed me to stop at Ganley's Bakery, nestled among souvenir shops on Main Street. He said the bakery had become a local favorite and a must stop for folks passing through town on the way to their lake cabins. The smell of fresh bread, cinnamon and coffee met me as we entered.

"Oh, my God!" A heavyset woman with a round pasty face rushed from behind the counter to meet Zenk. "For the love of Judas, look at ya." She gave him a big squeeze. Half a dozen patrons, some wearing ball caps with farm implement logos, swiveled off the counter stools and came over to greet him. Zenk knew everyone's name, asked about their families and made small talk about farming.

"Won't forget what ya did for us," a man in worn coveralls said. "Hope your health works out." He pushed a thick envelope into Zenk's hand. "We all want to do right by you and Riva."

"Give the man some air," the baker woman said, and ushered Zenk to a booth.

I hung off to the side of Zenk's reception, taking it in and recalculating my sense of who Zenk was.

"Pam, this here fella's Vince." Zenk nodded in my direction. "Got a background in philosophy and funny, too."

As I slid into the booth across from Zenk, Pam quickly dropped a pot of coffee on the table along with a whole strawberry rhubarb pie and two plates.

"Fresh this morning, don't ya know." Pam stripped off her apron and slid in next to me, across from Zenk. "Can't keep 'em on the shelf, almost as popular as those Zenk Cakes."

Zenk had told me on the way into town that he had worked an early morning shift at Ganley's Bakery three days a week, catering to the weekend traffic. He added Zenk Cakes to Pam's pie offerings and gained a following in his own right. Said he loved the creativity, and it gave him enough income to keep his farm going.

Zenk paused a fork over the pie and looked up at the walls. Oil on canvas portraitures of farmers, machinery and children stared back at him. The quality of the art defied its place in a small town bakery.

"Plenty of folks have wanted to buy 'em. Cept that one." Pam pointed at a plump baker woman covered in flour and let out a hearty laugh. "But with Riva and ya gone, never felt it my place to take money for 'em." Pam's eyes watered. "Had a hunch ya might be back someday."

"Riva was thrilled when you agreed to display her work," Zenk said. "I'm just lucky to see them again, as close to being fertilizer as I am." He pointed at a portrait of a thick farmer with a John Deere tattoo on his bicep. "Bill Knudsen, heard he passed. Appreciate it if you'd give it to his wife. It might be worth something, and I reckon that like most folks around here she could use the money."

Pam nodded.

"I'd like you to contact one of those art auction places in the city and see what you can get for the rest of them," Zenk said. "Take whatever you need for your troubles and donate the rest in Riva's name to the local school for some art classes."

"Always the savior," Pam said. "Have some more pie. You too, Vince."

"Thanks, but we gotta get on down the road. Want to give Riva's storyteller," Zenk nodded at me, "a look at Riva's last stand."

CHAPTER 35

HAZARDOUS

Zenk called out directions as we drove toward his farmstead near Baxter. Something seemed off after the bakery encounter and it nagged at me. Finally, I brought it up. "It seemed during our visit with Pam that Riva had some friends that cared about her. Why didn't anyone come to visit her at Angels of Mercy or catch wind of the funeral?"

"We'll get to that. Now turn here." He pointed.

I pulled onto a washboard gravel road that ended at a bullet-punctured, rusted mailbox. "We're here."

A posted sign read: Keep Out. Hazardous Property. Danger. I raised an eyebrow at Zenk.

"DEA covering their asses in case of chemical runoff." Zenk waved me on.

The deeply rutted driveway scraped the Toyota's undercarriage, leading me to keep my eyes on the rearview mirror to make sure we weren't leaving a trail of oil. The cautious, slow drive ended at a dilapidated house. Birds freely fluttered in and out of broken windows. A faded yellow crime scene tape, tied to a porch rail, blew in the wind like a party streamer. Behind the house stood a large barn, two implement sheds and a concrete silo banded with metal hoops. The painted sign on the silo read, 'Art Studio.'

Zenk got out of the car, without the oxygen tank, and walked the property. He waded into a fallow field taken over by prickly burdock and orphaned cornstalks. I took a deep breath and let my shoulders drop. The midday air revealed a mix of sage, honeysuckle and a distant skunk.

Zenk stopped, pulled a pointed leaf off a straggler stalk, and turned it in his hand. "Soil isn't good for much, but I made it count for something." He handed me the leaf. I turned it over in my hand. Cannabis.

"Maybe I wasn't patient enough, but I never took a handout." I detected a somber note in Zenk's voice—sadness. "Couldn't see a future beyond this place. It cost me my Riva." Zenk's eyes moistened, and he wandered off and sat under the lacy canopy of a black willow.

I followed. "How did you meet Riva?"

"She showed up at Ganley's Bakery one day, in a van full of musicians who were crisscrossing the country. The band played a mix of reggae, bluegrass and rock. Somewhere along the way, Riva hitched a ride with the minstrel vagabonds, and when they arrived in Nisswa there seemed to be a falling out of some sort in progress."

"A boyfriend?"

"Never sure about the relationship, but it was clear from the start she didn't suffer fools easily. In a scene that played out for Ganley's patrons to enjoy, Riva had a fight with her bandmates and refused to get back in the van. Said the only reason she signed on is that they would land in St. Paul. A change of plans had them traveling to Thunder Bay by way of Duluth. She told the group to buzz off. The band left her stranded in the bakery, broke and without a plan. Pam had a spare room and put her up while Riva figured out her next move."

"So that's how you came to know her?"

"We didn't exactly hit it off right away." Zenk let out a little snort.

"She came into the bakery every morning and spent most of the day reading and doodling. One might not consider her classically good-looking, but there was a soulful depth to the woman I found attractive."

A rattled hack erupted from Zenk's lungs. When the cough had settled, he shook his head. "I was twenty years older than Riva. Before my lungs turned to soot, I was a much healthier and more worthy man than I am now. I tried to play the world-weary vet who'd seen something of life. She saw right through my hogwash. She'd been around and had her own street cred. When I got up on my high horse, trying to leverage my age and experience to blow hot air about politics, religion or the way things should be, she cut me off at the knees."

A sudden plume of dust erupted from a neighbor's nearby field, under plow, and cast the sunlight into a tawny haze. "Better fetch the tank from the car," Zenk wheezed.

I used the break from Zenk to retrieve my phone. I turned it on. Mercifully, I got a cell signal. There were six calls from Toby. The guy was like a dog on a bone, trying to nag me into submission. He could wait. I called the mortuary and Winona picked up.

"Where are you?"

"Nisswa ... no Baxter, near Brainerd. I tried to call you but couldn't get through the answering machine."

"I know. I heard a garbled message with you and Truss talking over each other. What are you doing in Baxter?"

"Visiting with Jacob Zenk, O'Malley's boyfriend."

"Are you out of your mind? He's a violent criminal who bludgeoned his girlfriend and is now a prime suspect in her murder at Angels of Mercy."

"I'm not getting a violent vibe from him. He's broken down, weak, and has a terminal illness. He wants to share what he knows about O'Malley. I think I'm finally onto her story."

"You know who's onto you—Madelyn Dalton. She stopped by the mortuary and raised holy hell. Ross Dalton is missing, and she wants answers."

"He's probably on some bender. Who cares?"

"He's been missing for two days. Apparently, his mother has access to his phone and credit cards. There's been no recent usage or transactions."

"And this is our problem? Why, exactly?"

"She claims the last call received on Dalton's phone was from you."

"I called him to apologize per Truss' instruction. Dalton said Truss Mortuary was going under, then offered me a job and promised I'd make a boatload of money. I told him to forget it."

Winona made a gagging sound. "Look, you need to get back here now. Madelyn can be big trouble. We've got to deal with this."

I held my silence, knowing she was right. But I was so close to hearing who Riva O'Malley really was. I couldn't let it go.

"Are you there?" Winona's voice had turned desperate.

"I've . . . I don't know. I've been called. Riva spoke to me. My work is not yet done."

"Have you effing lost it? Get off whatever you're on and get back here."

"Seriously, I need just a little more time with Zenk. Have to go. Call you on my way back."

I hung up in the wake of Winona's protest and tossed the phone back into the glove box.

When I returned with the oxygen tank, Zenk was gone, but his cough hung in the air. I followed the hacking sound into the weather-worn post and beam construction barn, with a hayloft door in the gable.

"Riva's studio." Zenk waved an artist's paintbrush. "We remained worlds apart until she overheard Pam shag me on an errand into Bemidji and asked if she could hitch a ride. On the way back to the bakery, I stopped at a flea market. Riva wandered off to a table with art for sale. I let her be as engaged as she wanted with the paintings and such. When Riva found her way to my pickup, she had a bag of art supplies. She brimmed with excitement, like she found a buried treasure."

I spotted a dust-covered canvas on the floor, picked it up and set it on an easel ledge. It was an oil of Riva, Zenk and a dog, walking out of a tasseled cornfield. Riva appeared tall and thin, with dark hair and skin the color of autumn wheat. The dappling of freckles sprinkled on her sharp cheekbones reminded me of a spring fawn.

"She did most of her artwork at a table in the bakery or in the park, if the weather was agreeable." Zenk stood in front of the portrait and just shook his head. "Didn't quite know where I stood with Riva. Some part of me thought she wanted the counsel of a father. At other times, I could feel the spark of a lover. I kinda bribed her to move in with me. Offered to build her an art studio."

Zenk looked tired and started to shake.

I grabbed an arm to steady him. "You okay?"

"Need to sit a spell."

I helped him walk back to the farmhouse, tested the floorboards on the porch, rolled up an old newspaper and dusted off a tired rocker so Zenk could sit. I found a sturdy enough porch column to lean against. Zenk inserted the oxygen tubes and took a deep breath.

"Mostly, our relationship was easy, and we enjoyed each other's company, until I rolled the tractor. Then things turned to shit." Zenk shook his head. "Rear wheel dropped into a sinkhole. Crushed three vertebrae and left me as helpless as a new foal. Any money I had went to doctors, treatment, and useless medications. Should have given the farm up. If it weren't for Riva's insurance policy, we would have moved on. She was more determined than I was to save the place."

My ears perked right up. "What kind of insurance?"

"Life insurance. Never got a good look at the paperwork. Riva had it in play before she met me. Never knew about it. Desperate, she found this slick fella who offered her cash on the barrelhead if she turned over the policy." Zenk paused, lit a cigarette, turned his head sideways and blew out the smoke. "She should have walked from the deal. The insurance guy was clever. He knew we were out of financial options and knew exactly how much debt we carried. He made Riva an offer that would bring us even plus a couple of months forward." The light died in Zenk's eyes.

This sounded like a Reliance Funeral Home deal, but I needed to hear more and held back on a confirmation.

Zenk scratched his cheek. "I made two mistakes, one stacked on top of another. Not only did I allow Riva to take a bad deal to bail us out, but it also seeded my next move. After the back injury, I was in severe pain and couldn't drive a tractor to save my life. I tried medical grade marijuana, found it gave me some relief, but I couldn't afford it. So I turned my attention to processing cannabis oils and extracts on my own. Riva wanted no part of it, but I figured I was onto something. The truth of it is that, along with digging myself out of a hole, I was looking for some easy money. I converted an old tornado storm shelter into a lab. My neighbors grew the pot, I did the processing. It helped those farm families make up for a lot of poor years and got the creditors off their backs, too."

"A drug lab? Where?"

"As the crow flies." Zenk pointed at a blackbird that had just erupted from a cottonwood and flew across the fallow fields. "About fifty yards in that direction."

I scanned the field, looking for a structure in the gauzy, humid afternoon light. "Not seeing anything."

"When was the last time you saw an above ground storm shelter?"

I ventured toward the field for a closer look.

"I don't advise you go out there. Nothing but a burned-out hole and for all I know, it could be contaminated."

I put the brakes on with Zenk's warning and retreated to the porch.

Zenk knitted his gnarled fingers together and rocked in the chair slowly. The almost imperceptible action emitted the sound of squeaky wood, like crossed tree limbs rubbing in the wind. "That life insurance policy always nagged at me. Felt no good would ever come of having someone invested in Riva's timely demise. Once I got on my feet from the medical pot trade, I tried to buy that life insurance policy back, but the insurance guy would have no part of it. I threatened to call some regulator, although I didn't know who that would be." Zenk shook his head.

I took a seat on the porch steps. "What caused Riva's injuries?"

"My stupidity, at least in the end." A few heartbeats went by before he spoke again. "In hindsight, I'd been given a sign but missed it. One day, from the Nisswa bakery window, a yellow flash caught my eye, like a flicker of light. It was out of sight before I could get a mental purchase on the sudden splash of color. I let it go but felt uneasy. Turned out to be the insurance guy's yellow sports car."

"Dalton!" The name exploded out of my mouth.

"Oh, you're familiar with that earth worm?"

"I met him through Truss Mortuary. He was being disrespectful towards Riva and I gave him a shove. Now he's threatened to charge me with assault. I should have popped him one and really earned it."

"Wouldn't give him much worry." Zenk turned his attention to field stripping the spent cigarette and let the tobacco blow away.

CHAPTER 36

ANNIVERSARY

I heard what sounded like a car door slam. "You expecting someone?"

"No, why?"

"Thought I heard a car nearby."

"Maybe." Zenk pulled on his ear. "My hearing ain't so good."

I waited and with my attention focused on the driveway, alert for sound or movement. Silence. I turned my attention back to Zenk. There was a weathered coarseness to his skin, his whiskers as gritty as sandpaper. But I found a contradiction in his rough-hewn physicality and his sensitivity toward O'Malley.

"After my bakery shift, on the day the insurance guy sped through town," Zenk said, "I drove back to the farmstead with a cake box on the front seat. We had planned an anniversary celebration. It was a year to the day Riva took up with me on the farm. Fifty feet from the farmhouse, I spotted my black lab lying in the driveway—bled out, covered with flies. I jumped out of the car and ran into the house looking for Riva. I ran into the art studio barn. Nothing. Back outside, I saw smoke leaking out of the underground lab. I opened the door, but a hot, black plume pushed me back. Using my cell phone as a flashlight, I held my breath, rushed down and cast the light beam. Behind a metal drum, I glimpsed a leg. Blood pooled on the floor. I wanted to scream, but fought to keep my mouth clamped shut. I grasped Riva under the arms and carried her out into the light of day."

He coughed into his sleeve. "Before I could get to the surface, I gulped a lungful of toxic air."

I could see the recounting of events take a physical toll on Zenk. His hands were locked down on the chair's arms, his eyes fixed. I found myself listening to his labored breathing and found the pace of my breath had matched his. Mercifully, his cough broke the synchrony and saved me from hyperventilating.

Zenk continued, his voice now more anguished than agitated. "I felt for a pulse in her neck and put my head to her chest. With the blood pounding in my ears, I couldn't tell whose beat I was hearing. Emergency services are limited and slow in these parts. No telling how long an ambulance would take. I loaded her into the back seat of my car. Her eyes were half shut, and she was bleeding from both nostrils. It was as though the sudden deflation of life instantly added years Riva hadn't earned. As I drove away from the farm, the anniversary cake bounced on the front seat."

I heard voices and turned my head toward the driveway. Zenk didn't hear it. Perhaps it was just the heat making a strange noise. The day had turned into a low-hanging steam bath and contributed to my overall sense of disorientation.

"We should head back to town." I had enough of the picture for now. If there was more to O'Malley, Zenk could fill me in along the way.

"Come inside, I want to give you something." Zenk stood up and pushed through the unlocked farmhouse door.

I followed him into the house and batted away the cobwebs that ensnarled my hair and face. Someone had ransacked the place. The furniture was upended and kitchen cabinets rifled. Curiously, a small trophy sat on a bookshelf covered in dust, untouched. I blew on the nameplate—it read 'Best Duet'. An upright piano stood against the wall. I plucked at the keys, resulting in discordant notes.

"That was my aunt's piano," Zenk said, on his way to a pantry off the kitchen. "Riva played it, too."

I moved off the piano and followed him. "Did Riva ever talk about her life before she met you?"

"A woman like that doesn't just show up on your doorstep without some connections. And I was certainly curious. But right from the start, she let it be known that her past was none of my business. I thought she might be hiding out from some domestic trouble or the like. I took to looking her up on the internet—a violation of trust that left me ashamed but didn't stop me—but I never found anything on her. She knew I was probing, told me she cared too much about me to share her past and said if that wasn't enough, she'd be moving on."

"Nothing about family or friends?"

Zenk removed the cap from his head and swiped a sleeve over his forehead. "From prison, I tried to find someone who could assume legal responsibility for her. Riva, alone, and without advocates at Angel of Mercy? I couldn't stand it. I made contact with one of her old bandmates, but he wasn't much help. He thought she was from New Orleans, or Houston, maybe went to art school in California. Offered that Riva O'Malley could have been a stage name."

"What was so important about her going to St. Paul?"

"Don't know, although I was aware of at least two trips she made to the Twin Cities."

Zenk kicked away the debris on the floor and raised a trapdoor. With an adeptness I didn't think possible from someone in his condition, he dropped through the hole into a crawl space. When he reappeared, he slid a backpack onto the floor. I held out a hand and pulled with all my strength to haul him up and over the lip of the trapdoor opening. Once Zenk got upright, he picked up the pack and extracted a bronze colored, cylinder-shaped object. At first glance, I thought it was a bullet casing.

"If Riva taught me anything," Zenk said, "it's that you really never know someone. When I rescued her on the lab floor, she had it curled tight in her hand. She had worn that pendant around her neck from the day I met her. Meant something to her." He handed it to me.

The bronze pendant had bands of intricate zodiac symbols inscribed all around it.

"It was totally Riva to put up a fight." Zenk shook his head. "Perhaps, too much of one. She wouldn't give it up for the life of her. I think it's a clue from the time before I met her. Maybe it'll help you set her story straight."

While Zenk dug into the pack for more items, I heard quick thumps on the porch. Then the farmhouse door crashed open, and a man rushed me, drilling the barrel of a pistol into my skull.

CHAPTER 37

MUMMY

Zenk and I complied with the sharp order to move outside and kneel on the ground. It took me a minute to recognize the figure I saw standing in the middle of the farmyard.

Madelyn Dalton.

"Watch that one, Tommy." Madelyn pointed at me. I remembered Tommy from Madelyn's political fundraiser at the gun range. He appeared to be her personal attendant or maybe a bodyguard. That same necklace, a hog's tooth hanging a green cord, encircled his neck.

Madelyn stepped up to me. "Where's my son, you lowlife? His cell phone is obviously here."

"I don't know where Ross is. I'm just here on a eulogy assignment."

Madelyn pointed at Zenk. "Who's this piece of trash?"

"If it's introductions you're looking for, my name's Jacob Zenk. And you're the bitch who bore that insurance scammer."

Tommy stepped in and cracked the pistol alongside of Zenk's head. Zenk staggered but didn't drop, despite the blood dripping down his face.

"You sick son of a bitch." Madelyn's anxiety turned to aggression in an instant. "Where's Ross?"

"Turned him into a vegetable, same as he did to my Riva." A smirk formed on Zenk's face. "On his way to being worm grub."

I had no idea what Zenk was talking about, but I needed to deescalate the situation, and fast. "Listen," I said, "this place is contaminated—the land, buildings, everything. You saw the sign, 'Hazardous Property'. For your own health and safety, please leave."

Tommy tilted his head toward Madelyn to consider the warning. He opened his mouth, but before he could speak, Madelyn grabbed me by the ear. "Cut the crap or you won't have any health to worry about." She pivoted toward Zenk and kicked him in the gut. "Where's my son?"

Zenk gasped for breath as he raised a hand and pointed. "Just beyond the shed."

Tommy ordered us to our feet.

"He needs his oxygen tank," I said. "It's in the house."

"Negative." Tommy gave him a shove. "Let's go."

I felt a heaviness in my legs, as if they were filled with concrete, and had to will my body to move.

Zenk stopped at the shed and pointed at a shovel. "You might want to bring that along."

"What have you done?" Madelyn shouted and pounded her fist on Zenk's back.

Zenk seemed oblivious to the attack and continued his slow walk across a field and onto a sun-dappled path through the woods. There was no movement in the trees, no sound, not even a leaf quaking. Sweat beaded my forehead and ran down my face.

We would have missed it if Zenk hadn't pointed at a freshly disturbed patch of ground with a protruding rubber hose. "There's your insurance man." Zenk sat down with his back against a tree.

Madelyn ran to the mounded dirt and frantically clawed at the earth with her hands, screaming wildly, "No, no!"

I dropped to my knees. What was happening here? I'd thought

A COMEDIAN WALKS INTO A FUNERAL HOME

Zenk was harmless, I thought Dalton was crooked but not evil. Now, suddenly, I was in the middle of an episode of *Criminal Minds*.

Tommy grabbed Madelyn under the arms and pulled her up. "Let me handle this." He walked her back from the grave and handed her the gun. "If either of these low life bastards moves, shoot them."

Tommy knelt and put his ear to the rubber tube. "He's breathing." With the aid of the shovel, he carefully began the excavation. The grave was shallow and the dirt soft. The soil gave way to a duct tape bound body. Tommy worked enough dirt away to reveal what looked like the head of an elephant rat. I recognized the headgear as an old military style gas mask, with goggles and a long dangling oxygen air tube. Tommy rolled the body out of the hole, removed the mask and unfurled the duct tape. Tommy recoiled from a sickening stench that arose from Dalton and permeated the air.

Zenk was unmoved. "Pretty ripe for only being in the ground for two days, but he was garbage to begin with."

"Let it go," I yelled at Zenk. Madelyn had already turned into a feral animal. Poking her only irritated an impossible situation.

Ross Dalton gulped air and thrashed about on the ground in a spasmodic fit. He gave off a low growl, a sound that escalated into a full-on scream, a siren from someone whose brain had been blown away. His eyes bounced about, unable to focus. Madelyn tried to console him, but he pushed her away. I had to admit Dalton was a total nutcase, but he didn't deserve to be broken like this.

"I'm going to get him to the car," Tommy said. He stripped off his belt and bound Ross's flailing arms. He extracted a cell phone from Ross' back pocket and held it up for Madelyn to see. "Hold the gun on these creeps. I'll be right back to deal with them."

"Thank God you found him." I said.

"Too bad the same won't be said for you."

173

"He's not in on this," Zenk called out to Madelyn. "Suggest you consider the facts of the matter."

"Enough with your twisted blather."

"Desperate to cash in my Riva's life insurance policy, he bludgeoned her and left her for dead. But she proved to be a real survivor, if you call rotting away in a squalid care center, survival. When sonny found out I'd been released from prison, he figured I'd pay her a visit and end her life, as an act of mercy. Said he could see where that might be hard for me, as emotionally involved as I was, so he killed her as a favor to me."

"Shut up," Madelyn said.

"He pointed out that Riva was virtually dead already. You sure raised one considerate son."

"Shut up, shut up!"

"Your gopher dug his own grave, but not before he pleaded and whined. Even tried to cut a generous deal to save himself. He said I could have the full benefit of the life insurance he held on Riva O'Malley—two million dollars, thank you. No hard feelings. Just one minor detail. The death certificate was being held up, but as soon as it was registered, I'd be in the money."

"All lies!" Madelyn's hand trembled as she tried to steady the gun.

I was really wishing Zenk would just shut up, but of course he wouldn't. What did he have to lose?

"So as to make sure mommy's boy followed directions, I dragged the butt end of a shotgun along the ground and cut a rectangle in the turf. He struggled with the dig, at first. But once he got past the compacted topsoil and the excavation began to take shape as a grave, he mentioned you. Said his family had money and political connections, and whatever it took to make things right, he'd square it with me. Is that so, mommy dearest?"

"As soon as Tommy comes back, it will be the last anyone will hear from you."

"You sure about that?"

She pointed the gun at me. "I'm not stupid enough to let a witness live."

I didn't have the time to appreciate the terror this inspired, because while Madelyn's attention was on me, Zenk snatched the discarded shovel and swung it at Madelyn.

She instantly buckled with the crack of the spade against her shin, but hung on to the pistol. She fired wildly in Zenk's direction.

A round caught Zenk in the forehead and parted his skull.

Acidic bile welled up in the back of my throat. I looked at Madelyn, frozen in place, stunned by the kill shot.

A sudden rush of survival adrenaline propelled me into her space. I twisted the pistol out of her hand and pointed it directly at her face.

"What the hell!" I shouted, the smell of gunpowder searing my brain. Staring deep into her eyes, I felt the power of the executioner mixed in with my own pathetic desperation and weakness.

"You're dead meat." She squeezed the words out through a painful grimace, then caught me by surprise with a backhand strike that nailed me square in the mouth. I felt gritty bits of broken tooth enamel and my upper lip stun from her fat diamond ring.

Three blasts from a car horn riveted my attention, a signal from Tommy that he was on the move. Madelyn looked up the path. I took a quick look at Zenk's shattered head, holding my breath to keep from vomiting, and bolted into the woods.

CHAPTER 38

ESCAPE

The wooded thicket tore at my clothes and arms. Exhausted, my lungs on fire, I found a ravine bordering a shallow creek and dug myself into a muddy pocket of earth along the bank. I sat motionless and listened to the sounds of crickets, cicadas and frogs come to life beyond my circle of sight. I still had the gun. My fingerprints were now on it, along with Madelyn's and Tommy's, which opened me up to the possibility of a concocted story whereby I killed Zenk. I stashed the gun under a nearby boulder.

As darkness settled in, I saw passing headlights in the distance. I left my den, headed toward the road and followed it, walking along the drainage ditch, back to Nisswa.

The sign at Ganley's Bakery said *Closed*, but a light in the kitchen remained on. I went to the back door and knocked. The door opened and a woman with a stack of white hair peeked out. "We're closed. Open at six in the morning."

"I need your help. I'm Vince, the eulogy guy. I was with Zenk."

Pam paused and looked me over—swollen lip, scratches and bug bites in evidence. "Somebody punch ya into a raspberry patch?"

Before I could answer, she ushered me into the bakery and over to a table in the food prep area. "Still got some coffee on." She set down a mug. "Got a First Aid kit round here someplace."

"Thanks, but I can manage. Zenk's dead."

Pam gasped and sat down.

She listened to my account about Riva's insurance policy, Zenk's kidnapping of Riva's assailant, Ross Dalton, and Dalton's rescue by his mother. I attempted to put events in the proper order, but terror doesn't inspire clear thinking.

When I was done, Pam sat for a while, taking it in while I downed coffee and day-olds. "Madelyn Dalton, the woman running for Governor?"

"She killed Zenk, shot him in the head."

"Jesus, save us all." Pam traced the sign of the cross along her ample bosom.

"I think Madelyn's thug friend, Tommy, might have buried him, but I'm not sure. I should call the police."

"Of course, but dead is dead, so let's take a breath before ya jump in with both feet. Trust me, this ain't my first smorgasbord." She poured more coffee. "I'd say Mrs. Dalton and company had plenty of time to cover their tracks. No telling how it will play out from here. Could be they might just call in a tip that ya murdered Zenk. Get ya tossed in jail. Or they might come lookin for ya on their own account. Either way, yer in danger. Ya got folks who can keep ya safe for a bit while things get sorted out?"

I called the mortuary. Truss answered. I didn't know why I sought out Truss at this juncture, but the old man's steady hand was just what I needed. I gave him a play-by-play account of my afternoon with Jacob Zenk.

Pam waited eagerly to hear my next move and asked how she could help.

I related that Truss said he'd contact Agent Kirchner from the BCA. The BCA would follow up with the Daltons and send the local sheriff out to Zenk's property. Truss also told me to lie low until arrangements were in place for me to give my side of things to the authorities. Winona was coming to pick me up. Where to, from here, he didn't say.

I thought I'd feel better when I talked to somebody, yet the tight band that gripped my head wouldn't release. Zenk's frozen gaze ran a continuous loop through my brain. Adrenaline and caffeine had powered me through the night, but now it was dawn and I was crashing.

Pam stood behind my chair and gently kneaded her baker hands into my shoulders until they gradually deflated.

"Can I do something for ya?" she asked.

I reached up and tapped her on the hand to signal my appreciation for her help. "There is something very important I'd like to entrust to you."

"You betcha!" Pam came around to the table and sat.

I pulled Riva's pendant from my hip pocket and handed it to her.

"That's Riva's." Pam rolled the piece of jewelry in her hand. "Never saw her without it."

"I need you to get this to my brother as fast as possible. He's a pain in the ass, but he's also a genius. If this is the lock to Riva O'Malley, he'll find the key."

CHAPTER 39

TWOFER

I spotted Winona's car from inside the bakery. Along with a crushing hug, Pam sent me off with a fresh pie.

"Are you all right?" Winona took in my scratched arms and face. "Hey, that puffy lip sure is sexy."

"Right now, I feel like a total nutcase." My words came out in a spittle spray. "Zenk said Dalton tried to kill O'Malley over some insurance scam, left her for dead on his farm, then finished her off at Angels of Mercy. Next thing I know, Madelyn Dalton and her thug Tommy show up looking for Dalton. Zenk had him stashed in a shallow grave—buried alive. Zenk gets a bullet to the brain and I'm within a finger's twitch of being executed. Oh, did I mention I spent three hours burrowed into a mosquito infested hole fearing for my life?"

"Dalton, that scumbag!" Winona put a stranglehold on the steering wheel. "He showed up on Truss Mortuary's doorstep just as we took O'Malley in." I could almost hear the puzzle pieces in Winona's brain click into place. "He wanted her buried pronto! When he caught wind that Truss was contesting the ME report, he harassed and threatened to take us over or shut us down, anything to get O'Malley's interment finalized and her death certificate issued so he could cash in on her."

I instantly regretted dumping my pent-up rage on Winona and

escalating her Dalton obsession. I rolled down the window to feel the slap of air against my face. She kept her attention on the road and we let things settle. Traces of magenta streaked the pre-dawn sky. I quickly recognized we were not heading back to St. Paul. "Where are we going?"

"A twofer. Tamarack Lake Rez. Truss thought you should stay off the radar for a couple days, out of harm's way, while he sorts things out with the authorities, and I get to visit my family."

"A twofer." I scratched at the mosquito bites, too exhausted to argue the plan, and watched the shadowy glacier scrubbed Plains of central Minnesota transition to thick stands of forest pines.

Still, my brain wouldn't let it go. Ripples of fear kept bouncing off the sides of my skull. "Did Truss hear anything about finding Zenk?"

"He said Agent Kirchner had the BCA and the local sheriff scour the property. No body has been found."

So they moved it. "What about the shallow grave, duct tape, oxygen hood?"

"Nothing—but there were signs of tampering at the site where you claim Zenk was killed. Someone had spread lye and an oxygen-based detergent all over the suspected crime scene. Chemicals Truss claims destroy DNA."

"That would have been Tommy covering their tracks. I'm not at all surprised that's part of his skill set. What about the gun?"

"Don't know."

"So, it looks like they're planning to say I fabricated the encounter with Zenk, and worse yet, the police probably think I covered up the crime scene." I pulled at my hair. "Somebody please let me out of this nightmare."

"Truss said you're not a suspect, but . . ."

"But?"

"Agent Kirchner says you're a person of interest, and it's important that you talk . . ."

"Deer!" I braced my arms against the dashboard.

Two brightly dilated eyes stood dead ahead in the road. Winona swerved, narrowly missing the hindquarters of a large doe. I heard the click of hooves on the asphalt as it bounded into the woods.

"Oh my God. Are you okay?" I'd broken a sweat.

"Just startled. I need to pull over and catch my breath."

We sat and listened to the call of croaking frogs and crickets. With our nerves settled, Winona cautiously pulled back onto the road.

"Why should I trust Agent Kirchner to operate in my best interest?"

"All I know is that he's loyal to Truss. That makes him trustworthy in my book."

"Loyal why?"

"Truss told me he buried Agent Kirchner's father, a St. Paul cop killed breaking up a domestic dispute. In the aftermath, Kirchner, the son, fell into a bleak period, steeped in depression and booze." Winona shook her head. "Boy, do I know what that's like." She took a deep breath. "Kirchner would show up at the mortuary from time to time, as he seemed to find solace in the place. Truss steered him into a treatment program."

I thought about my plight and Winona's and now Kirchner's. So Truss saves souls and then has them do his bidding.

No, that was the cynic in me talking. I pushed it away. I could only hope Kirchner's debt to Truss extended to me. "Any information on Dalton? He was in terrible shape."

"Truss said he heard his mother checked him into a private mental health facility. Nervous breakdown."

I rubbed my eyes. I couldn't get Zenk's bullet-punctured skull out of my head. "Madelyn will do anything to keep her political campaign on track."

"Yep, murder, life insurance and politics, all on their terms. Pretty much how the Daltons roll." Winona cocked an exaggerated eyebrow. "Did Zenk share anything with you about O'Malley's mysterious background?"

"He gave me something, said it was a clue to O'Malley's past, a pendant. It meant something to her. I sent it to my brother. Hopefully, he can figure it out."

CHAPTER 40

SECRET PIE

As we pushed on through the night, a flash of light, like a wink of an eye, broke from the eastern horizon. I asked Winona if I could use her cell phone to call my brother. I had left my phone in the glove box of my car at Zenk's farm.

"Ray, it's me. Did you get a package?"

"Yeah, a pie. Gave it to the neighbor's dog, compliments of Ganley's Bakery, whoever that is."

"You didn't?"

Winona looked over at me, her face a question. I raised a finger to signal her to give me a moment. I had to keep Ray on task.

"Should have. I found a note from you taped to the bottom of the pie tin—some bull about a mystery pendant. I've left you messages, but you didn't get back to me. That's totally rude, dude."

"Can't get at my phone, long story."

"Like I don't know. Some Toby guy stopped by, all bristled up about getting hold of you. Says he's your comedy agent. Told him to get lost, I'm not your receptionist."

"What about the pendant?"

"Why are you dragging my ass into this?"

"Because I have no one else to turn to."

"So you finally admit I have some value. Red-letter day. Whoopee!"

"Ray, what did you find?"

Winona looked at me in nervous anticipation, barely able to keep the car on the road. I listened for a response from Ray.

Silence.

"Ray, you still there?"

"A forest berry pie with a crusted top. Looked amazing, but you had to bury some foreign object in it and ruin it for me. Found the pendant in a plastic bag. I made a mess getting at it. The kitchen cleanup is on you."

"Ray . . . the pendant?"

"A vintage combination padlock with four rotating brass cylinder-shaped bands with carved zodiac characters."

"Can you get it open?"

"Contact an astrologer."

"Ray!"

"Each of the bands have five unique zodiac characters and spin freely on a center shaft. Like any combination lock, the correct characters from each band must be aligned in the proper order for it to open. My guess is that once it opens, the center shaft drops out to reveal a secret compartment."

"Can you open it?"

"What am I, Houdini? There are over fifty thousand combination possibilities, which I don't have time to twiddle my thumbs over, but a good whack with a hammer should do it."

"Don't, you could damage the contents."

"So what's the big deal?"

"I'm hoping the pendant reveals something about its owner, Riva O'Malley, a murder victim."

"Murder? No way."

"Ray, this is important. Call me on this number when you've got something. Thanks, bro."

CHAPTER 41

SWEAT

As we drove toward Tamarack Lake, we entered the town of Bemidji. "I've got to make a stop," Winona said.

To my surprise, she pulled up in front of the Bemidji municipal liquor store. She pulled a wad of cash out of her pocket and handed it to me. "I'd be grateful if you'd buy a jug of good bourbon."

"Kind of a thing with you, send people into liquor establishments to do your errands?"

"I don't drink anymore. It ruined my life, that and other things. This is for someone else."

The day had broken wide open when we arrived on the reservation. Winona drove down a winding road, through a stand of birch and pine trees, over a wooden bridge and into a small clearing. Smoke rose from the chimney of a tar-paper cabin. Cords of cut firewood were stacked crosshatched in neat piles around the property. A basketball backboard with a bent hoop was nailed to a tree. Two barking, blue-eyed malamutes ran for the car, stood on their hind legs and scratched at the car doors.

Two women in sweatshirts exited the cabin door, walked toward the car, and shooed the dogs away. A barrel-chested man stood on the cabin steps, pulling up dangling suspenders over a mackinaw shirt. He slapped a ball cap into shape against his thigh and put it on his head to gather in his shoulder length, gray-streaked hair.

"Those are my cousins." Winona pointed at the women. "And that's my grandfather, Jordan. He's a shaman, the tribe's spiritual guide." She reached into the back seat before exiting the car and grabbed the Ganley's Bakery pie and the jug of bourbon. She handed both items to me. "Presents from you." She winked and left to join the women.

I approached the grandfather, held out the gifts of pie and bourbon, one in each hand. I cocked my head to set up the punch line. "You decide."

"Ha!" The old man cracked a smile, revealing missing teeth and gums like black licorice. "Good one." He motioned me inside.

Over coffee spiked with bourbon, Jordan inquired about Truss. I explained that I was new to the funeral business and had only recently met him. Jordan forged ahead as if he didn't hear me. He spoke as though we were two men who shared a vocation in the preparation of the dead. He confided that many of the old Indian practices of returning the dead to the spirit world, although now banned, were still in evidence. Rickety burial scaffolds still swayed on the plains, and mounded burial grounds were prominent features throughout Indian land.

Jordan took a long pull of coffee and let the conversation settle into silence and memories. He looked out the window, past a pot brimming with red geraniums on the windowsill. I could feel the mood shift.

Jordan poured more whiskey. "My son was a great warrior, a decorated marine with three tours in Iraq. But once home, he could not make peace with his spirit and was lost to the demons of racism and addiction. My granddaughter Winona, like many young people, was scrubbed of her Indian identity and tried to fit in with the city ways. Winona's son, the second great-grandson of White Cloud, returned to us along the well-worn trail of sorrows, never to sit under the Ahnunggokwan, the star world."

Winona's son? Something she hadn't shared with me, but hearing the depth of sadness in the old man's voice, I let it be.

Jordan dropped his gnarled, thick hands on the table and pushed himself out of the chair. "Come join me in the sweat lodge. I would be honored."

I followed Jordan along a path away from the house, past an old car graveyard and into the woods. As we approached a domed lodge on the banks of a narrow river, I could smell smoke, mixed with the scent of pine and boreal decay. The lodge's frame, formed with supple aspen saplings and lashed together with rawhide, was covered with deer hides. The entry, a loose flap, faced east.

Jordan tended to the fire pit alongside the lodge. He dug two branches into the embers and retrieved hot, round stones and carried them into a shallow pit in the center of the lodge. After several trips, he signaled the lodge was ready. Jordan struck a match to a bundle of sage and wafted the smoke over himself. As the sage burned out, Jordan smudged his face with the charred grass and did the same to me. He removed his clothes, bowed in the direction of the sun, opened a loose flap, and entered the lodge.

How strange was this? Getting naked in the woods with an old man and crawling into a man-made cave with fire. Ever since I met Truss, it's as though I'd fallen down a rabbit hole into an alternate universe.

I stripped down and followed. Inside, woven mats of sweetgrass covered the dirt floor.

Jordan closed the flap and dropped the lodge into black. As my vision adjusted, I could see Jordan's silhouette in the red luminance of hot stones. He dipped a bundle of sage grass into a bucket of water and sprinkled the rocks. Hissing steam erupted and Jordan chanted something deep and sonorous.

In the steamy blackness, I felt light-headed and disoriented. Then all separation vanished. I became the radiant stones, the hissing vapor, Jordan's chant and the darkness. The earth's gravitational pull released me and I drifted through the vast cosmos. Expressionless human forms swept past me. The numbers grew, swarmed, circled and bound me to their wheel. The thunderous whirlpool of human spirits sucked me through their mass to the center of its starry eye. I floated among ten thousand glowing souls, each one leaning against one another in absolute dependence. Voices called to me in strange languages I somehow understood as they cycled through birth and death. Memory fragments appeared from realms I never visited. Sinking deeper into the vortex, I gave myself over to be breathed by the pulsating abyss, watching the intensity of the heated stones drain my life away. Into the darkness of the lodge came a bright light.

A cold shock of water suddenly splashed my skull, and a heavy hand dropped on my shoulder.

"Breathe. Not your day to die." Jordan threw open the flap. "It is time for you and the ancestors to go."

My eyelids squeezed to a squint as I crawled out of the lodge into the harsh light of day. My scarlet-red skin radiated heat. The boreal colors, quaking leaves, and the touch of a breeze upon my skin all seemed amplified. Somewhere in the distance, I heard wind chimes tinkle. A fractured sun appeared through the latticework of overhead branches.

When I turned my attention to Jordan, the shaman was gone.

I took stock of my smoke-infused hair and salty skin. The sound of the river beckoned.

I dropped my bunched clothes under a weeping willow, walked

down the sandy riverbank and into the swirling black current. The cold water triggered short huffs of breath. After a few minutes, I acclimated and relaxed into the current's caressing massage.

"Wooh-wooh-wooh!" Winona, with a basket in hand, suddenly appeared and stood over my clothes. A good-natured laugh followed her Indian war cry.

I crossed my hands over my crotch, which only made my nakedness seem even more ridiculous. Winona erupted in an infectious laugh.

I picked up on her playfulness and flailed my arms, splashed at the water, let out a maniacal howl and felt the tension of recent events drain away. Winona spread a blanket on the ground, and to my surprise pulled off her boots and unbuttoned her shirt and pants. She let them drop to her ankles and kicked them out of the way. I watched as she entered the river and lay down in the sandy shallows. The current floated Winona's hair in undulations and eddied around her dark-nippled breasts. A whirlpool formed at the triangle of her legs.

I felt a stir too strong for the chilly water to suppress.

Not wanting to be that guy, I dashed for the shore. As I pulled on my trousers, I watched as Winona emerged from the water, the sun glistening off her smooth skin, her ripe lips stretched in a smile.

How could I have been so blind to her radiance? Maybe nature had a way of opening one up to beauty. She plunked down on the blanket next to me, content to air dry.

"It's been a long time since I loved someone," Winona whispered, as she watched a fawn tiptoe into the water upstream.

I felt an electric shock course through my body. Was that meant for me? Tentative, and with the adeptness of someone trying not to wake the baby, I touched her hand. In a seamless motion, she lay back on the blanket and reached for me.

Our bodies quickly took over. Her eyes closed and her mouth opened. The adrenaline rush blocked the pain of my swollen lip as I tasted the salty passion of her kiss and felt her grasping breath pull air from my lungs. Our stomachs pressed together, her hands clutched at the small of my back and pulled me closer. Her hips rose in smooth undulating waves, swelling and cresting in surges of pleasure. She let me know what she wanted and cascaded in a seismic climax with pulsating tremors.

Breathless and spent, we held each other. With Winona, I felt more than simple physical pleasure. Making love to her was a spiritual experience.

We sat for a long while sunning, then lazily got dressed. Winona opened the basket she had brought. She unwrapped wild rice flatbread, fried venison sausage and freshly picked raspberries. I grabbed at a plate of food, suddenly starving.

"If I knew you were so voracious, I would have strung the basket up in a tree," she said.

As we sat and ate, I took stock of Winona's tattooed arms with images of animal tracks, flowers, stars and curious symbols. "Are those petroglyphs?"

"Like the rock carvings of my ancestors, these tats tell my story." Winona extended her arms, allowing me to inspect the art.

I pointed at a turtle set in a circle. "What does this mean?"

"The Tortoise Umbilical Bag carries the world on its back, as do women who bring babies into this world." She stood up. "Come meet my son."

CHAPTER 42

TAMARACK

I followed Winona away from the river to a cemetery on a ridge-line above Tamarack Lake. A burial ceremony was in process. In the distance, I spotted a backhoe tucked behind a shed. Just past a stand of red pines, we arrived at a large granite boulder etched with symbols. Winona stopped, folded at the knees, and crossed her hands over her heart.

"This is Little White Cloud," She said.

I gently touched her shoulder. "I'm so sorry for your loss." Once again, I felt the inadequacy of words. I had never lost a child, but I had been a lost child, the recipient of platitudes that fell short.

"Thank you." She stood and took a deep breath. Then with out-reached hands, she raised her head to the late afternoon sky and chanted.

Her voice was both haunting and spiritual. In the harmonic over-tone of her native tongue, I felt the vibrations of her emotional healing. She was the granddaughter of a great tribal shaman.

We stood motionless and let the song fall away into silence. Then she said, "Let's walk."

The path led through a stand of fuzzy tamarack onto the shores of Lower Tamarack Lake. The pebbly beach squished and grated underfoot. The stained black water lay flat and reflected the layered rays of sunset. We sat on a log and watched mayflies hover over the water. A hungry walleye broke to the surface and sent concentric ripples into infinity.

"When I told you how I met Truss, I didn't give you the full story," Winona said. "I arrived at his door, bleeding, holding my lifeless son, Little White Cloud. I was a mess. Truss helped me clean up my baby and prepared him for the journey into the spirit world. He drove us back to the rez, a five-hour ride, to the care of my grandfather. Before he left, he told my grandfather he wanted to help with the expense of putting me in a treatment program."

"I can see how you'd want to give something back to Truss, but doesn't being around death all the time make it all the more difficult to deal with the loss of your son?"

"In my tradition, the deceased stay alive as long as someone tells their story." Winona tilted her head to the evening twilight. "Children who pass from us without a story become part of the collective story of all our ancestors. Little White Cloud came into this world without a cry. He had entered the realm of death before I knew him. He now stands at the gateway of the Great Spirit and guides others on the only journey he ever knew. I meet him at death's doorstep with each passing person and in the grief and loss they leave behind."

In Winona, I felt the weight of history, hardship and oppression of the native people. Yet she carried on with a soulfulness that accepted the tragic past and her present station. I wondered if that enduring acceptance could extend to me, a self-indulgent, privileged white guy who sabotaged his own life.

I put my arm around Winona, and we walked back to the cabin. Inside, Jordan sat at the kitchen table and worked a crossword puzzle. He removed a pair of reading glasses taped together at the nose bridge and looked up at me. "You brought the mystery of your father into the sweat lodge."

What?

I sat down across from him in a buzz of confusion. "How did you . . . how do you . . ."

"You spoke the name of Earl Locker and called after him."

I searched Jordan's dark eyes for more information. They seemed to see everything and nothing.

More information was forthcoming. "Your father was not among the ancestors."

"I don't understand. How do you know this?" I wasn't sure whether to be angry or hopeful.

"It is easier to forgive an enemy than one you love."

CHAPTER 43

CARLIN

As we barreled down the highway, away from the reservation, the night felt heavy. Heat lightning leaped from the night sky and flashed the landscape.

Winona checked her phone. She had received two voice messages, both related to me. The first was from Agent Kirchner, who wanted to meet regarding my account of Zenk and the Daltons. He could wait. The second was from my brother, who said he'd opened O'Malley's pendant, and also mentioned somebody had been watching the house.

We arrived at my mother's house at five a.m., just as the night canopy opened to the light of day. I told Winona to park the car two blocks away in an attempt to skirt any possible surveillance, per Ray's assertion. I got out of the car and told Winona to wait. She ignored the directive and followed me through an alley and into my mother's backyard. The door squeaked like a nail being pulled out of green wood.

"Ray?"

"Down here."

The unfinished cinderblock basement exuded a musty smell. Ray sat at his computer under a single overhead light on a pull chain. The make-shift desk consisted of two sawhorses and a sheet of plywood.

"What's with the sausage lip?" Ray pointed at my face. Then, "Who's this?"

"Winona. We work together at the mortuary."

"And you must be the genius," Winona said.

Ray had a highly sensitive bullshit detector. He looked Winona over, giving her greeting the sniff test.

Then he noticed her arms, which were covered with tattoos of Native American glyphs. "Wow!" He scooted his desk chair over to Winona to look more carefully. "Indigenously cool symbols." He then rolled up a shirt sleeve to reveal a green and red swirling river serpent tat, a tribute to our dad.

"Ray, knock it off." I said. "You said someone's watching the house. Did you pick anything up on the security camera?" Somebody rifled through our mailbox three or four years ago when mom was still living at the house. They ripped off a package she had ordered from the Home Shopping Network. Shortly thereafter, Ray installed a security camera over the front door.

"Not on the camera, out of range, but I got a look at him." Ray held his cupped hands up to his eyes, feigning binoculars. "This dude kept cruising by the house and parking halfway down the block. Yesterday, he tailed me into the liquor store. I stared him down, but he looked mostly disappointed, most likely because it's you he's after. I haven't seen him since."

"What did he look like?"

"Tall, cropped hair, kinda good-looking, if you're into muscle freaks."

"Oh my God, Tommy." Winona shivered. "He's muscle for Madelyn Dalton, total creep."

Ray cocked his head. "Is he tied into this secret pendant lock you laid on me?"

"No, well maybe. Hell, I don't know." I realized I was grinding my teeth and deliberately stopped. "You said you got the pendant opened.

Where is it?"

Ray pulled it out of his pocket and held it up in front of my face. It looked locked.

"What did you find?"

"Do you know how long it took me to build a random number model to identify all the probable combinations and then manually diddle with that el cheapo pendant until it finally opened?"

"Ray, I appreciate your help. What did you find?"

"What's it worth to you?"

"Give me the goddam combination and I won't kill you." I lurched for the pendant. Ray closed his hand around it and we grappled back and forth.

A loud whistle pierced the air. We froze as if a referee had stopped play.

Winona removed the two fingers from her mouth. "What are you guys, six?"

I backed away from Ray. "Butt head."

Ray let out a devilish laugh and pointed at me. His amusement at my expense ended in a full body coughing fit. "I wrote the combination inside your George Carlin book, page 211. Too bad you were never that funny."

I had to restrain myself. Ray always found a way to push my buttons.

"Ray, we appreciate your help," Winona said. "Hopefully, there's something to this that will give us a clue to the life of Riva O'Malley."

"At your service." Ray gave a slight bow and bounded up the stairs.

I quickly located the George Carlin book, and with Winona at my side, I took a deep breath and spun the pendant's zodiac wheel symbols until they matched Ray's pattern. A sealed cylinder dropped out of the center shaft.

I carefully opened it up.

"Oh, my God," Winona said, as a slate gray powder poured out. "Cremation remains."

We sat quietly for a moment in reverence for the unknown person whose eighth of a teaspoon of dust had spilled onto the plywood tabletop.

I held the cylinder up to the overhead light. "There's something else in here, a piece of paper." I carefully worked the scroll out into the open.

Winona read the tiny handwritten inscription. "Sarah M. O'Malley, June 5, 1978—October 30, 2018."

I rummaged around to find an envelope to capture the pendant and contents. "A relative, maybe her mother?"

Winona's phone chirped. She handed it to me. "It's Jessica, for you. Got my number from Truss. She sounds panicked."

"Hi Jess, sorry. Lost my phone. Everything okay?"

"You tell me. On the way to taking Claire to school, some creep walked up and threatened us. Said my funny funeral guy ex has a big mouth and if he doesn't keep it shut, things would not go well for the loved ones."

"Oh, my god, what did he look like?"

"Big brut, wore a necklace with a tusk or tooth on it. Scared the hell out of me and Claire. What in God's name is going on?"

The background noise of passing cars and kids' voices sounded as if she was in a busy place outside. "Where are you?"

"Standing outside of the school."

"Have you called the police?"

"I called Pete."

"Your brother? He's not stable, basically useless. You need protection."

"Don't talk to me about useless."

I wanted to ask about the status of her Wisconsin boyfriend, but that was a land mine I didn't need to step on right now. "Listen, Jessica, these people are dangerous. Keep Claire close. Have her skip school today. I'll have Agent Kirchner from the BCA get in contact with you."

"Whatever thoughts you had about being part of Claire's life are over. I don't even give a damn about the child support. Whatever mess you're in, we want out."

There was a pause, room for me to say something that would make the situation better. "I'm sorry," I finally said.

She hung up.

I squeezed my skull with both hands. "Tommy's threatening Jessica and Claire to keep me quiet."

Winona swept her hair into a ponytail and knotted it with an elastic hair tie. "You know what?" She shuffled her feet and threw punches in the air like a shadow boxer. "We are going to go after the Daltons, meet them head-on and kick some ass."

"Nice thought," I said evenly. "But I'd like to think a bit before risking my daughter. Here . . ." I picked up the envelope with the pendant in it and handed it to her. "See if this leads us anywhere and take this." I handed her the Carlin book. "In case you need the combination." We hugged, and I watched her slip into the alley toward her car, to the sound of barking dogs.

CHAPTER 44

HILLBILLY

Agent Kirchner came through and provided protection for Jessica and Claire. The St. Paul police were routinely checking on them and patrolling their neighborhood. I now gave my full attention to the throbbing pain emanating from a broken tooth, compliments of Madelyn Dalton.

After three days of gulping down Tylenol and coming to terms with the out-of-pocket expense, I visited a dentist. An X-ray determined the root was intact, but the tooth above the gum was beyond repair. It needed to be ground down in preparation for a crown.

The dentist produced a large syringe and jabbed my gum with Novocain. "Let that numb up, I'll be back." She patted me on the arm and left the room.

"Jesus, you're harder to find than the Holy Grail." Toby's voice came from behind the dental chair.

I struggled to sit up. "What are you doing here?"

"The National LaughCom Contest—drum roll!" Toby pounded the padded back of the dental chair, adding to my tension-filled headache. "I can't believe I haven't heard from you."

Toby's pronouncement boomed off the walls and drew the attention of the dental assistant. "Sir, I will have to ask you to leave."

"Sorry, just delivering good news. Give me two minutes."

"Keep it down." She eyed Toby wearily and retreated.

"How did you find me?" I could feel my tongue thicken.

"Stopped by the mortuary. Winona put me on to your dental appointment. Cavity?"

"No. Long story. Complicated." My words tumbled over fat, drooling lips.

The back of the dental chair moved, elevating me into a sitting position. Toby had found the chair's foot pedal.

"Knock it off!" I batted him away.

Toby peered into my face. "Wow, cracked tooth. Get the dentist to pull it and maybe we can work you into an 'ah-shucks' hillbilly set."

The dental assistant stuck her head in the room. "Starting to numb up?"

I nodded. "Not soon enough."

"Let's give it another five minutes. When the dentist comes back, your friend can wait in the reception area." She shot Toby a look of disapproval, turned on her heels and left the room.

Toby picked up the dentist's hand drill, made a contorted face, and pretended to come after me like in Marathon Man.

"Cut the crap!"

"We've got to get the contest entry paperwork submitted. Louie's signed off. I just need your signature." He pulled out a folded sheet of paper and pen from his jacket.

The dentist entered the room, followed by the dental assistant.

"I'll wait in the reception area," Toby said, and shot me a thumbs-up.

Through the vibration and grind of the drill, I tried to process my backdoor entry into the Nationals. I should have been over the top about it. After all, I almost killed myself because I'd lost it. But now, so much had happened that I wasn't sure who I was. Was I a comedian doing eulogies, or had I become a eulogist with a comedic angle? Was

I pretending to be someone else, or had two halves blended into something synergetic?

Why was I even thinking about this crisis of duality? My family was being threatened by the Daltons, and if Zenk's body were ever found, I could be framed for his murder. Performing stand-up was beyond consideration.

I walked out of the dental office with Toby on my heels. "Laugh-Com Nationals, here we come." He waved the contest paperwork in my face.

"Toby, I'm sorry, but that ship has sailed," I mumbled through a lopsided face, pushing the paperwork away.

"But this is your ticket, everything you ever wanted." Toby kept pace with me as I headed for the bus stop. "You can't just piss this away!"

I sat on the bus stop bench with my back to a realtor advertisement offering to 'Buy Ugly Homes'. Toby plopped down next to me.

"Even if I could go to the Nationals," I said, "which I can't for reasons I don't want to get into, I'm not in stand-up shape. I haven't performed my material since the debacle at Louie's."

"We've got time to work on the set list. The thing is, your stage presence is sharper and more poised than ever. I've seen it."

I stood up as I saw my bus approach. "I'm not tracking."

"Your eulogy work has made you a better performer. You're teeing up a new routine every time you memorialize somebody. The material is always fresh and you connect with an audience that's not predisposed to humor. There's nobody, and I mean nobody, doing stand-up who's that creative or brave. Plus, you love it."

I had to admit I craved the attention of an audience—the instant gratification; the heart pumping immediacy of it.

I boarded the bus and leaned my forehead into the window. I tried to put the Nationals out of my mind along with the fantasy as to where that might lead. But dreams don't suddenly disappear. They just slowly get smothered by the weight of the odds against you, and this one was clawing its way back to the surface.

A group of kids with backpacks boarded the bus.

BACKPACK!

Back at his farmhouse, Zenk had emerged through the trapdoor of the crawl space with a backpack. I helped him up. He picked up the pack and handed me Riva's pendant. That's when Tommy stormed us like a blitzkrieg. This was the fuzzy part, but I think Zenk dropped the pack back into the crawl space and, in the scuffle, kicked the trapdoor shut. If there was more to O'Malley, it was in that backpack.

I thought about borrowing someone's car and driving to the farmhouse to retrieve it, but that was a risky proposition. The property could be under surveillance to see who returned to the scene of the crime, or to keep people from tampering with evidence.

I pulled out my newly refurbished cheap phone and called Pam at Ganley's Bakery for help.

CHAPTER 45

RED DRAGON

Winona called to check up on me. "You ready to chew a bone?"

"Not yet. Still sore, but I am hungry." I ran my tongue over the new crown.

"Great, meet me at the Red Dragon. Lots going on here. I located Sarah O'Malley's obituary and you'll be happy to hear someone dropped off your car."

I wondered if Pam, along with retrieving my car from Zenk's farm, had also found O'Malley's backpack?

The Red Dragon occupied a building just two blocks from the mortuary. The essence of ginger and soy invaded my senses as I entered the restaurant. A slight Asian woman guided me past photos of Chinese ancestors, jade figurines, and paper lanterns to a booth toward the back of the restaurant where I found Winona.

"Family style," Winona said, and before I could make a menu choice, she ordered food for the table. "Also suggest you use the chopsticks. Muqin Tang finds forks disrespectful, and she's good with a saber."

I picked up the chopsticks to signal compliance.

"Toby, your comedy agent, sure has been persistent."

"Yeah, he showed up at my dental appointment." I opened my mouth and tapped the new crown. "He's trying to plug me into the National LaughCom Contest. I'm supposedly a default winner in the regionals, as the declared winner has bailed."

"Sounds like a wonderful opportunity."

"Except that I'm done chasing rainbows, and if you haven't noticed, I'm trying to make this eulogy thing work."

"Can't you do both?"

"Didn't work out so well for Buridan's ass."

"Whose ass?"

"It's an example from ethical theory."

"Yeah, almost forgot you're a professor."

"Teaching assistant."

"So something about an ass?"

"Buridan's ass is a hungry and thirsty donkey. The assumption is that it will always go to the closest source of food or water. However, when placed equidistant between a hay bale and a water trough, the donkey can't decide and it dies."

"Harsh," Winona said, "but it is true you can be a horse's ass." She laughed.

I let Winona's amusement at my expense settle. She had become my moral compass, someone to lean on in a hopeless storm. "I'm doing everything I can to support my daughter, but I still feel like I'm losing her. It doesn't help that my family is being threatened by the Daltons."

Winona reached over and touched my arm. I felt its warmth through my sleeve.

"What do you have on Sarah O'Malley?" I asked.

"I found her obit in the Baton Rouge Advocate. The only surviving relative listed is a daughter identified as Maureeva O'Malley. There was no mention of a spouse, so it's possible she never married. It listed an Audrey Ardoin as a special friend."

"Maureeva to Riva. Probably explains why she's been so hard to track. And this friend, special how?"

"I had a phone conversation with Audrey Ardoin. She's a lifelong friend of the family. She said Sarah died of cancer. When I informed her about Riva's death, she was terribly upset."

Muqin Tang approached with bowls of steaming food. I pulled apart the wooden chopsticks and held them up for her to see.

"You going to eat that?" Winona pointed at the seafood bowl.

"No. I've got a shellfish allergy."

"Sucks being you." She dragged the bowl over to her side of the table.

"Did this Audrey Ardoin say anything about Riva being missing or in hiding?"

"Audrey called her a bohemian, a free spirit who loved art and music. Oh, and she had run away multiple times starting in her early teens. Audrey didn't consider her to be a rebel—more of an explorer looking for something, perhaps a father or maybe, now orphaned by her mother's death, someone to claim her."

"Amen." I tried a bit of the Kung Pao chicken but found it too crunchy.

"Audrey also claimed Riva got caught up in an abusive relationship with a Baton Rouge cop. She tried to cut it off, but he kept stalking her. One day she just picked up and left."

"Maybe that explains not wanting to be tracked."

"What, you don't like Kung Pao chicken? Unbelievable." Winona scooped a helping onto her plate.

"Mouth is still a little sore."

"So, are you ready for the big reveal?"

"You sound like Oprah Winfrey. Should I look under my seat?"

"You know how some families and friends buy a newborn a savings bond that increases in value over time?"

"Not in my family, but yeah."

"Audrey's husband was an insurance salesman. When Riva was born, the Ardoins purchased a life insurance policy for her. A gift that Riva could convert to cash in time of need, or as a safety net for her family should she get married and have children. When I explained the role life insurance may have played in Riva's death, Ardoin blamed herself and broke down in tears."

A man approached the table. "Well, if it isn't the Trouble and Strife."

"Agent Kirchner," Winona said, "what are you doing here?"

"Hopefully, eating." Kirchner pointed at the Cantonese sweet and sour pork. "One of my favorites. Mind if I join you?" Winona moved over to my side of the booth to make way for Kirchner. "Truss said I'd find you here."

Although I had spoken to Agent Kirchner by phone, I had never met him. He was totally what I had expected. A cop with closely cropped hair and a steely face that looked like it couldn't take a joke. And not much for fashion with his off the rack Macy's gray suit that came with two pairs of pants.

Kirchner scissored two fingers at Muqin Tang to signal he needed a plate and chopsticks. After a couple of mouthfuls, he paused. "Vince, I want to let you know we've given the matter of malicious harassment against your former wife and daughter our utmost attention. Along with providing around the clock police protection, we've issued an arrest warrant for the suspected perpetrator, Tommy Stoltz. Your ex picked him out of a photo array."

"Tommy works for Madelyn Dalton. Have you questioned her?"

"She lawyered up, so it's slow going."

"Did you look at her leg where Zenk hit her with the shovel? Or did she lawyer that away?"

Kirchner was silent as a sphinx.

"So, you've got nothing and my family continues to live in terror!" My outburst drew a stern look from Muqin Tang.

"Agent Kirchner is here to help," Winona said.

"What about Ross Dalton? Has he lawyered up, too? Oh, that's right, he's indisposed, getting his brain aired out at a mental institution that most folks would recognize as a fancy health spa."

"I've spoken to Ross Dalton. He's been released from the mental care facility." Kirchner pushed his plate away. "He claims you deliberately sabotaged a Reliance funeral, that you physically accosted him, and now are attempting to involve him in O'Malley's death through a fabricated account, all in retaliation for his efforts to take over Truss Mortuary."

"Bullshit." I leaned into Kirchner. "Dalton admitted to O'Malley's murder to cash in on her life insurance."

Kirchner held up his palm. "The county medical examiner's forensic work up on O'Malley attributes her death to natural causes, Truss' opinion notwithstanding. There is no witness tying Dalton to her death and your report from Jacob Zenk is hearsay, as he remains unaccounted for."

"So Dalton gets away with murder, unbelievable." I propped my elbows on the table and held my head to keep it from rolling on the floor. Winona put her hand on my neck and gave it a gentle squeeze. I found her ability to tame me both attractive and annoying.

"If you've spoken to Truss," Winona said, "I'm sure he informed you we found Riva's mother."

Kirchner nodded. "I've put in a request for the bureau to obtain Sarah O'Malley's and Maureeva O'Malley's vital records."

"So you're just going to shuffle some paperwork and build a nice thick file so it looks like there have been investigative resources spent on O'Malley's behalf, case closed?"

"I'm not here to defend the BCA or myself. I just wanted to keep you up to date."

Muqin Tang appeared and set the bill on the table along with three fortune cookies.

Kirchner cracked open a cookie and read the fortune out loud, *'You'll die alone, poorly dressed.'* Kirchner looked off in the distance as if observing himself in a mirror, then turned his attention to a spot on his shirt.

"Looks like you're halfway there." I chuckled. Winona gave me a soft, admonishing slap on the arm.

"One more thing." Kirchner looked at me. "As a person of interest in Jacob's Zenk's disappearance, you will need to make yourself available for formal questioning at the BCA. Call me within the next twenty-four hours." He dropped a twenty-dollar bill on the table and left.

I felt sick, beaten and scared.

Winona handed me a fortune cookie.

"You first," I said.

Winona read her fortune message. *"'Don't fry bacon in the nude,'"* She laughed. "I guess I'll have to forgo my bacon strip."

"Cute and quick." I cracked my cookie. *Drive like hell, you will get there.* I ate the cookie and thought for a moment. "Hey, my car. I'm dying to get my ride back. Let's go."

CHAPTER 46

CRUSHED

When we arrived back at the mortuary, I looked for my car. No luck.

"It was here this morning." Winona dug into her pocket. "And I still have the key."

I searched for a sign that would suggest a parking violation, but saw none. "I can't believe someone would steal that rust bucket."

"In this neighborhood, they're not picky."

I called the police. "When? Why? How much?"

I clicked out of the call. "Can you believe this lunacy, I got towed because someone called it in as an abandoned car. It's being held for ransom at West End Impound and Auto Salvage. If I don't pick it up within twenty-four hours, they'll turn it into scrap metal. I'd let them have it if I had a better transportation option."

"Let's get this over with." Winona pointed at her car. "I've got cash."

The route to West End Auto Salvage took us across the Wabasha Street Bridge over active railroad tracks, through an industrial area to a gated junkyard. A ten-foot-high chain-link fence surrounded the entire yard, with an aggressive German shepherd running back and forth to remind us we weren't welcome. Winona hit the intercom button on the gate and yelled into it as if ordering a burger. The electronic gate opened and quickly closed as she drove into the property and followed a sign to the yard office. We passed compacted cars stacked on top of one another like Jenga blocks.

At the office, a heavyset yardman met us and asked for identification. He reeked of dill pickles and pastrami. A half-eaten sandwich, wrapped in greasy paper, sat on the counter.

"Vince Locker," I said and handed over my driver's license.

"That will be a hundred and fifty dollars in fines and towing fees. Cash only."

"Total robbery." I slapped the counter. "My car was not abandoned."

Winona forked over the money.

"You got the key?" the yardman asked.

I dangled it in his face. The yardman handed me a clipboard with a form attached. "You're required to inspect the car and sign the claim form before we release it. It's in the back, third row."

"There better not be any damage." I turned to Winona. "I've got it from here. See you back at Truss'."

The car's exterior didn't appear to have any new dents, though I'd never actually kept score. I opened the driver's door and dropped into the seat. I fired up the car to make sure they didn't put a hole in the muffler or something else. The Toyota let out a sudden farting burst of exhaust, but that was normal.

I looked behind me as I prepared to back the car out when an arm reached through the window, across my chest, and snatched the key out of the ignition. "You got a big mouth."

I saw the hog's tooth necklace around the man's neck first. I jerked on the door handle.

Tommy put his weight against the door. "Mrs. Dalton says you don't impress her as a guy who can leave well enough alone." He held the car key in front of my face, then pitched it into a scrap pile. "She considers you a liability in her run for governor and she's out of her mind angry about the torture you put her son through."

"I had nothing to do with her son being buried. The police know you've threatened my family so back off!"

"Yeah, I should believe a first class bullshitter. Comedy act, eulogies, whatever, anything to be the center of attention."

I quickly slid to the passenger door and swung it open.

The junkyard dog attacked.

I jerked back into the car, leaving behind a patch of fabric ripped from my pants.

Tommy circled a hand overhead and stepped back from the car. A giant mechanical claw came into view. For a moment, it reminded me of the claws on an arcade game, operated by a joystick in pursuit of useless toys.

Thoughts of play vanished as it plunged and the steel jaws crashed through the car's front and rear windows, blasting me with shards of glass.

Before I could move, the crane swept the car into the air and hovered it over the maw of a four-direction compactor. I threw my shoulder against the door, but the frame had flexed with the impact, trapping me inside.

I stuck my head out the side window. Suspended thirty feet in the air, I yelled and flailed my arms to get someone's attention. Tommy had disappeared. I pulled out my phone to call for help, but the shudder of the crane jostled it out of my hand, and it fell into the compactor.

In desperation, I crawled out of the passenger window and onto the suspended car's roof. I stepped up onto the claw's arms and held onto its greasy support cable.

The blare of a car horn momentarily distracted me. Winona had parked outside the gate, no doubt waiting for me. The movement of an overhead crane with a car in its grasp and me waving on its roof must have caught her attention. Locked out of the yard, I watched as she put the car in reverse, peeled off twenty-five yards, then charged forward into the chain-link fence.

The snared, entangled car erupted in a shower of steam, but she was through.

The operator swung the crane's arm erratically, turning my perch into a mechanical bull. But I was motivated to hang on.

Then the operator suddenly popped the claws open. My car plunged out from underneath me and, after a moment of fumbling with the greasy cable, I followed it down.

Into the compactor box.

The hydraulic driven compression walls began to move. I felt the Toyota's frame buckle under the pressure. Car parts exploded around me. Too panicked to take an inventory of my injuries, I leapt from the top of the car, caught the lip of the compactor wall, and swung my body over and out of the box. I felt the sickening crunch of flesh and bones as my body bounced off machinery on the way to the ground. The landing sent a flash of searing pain up my spine.

I saw Winona running toward the crane as the door to the yard office opened. Tommy and the junkyard dog appeared. The dog made a dash for Winona and brought her to the ground. Tommy made a run at me. Barely able to stand, I picked up a piece of scrap metal, a steel rod, and waved it at him. "Call the dog off," I screamed and staggered toward Winona.

Tommy cut me off. I swung the metal club at him and missed. He countered with a kick to my chest and knocked me down. I saw the hog's tooth necklace jiggle over me as his hands gripped my neck.

A shot rang out, followed by a high-pitched whine. Tommy released his grip, and we both turned our attention toward the blast.

A policewoman stood over Winona and the dead dog. Her partner came toward Tommy and me with his gun drawn. He was joined by the policewoman, who took charge.

"Cuff these two," she said, "and corral that crane operator. I've got backup and medical personnel on the way. The girl is pretty beat up and so is this one." She pointed at me.

"Hey, I'm the victim here," I protested.

"Zip it and huddle up." She ushered Tommy and me toward Winona and the dead dog in the middle of the yard. The policeman brought the crane operator into the circle. "We got a call about someone being crushed in a car."

"I made the call," Winona said.

"I was the crushee." I pointed my chin at Tommy and the operator. "They're the crushers."

"Check it out," the policewoman said to her partner.

The policeman scampered up the side of the compactor and looked into the box. "Got a crushed car, can't determine the make."

"That's my Toyota," I shouted.

The yardman came out of the office in a huff, waving his arms. "You killed my dog," he shouted at the police. "I've already called the yard owner, Madelyn Dalton. She said you better have a warrant to be on the premises."

"Shut up," Tommy growled.

"Call Agent Kirchner from the BCA," I said to the policewoman. "This guy, with the hog's tooth necklace, he threatened my family."

The police separated Winona and me from Tommy, the crane operator and the yardmen, and released me from the cuffs. As we waited for Kirchner and the paramedics, Winona tenderly touched the wound on my forehead, like a parent soothing a fevered child.

I leaned into her. "I always knew you had a crush on me," I said in a raspy voice, my windpipe sore from Tommy's grip.

She gave me a wan grin, then burst into tears.

CHAPTER 47
CANDIDATE

I sat at home nursing my wounds. A gauze bandage on my forehead concealed a horizontal cut that looked like the work of a self-inflicted lobotomy. An elastic girdle around my chest held two cracked ribs in place, and one ankle was wrapped. With my brain hazy from Percocet, I fell into a three-hour TV binge watch. The National Geographic Channel had hooked me into a series with the existential question: Do nonhuman animals have the emotional capacity to grieve?

A marble colored orca killer whale carried her dead infant through the icy gray waters of the Puget Sound, keeping it afloat for fifteen days before finally dropping the dead calf into a watery grave. In northeast India, in the shadows of the Himalayas, a dusty Asian elephant family holds a funeral vigil. They repeatedly pass by the body of a deceased matriarch, smelling, touching and weeping over the corpse. Betty, a prominent chimpanzee of twenty-five years, has just died at the Jane Goodall Rehabilitation Centre in the dense forested reaches of western Tanzania. Her chimp family suddenly appears from out of the bush and stands in quiet reverence as Betty's corpse is wheeled past them. The chimps place their hands on one another's shoulders, comforting each other, and watch in complete silence, a rare occurrence for these usually clamorous animals.

I hit the pause button to freeze frame the faces of the fuzzy chimps. I recognized their wrenching sadness of abandonment and desolation as my own. Long held tears from deep inside streamed down my face. I crawled up to the TV and touched the screen. "You're not alone, you're not alone . . ." I whimpered until my phone buzzed.

I swiped at my eyes and blew my nose. It was Agent Kirchner. As instructed, I had met him at the BCA and gave a formal account of Dalton's kidnaping and Zenk's murder. He said he'd keep in contact with me as the investigation developed. I clicked him in.

"Turn on Channel 11."

"What's going on?"

"We got the crane operator from the auto salvage yard to flip."

Kirchner hung up. I switched on the channel. A woman reporter stood in front of an office building and spoke into a handheld microphone.

A swarm of local and national media has descended on the Ramsey County Courthouse in St Paul as gubernatorial candidate Madelyn Dalton awaits an appearance before a judge to enter a plea to charges tied to the apparent murder of Jacob Zenk from Baxter, Minnesota. Also, being arraigned as a co-conspirator is Tommy Stoltz, a former Navy SEAL and a longtime Dalton political operative.

"Holy shit!" I circled around the couch, not lifting my eyes off the TV. The streets outside the courthouse were lined with satellite news trucks.

The investigation led by the BCA has alleged, after the murder of Zenk, Dalton and Stolz stashed Zenk's body in the trunk of Dalton's late model Bentley. Based on a tip from an employee at an auto impound and salvage yard owned by Dalton, the Bentley, worth an estimated one-hundred and fifty-thousand dollars, was crushed and transferred to a scrap metal barge awaiting shipment to China. In the remnants of the car, investigators found fragments of bone and teeth that matched Zenk's DNA. Prosecutors have stated that Zenk's murder may be related to a business transaction Madelyn Dalton's son, Ross Dalton, a high-profile aggregator of funeral homes, had with Zenk. Madelyn Dalton and Stolz allegedly further engaged in an aggravated assault on a witness.

"How about O'Malley?" I shouted at the TV.

Our legal analyst here at KARE TV has indicated that at today's proceeding, the defendants will be fingerprinted, have their mugshot taken, appear in court, hear the charges and enter a plea of guilty or not guilty. The court will then determine if the defendants are to be held or released on their own recognizance or are required to post bail.

It has been a stunning and unexpected fall from grace for Madelyn Dalton, who was the leading candidate in the upcoming race for governor with the election just a month away. Her get tough on crime campaign platform may result in a tragic irony if she's convicted.

The reporter held her hand up and touched her earpiece. *We've just received word that the arraignment has concluded. It's reported that defendants pleaded not guilty. Madelyn Dalton has been released after posting a bond against bail set at a million dollars. Her associate, Stolz, is being held without bail, on unspecified outstanding warrants.*

"Yes! Tommy's locked up," I shouted at the TV and pumped my fist.

Dalton and her attorney pushed their way through the crowd of reporters. Dalton held a sheet of paper over her face, a far different person than the candidate who had relished the press during her campaign.

Reporters began shouting questions.

Will you be dropping out of the governor's race?

Who is Jacob Zenk?

Was Zenk alive when he was crushed in your car?

Without saying a word, Dalton and her attorney kept moving and disappeared into a waiting sedan.

I called Jessica to share the good news. "Jess, Tommy, the guy who threatened you and Claire, is in jail. All good now."

"I heard, but I will not forget the terror you put us through." She hung up.

There was a knock on the door. It pushed open before I could answer it.

CHAPTER 48

TWISTED

Winona handed me a tray of coffee with three cups, released the backpack from her shoulders and set it on the kitchen table. "The coffee's the strong stuff, so buckle up. Got one for Ray, too, if he's around."

"Ray," I shouted down the basement steps, "Winona's here. She brings coffee."

He bounded up the stairs and accepted the cup from Winona's outreached hand. "Thanks, been going to get in touch. Is anybody still doing the indigenous nipple piercing ritual? You know, where the men push a bone through their breasts and hang by leather straps? Those scars are amazing."

"Ray, put a lid on it!" I said.

Winona grabbed Ray by the nipple and gave it a titty twist.

"Ow-ow-ow!" Ray yipped and bobbed, trying not to spill his coffee.

"It's a manhood ritual." Winona released the pinch. "Don't think you're ready."

I laughed so hard I had coffee in my nose. Ray, for once, was speechless and slinked off into the kitchen.

"The guy from Ganley's who dropped off your car keys also handed me this backpack." Winona pointed. "Said it was for you. I stashed it inside the mortuary, but we got a little distracted with the impound escapade. Here it is."

"It was O'Malley's. I never actually expected it to show up. Have you looked through it?"

"Nope, addressed to you." Winona moved to the table. "But I'm dying to have a peek."

Ray rubbed his breast and pulled up a chair.

I unbuckled the backpack straps and opened the flap. My hands were shaking. There was a stack of labeled envelopes inside and I pulled one out. "Photos," I said, and held my breath. We were finally going to get a glimpse into Riva's past.

We leaned in as I carefully placed each photo on the table. They seemed to be in chronological order: a bright-eyed toddler with a cherubic face smeared with ice cream, a young girl with pigtails holding up a drawing of a dog, a teen in a prom dress next to her date, a young pianist on stage accepting a bouquet, a cap and gown graduate with the carefree innocence of a promising future, and an evening silhouette of a beautiful woman looking out to sea. None of us spoke as we tried to absorb the missing pieces of Riva's life.

"She was beautiful," Winona said.

"And familiar," Ray added.

I shrugged and spilled the backpack contents on the table.

"Here's an expired Louisiana driver's license. Maureeva O'Malley, born in 1999. That makes her twenty-one when she died." Winona passed the license around the table.

"Here's a copy of a life insurance policy issued by BrightHouse Financial and Life. Maureeva O'Malley is listed as the sole beneficiary. Now, it's Ross Dalton." I shook my head.

"I've got a copy of a restraining order on some guy in Baton Rouge," Ray said, without looking up. "Hope they hang him by his nipples."

We found rent receipts from an apartment in Spokane, a poster of the band and its tour schedule, along with a Minnesota map with St. Paul circled.

Winona held up a little bell with a starry constellation inscribed on it.

"Let me see those personal photos again," Ray said.

I handed him the envelope, and he spread them out on the table.

"That one," he pointed, "the graduate." He stood up and retreated to his bedroom and came back holding a laptop computer. "When did you say this Riva arrived in Minnesota?" Ray fingered the keyboard.

"I think her boyfriend Zenk said just over two years ago. What are you after?"

"Security images."

Winona and I looked at each other, then turned our full attention to Ray as he toggled through month after month of archived security camera images that captured activity around our house.

"Bingo." Ray zoomed in on an image and turned the screen toward us to see.

A woman who looked just like Riva O'Malley approached the house and stood briefly at the front door, then left. The security images did not capture audio, so we're left not knowing whether she spoke to anyone inside.

Ray leaned into the computer and pointed at the date stamp. "Twenty-six months ago."

"Mom and that Jack ass were still living here," I said.

"Mom didn't pay any attention to the security camera," Ray said, "so I would periodically run through the captured footage to make sure nothing strange was going on."

"Could there be other images?" I asked.

"Don't recall any." He tapped the screen. "I remembered this one because it was so strange. I didn't know what to think. Wrong address, peddler, maybe a package pirate, but it's worth another look."

Winona left, and I grabbed a beer and set it in front of Ray, as he plowed through past security camera images.

Mom never mentioned anything about Riva, so that would suggest the connection must be with Jack. As a river barge tow hand, he made plenty of trips through Baton Rouge. Could be something there. I called my mother and got her voicemail.

CHAPTER 49

ELVIS

As I sat at Truss' desk in the parlor, I struggled to set aside the bizarre circumstances that would warrant a visit from Riva O'Malley to my mother's doorstep. I had a eulogy to prepare for, but I couldn't focus. I needed a distraction.

I noodled on some comedic material as though I was preparing for a stand-up gig. My comedic brain was hard-wired to be on the lookout for unusual personal quirks that I could use in my routines. Tonette, the roly-poly Angels of Mercy supervisor, unexpectedly popped into my head.

I found it odd, when Truss and I paid her a visit, that she touched her head when Truss asked about O'Malley's missing wig. To chase down my curiosity, I pulled O'Malley's file from the records room and called Angels of Mercy. It was Tonette's day off, but the person who took the call obliged me with her home address. I now had enough information to check the public records.

Tonette had a petty crime arrest record that included shoplifting, resisting arrest, and public intoxication. Not exactly someone you would entrust with your grandmother.

Truss entered the parlor and noticed I had a client file. "What do you have?"

Uncertain as to whether I had crossed a privacy line, I played to what Truss had called his 'sacred bond' between the coroner and homicide victim. I related my fear of Dalton getting away with the murder of O'Malley and my suspicions of Tonette.

"We'll, I'm afraid that if Ross Dalton is behind O'Malley's death, and he has a claim to her insurance as that fella Zenk told you, our leverage is gone."

"Gone how?"

"I had to release O'Malley's death certificate. I can't exhume a body without one, and that's what Riva's mother's friend, Audrey Ardoin, has requested. She has no legal standing, but if pressed, no one would deny the uniting of family members in death. The plan is to have Riva cremated and reunited with her mother at a cemetery in Baton Rouge. Ardoin will cover all costs associated with the process. Without a formal criminal probe, I have no standing in contesting the cause of death."

"So, Dalton gets a free ride."

"Perhaps. What's this about Tonette?"

I shared my observation of Tonette's response to O'Malley's missing items with Truss.

"That's been nagging at me, too," Truss said.

"Let's go nag Tonette about it."

"So back to Angels of Mercy?"

"Suggest a house call, a surprise visit, as it's her day off." I snatched up the keys to the Miller-Meteor. "I'll drive."

"Bring the O'Malley file along."

The late summer day felt gray and heavy. With bubbling raindrops on the windshield, I drove through St. Paul's West Side, District del Sol barrio, and along Cesar Chavez Avenue with colorful Latino storefronts.

The address I had for Tonette revealed a rundown, two story home on a narrow lot with a boarded-up window, faded wood siding and a sagging front porch. Truss gave the door a solid rap. From within the house came the sharp bark of a dog followed by a "Shut up!"

Tonette opened the door just far enough to get a peek at us. Through the narrow opening, I could see there was something different about her—same stout figure but a new hairdo.

"What do you want?" She snarled, but she allowed the door to open wider.

"For starters, where did you get the wig?" I asked.

Tonette instinctively touched her head, then caught herself. "None of your goddam business."

"We'd like to have a chat about Riva O'Malley," Truss said.

Tonette suddenly threw her weight against the door to block our entry. Truss held the door open. His arms swelled with blue veins, the same arm strength that kept me from going over the bridge rail.

"If this is what you're after, here," Tonette grabbed a fist full of hair from atop her head and threw it at us. "Not my color anyway." Tonette's dog squeezed past her, ran out onto the porch, pounced on the wig and shook it like fresh prey.

"Elvis, get back in here," she called.

I wanted to pop off with, 'Ladies and gentlemen, Elvis has left the building,' but I restrained myself.

"Leave." Her pouched eyes narrowed. "Or I'll call the police."

"I was just about to suggest that," Truss said.

I pulled out my phone.

"Okay, okay, put the phone away." Tonette moved away from the door, clearing a path for us to enter. The old house felt overly warm with the smell of stale perfume and spicy foods. I left the front door partially open as I wasn't sure what we were getting into. From the entry, a stairway ran to the upper level and was flanked by a kitchen and living area. Uninvited, I slipped past Tonette into the living room.

On the coffee table sat a box with a stash of jewelry. A sofa held a heap of clothing in an assortment of styles and sizes.

"What the hell do you think you're doing?" she yelled from behind me.

Truss split off into the kitchen. Tonette chased after him and I followed. The fluorescent tube above the stove blinked and buzzed like there were wasps trapped inside. A cluster of prescription drug bottles sat on the counter.

Truss picked up a bottle and read the label, "Stanley Hoyt, Angels of Mercy. Take two every four hours as needed for pain."

Tonette snatched the bottle out of Truss' hand. "What's it to you?"

Truss pushed the bottles of drugs aside and extracted a photo from the O'Malley file we had brought with us. The photo was from the BCA and documented the attack O'Malley had sustained on Zenk's farm. Truss set the black and white glossy on the counter. "This is the person you know as Riva O'Malley before she arrived at Angels of Mercy."

Tonette stood her ground and didn't look away. At a glance, the terrible nature of Riva's assault was clear. A deep head laceration had soaked and matted her hair into a bloody web. Her fixed eyes seemed to stare at nothing. Her contorted mouth hung open. The stark photo seemed invasive and degrading. As I looked on with Truss and Tonette, my thoughts on capital punishment began to shift.

"So what does this have to do with me?" Tonette said, but a little less anger.

"We need your help, Tonette," Truss said. "O'Malley needs your help. We both know nothing gets by you at Angels of Mercy, and this stuff…" Truss waved his hand at the table full of ill-gotten drugs, "doesn't interest me." Truss stabbed his finger at the photo. "The murder of this woman does."

"You people . . ." Tonette shook her head, turned and walked into a compact room off the kitchen. I figured she was either getting some evidence or a beer. She came back holding a shotgun.

"Get out!" She stood rigid, with knees locked and shoulders pulled to her ears. "You're trespassing, and you ain't got a warrant." She jerked the blue-black barrel back and forth.

"Easy, easy, we're leaving," I said and took a step backwards.

Truss held his ground.

Tonette opened her mouth to say something when the click of toenails on the Linoleum kitchen floor caught our attention. Tonette's dog still had the wig in its mouth and dropped it at her feet. "Git. Bad dog, Elvis."

Truss grabbed the barrel of the gun. Tonette reflexively jerked back during the tug of war and bumped into the refrigerator. The shotgun's discharge froze me in place and blew a hole in the ceiling. Sheetrock debris and dust rained down.

Truss secured the shotgun and, with repeated pumps, ejected the remaining shells.

"Call the police," Truss said to me, "and get hold of Agent Kirchner."

Agent Kirchner read Tonette her rights and leveraged her felonious theft of patient drugs and belongings to put the squeeze on her for immediate cooperation. She volunteered Dalton had paid her to monitor O'Malley's visitors. When Zenk showed up to visit O'Malley, she called Dalton.

"I didn't know Dalton would kill her," she said. Somehow, I think she thought that made it all right.

CHAPTER 50

DUET

I called Jessica. Her brother Pete picked up.

"Hey, Vinney."

"Why are you answering Jessica's phone?"

"She's out in the yard, left her phone in the kitchen and I saw it was you."

"Get her on the phone."

"Vin buddy, can you spot me two hundred bucks? I need new brakes."

"Brakes? Your driver's license is suspended. Are you driving?"

"Come on, Vin…."

Jessica cut in. "What do you want?"

"Your brother's a drug addict and a scammer. He shouldn't be around Claire."

"Is that why you called, to stick your face into my business?"

"I'd like to stop over for a visit with Claire."

"No."

"Why?"

"Because of your craziness, we're suffering from PTSD. My hair is coming out in clumps, and Claire's afraid to go to school."

"You're safe now. They've arrested Madelyn Dalton and the guy who harassed you. Ross Dalton is being held as a suspect for murder. Please let me . . ."

"Stay away!"

"You can't withhold my daughter."

"We'll see what the courts have to say about that." She hung up.

"Wrong, wrong, wrong!" I threw my phone against the wall. The screen cracked. I thought for sure I had killed the cheap refurb, but a wimpy ring tone emerged.

I clicked in the call. "Vince, Pam here. The folks around here been talkin. They always do. Anyway, lot of 'em feel as though they abandoned Zenk and Riva. Well, no one feels good about that. So, we all been thinking about a celebration of some sort for them in Nisswa. We got a hall rented and all. Being yer a eulogist, figured ya could take the lead."

★ ★ ★

Two days later, with Winona at the wheel, we headed out toward Nisswa. The drive skirted lakes bordered by a kaleidoscope of fall colors. I thought about fishing. The last time I went was just before my father disappeared. I directed Winona to exit the highway just short of Nisswa.

"This isn't the way to the Nisswa Legion Hall," she said.

"Just a quick stop outside of Baxter."

I retraced my previous trip to Zenk's farm. As we approached the farmstead, everything looked the same: the mailbox with bullet holes, the posted 'Hazardous' notice, and the empty rocker on the front porch.

"What is this place, Chernobyl?" Winona asked.

"Maybe. Wait here, I'll be right back." Inside the abandoned home, on the fireplace mantle, I spotted what I came for, snatched it and retreated to the car.

A half mile past Nisswa's town center, we located the American Legion, Billy Brown Post 627. The tires crunched on the gravel as we pulled into the parking lot filled with pickup trucks and SUVs. Under a tall flagpole, flying both stars and stripes and a black POW-MIA flag, stood a decommissioned tank. In the windows of the one-story building, a sign touted 'Meat Raffle and Bar Bingo.' Just inside the door, I spotted Truss.

The decorations in the banquet room seemed to have been left over from a wedding. On the small stage, a memorial table held matching urns of Riva and Zenk. Neither urn contained ashes—just dirt from Zenk's farm. Riva's body was still in the pauper's grave awaiting exhumation. Zenk's remains were entombed in Madelyn Dalton's crushed Bentley. I placed the small trophy I had picked up at Zenk's house, next to the urns.

Winona and I stood surrounded by locals eager to contribute anecdotal accounts about Riva and Zenk. Pam took charge of the event and passed around Swedish meat balls with toothpicks as a prelude to the generous buffet that was to follow my tribute. With a nod from me, she clanged a sturdy pie tin and asked everyone to take a seat.

I stepped onto the stage, tapped the mic and turned my attention to the gathering. "It's an honor to address the friends and neighbors of Jacob Zenk and Riva O'Malley." I cast a sweeping hand toward an easel mounted painting of Riva, Zenk, and their Labrador dog, allowing the guest to take in. Pam had rescued it from Riva's barn studio and cleaned it up as best she could.

"Zenk asked me to tell Riva's story, and I guess, as intertwined as they were, his too. For some, the story of Riva and Zenk might revolve around Riva's art on your wall, or a piece of machinery you might not otherwise have, thanks to Zenk. Community was at the core of who they were. Riva enlightened our lives with her creativity, and Zenk helped to support himself and friends in the medicinal drug trade. But even with our stories and observations of each other, we always wonder if we really knew someone."

The attendees sat respectfully, but I hadn't connected yet. Time to lighten up. "Turns out Zenk and Riva were closet rock stars."

Some snorts and a little chatter.

"Zenk said it started innocently enough. Riva would hum a tune and Zenk would absent-mindedly hum along. The humming turned into a song, here and there. On a dare, they went to a karaoke bar a few towns over, just to check it out. You know what they say about karaoke—it's an event that mixes people who shouldn't drink with people who shouldn't sing."

Heads nodded, some broad smiles of 'oh yeah, been-there-done-that.'

"Despite their better judgment, after a few drinks they decided to give it a go. They laughed all the way home. But something had clicked. Their harmony, chemistry and stage presence all seemed to work. They began to frequent karaoke bars and even entered a few contests, at a safe distance from the Baxter farmstead, where they could totally embarrass themselves and not be recognized. Duets became their thing, mostly country songs, and they took on the personas of original artists, such as Kenny Rogers and Dolly Parton singing "Island in the Stream". Zenk grew a beard, and Riva did a little front-loading."

Outright laughs, smiles, talking among the guests, trying to picture it.

"Riva and Zenk even won a county-wide contest and walked away with the top prize." I picked up the trophy off the urn table, held it up, and read the nameplate. 'Best Duet'. The trophy also had the name of the bar that sponsored the contest. I had called the bar owner on the drive over. He vividly remembered Zenk and Riva and was more than happy to describe their performance details.

"For their winning number, Zenk shaved, wore Johnny Cash black, and Riva sported a June Carter flip style wig and a red, fluffy sixties dress. They rocked the house when they sang "Jackson", adding a little personal 'Baxter' touch." I sang a few bars of the parody.

We got married in a fever, hotter than a pepper sprout
We've been talking 'bout Baxter, ever since the fire went out

Pam picked up on the burlesque chorus.

Yeah, I'm goin' to Baxter, lookout Baxter town

Her enthusiasm prompted the guests to join in. People were out in front of the stage, rocking side to side, clapping, twirling, singing.

I'm goin' to Baxter, let loose of my coat
I'm going to Baxter, that's all she wrote

With the celebration now on autopilot, I left the stage to get some fresh air. I checked my phone and saw a text message from Ray. "Found another image of Riva on the security camera."

CHAPTER 51

KARMA

The security image sequence showed Riva talking to Jack on the front steps of my mother's home. Jack's arms flailed, and Riva backpedaled into an abrupt retreat from the property.

"Has mom gotten back to you?" Ray asked.

"I've called four times, but Jack never lets her pick up the phone, and I'm sure he screens the voice messages."

"I don't know how she puts up with that control freak." Ray poked a finger at the security image of Jack on his computer.

"Time to call their bluff."

"Like what?"

"You know how mom's always inviting us to Florida, knowing we won't go anywhere near Jack? I'm going to pay them a surprise visit, drop in like a meteorite and find out what's going on. Mom knows something. There's no way that Riva's visit could have gotten past her. I'm sick of the secrets and cover-ups."

"I hear ya, brother." Ray snapped away at his computer keyboard. "Sun Country Airlines has forty-nine-dollar flights to Orlando."

"What's the next flight out? I on it."

As long as I'd known Jack, I'd hated him. It's not that I denied my mother a boyfriend, but he was a smug son of a bitch. He knew dad from working as a barge crew hand and moved in on my mother not long after the dust settled on dad's empty grave. Jack never showed any interest in Ray or me. His departure to Florida was a relief. I did, however, miss my mother and felt a mix of perverse guilt and delight in springing a surprise visit on her.

I picked up a rental car at the Orlando airport and asked the counter agent to get me started in the direction of Harmony Lake Village.

"Relatives staying out there?" His voice held a familiarity for the area.

"My mom and a friend."

"Lot of them fifty-five and older communities out that way." He unfolded a map and turned it toward me while he read it upside down. "Suggest you pay attention to the signage along the way. All those mobile home parks kind of look the same, easy to get confused. For instance, this here community," he dropped a tobacco stained finger on the map, "Magnolia Creek Park, right near to where you're headed, is a habitat for sex offenders. Some enterprising realtor figured out that most of these trailer parks prohibit felons and sex offenders, so he opened a park just for 'em. Charges the renters double what he'd get otherwise from civil folks and guess what? There's a waiting list to get in."

Harmony Lake Village near Westminster City was a landlocked giant patch of asphalt crammed with 500 trailers. I remember mom sharing with me the property's lifestyle brochure featuring a montage of sun-splashed photos of the pickle ball courts, swimming pools, fishing and boating activities, and a community clubhouse. She was beyond excited.

I drove through an open gate, past an unattended guard shack, and stopped at a large sign with the Harmony Lake Village master plan that included lot numbers. A banner at the bottom of the sign proclaimed, 'No Children, No Pets, No State Taxes'.

I proceeded into the community's labyrinth of roads, past row after row of single wide mobile homes with faded corrugated siding. The residents' landscaping of choice seemed to favor a resurgence of American kitsch. Plastic flamingos, fake rocks and mirrored spheres mounted on vases punctuated the vegetatively barren yards. The only recreational element in evidence was a dried-up lake bed, lawn chairs circling the perimeter.

I found my mother's place, stepped out of the car and took a deep breath. I wasn't looking for a confrontation, I just wanted to get some truthful information. I looked around. Not a person in sight. The weight of the late afternoon heat and humidity held the equivalency of a blizzard; no one wanted to be outside. The only sound was the humming of air conditioners that added to an overall eerie vibe.

I immediately recognized mom's handiwork. In the front yard, she had built a rock grotto around a statue of Saint Anthony, the patron saint of all things lost. After dad went missing, mom prayed to the saint for a divine intervention that would bring her husband home. Next to the trailer, under a makeshift carport, sat Jack's ride—a pickup truck on steroids with oversized knobby tires and a rack of headlights mounted on the roof.

Jack answered the door. "For Christ's sake, ain't you heard of calling? You trying to give your mother a heart attack?"

"Who's at the door?" My mom shouted over the TV.

"Your uninvited kin." Jack stepped out of the way. Mom rushed me with a hug and looked past me.

"Where's Ray?"

"At home, sends his love."

"I do so worry about him. Is he taking his meds?"

"He's fine."

"Is everything okay?"

"Fine, mom."

"Well, you scared the dickens out of me showing up like this."

"Sorry, but I left you voice messages. You never returned my calls."

"Let me get you something to eat."

"I'm good."

"Nonsense." She started pulling food out of the refrigerator.

Jack slumped into his recliner and turned his attention to the TV. I removed a stack of magazines off the couch and sat down. Mom had never been much of a housekeeper, but I found the place to be reasonably neat and almost cheery.

"Did you see the new pickup truck?" Mom said over clanking pans. "Jack, tell him about your new hobby, hunting alligators."

"You just did." Jack said.

"He's caught some, too. Taste just like rattlesnake, only a little gamier."

"You just happen to be in the neighborhood or you got something specific on your mind?" Jack asked.

"Came to find out what your connection is with Riva O'Malley."

The kitchen clatter fell to silence. Mom froze.

"Mom, you know something. No more secrets, please."

"Let's take this outside, sonny. Your mother doesn't do well when she gets stressed."

"The mosquitos are terrible this time of day." Mom spoke with her back to me. "Put on some mosquito lotion."

"I don't need any goddamn lotion." Jack got out of his chair, grabbed a beer out of the fridge and walked outside. I followed. He pulled out a folding chair from under the steps and positioned it in a patch of shade next to the trailer. I stood and leaned against the siding.

"For Christ's sake, why can't you leave well enough alone? I suppose that pot smoking knucklehead brother is in on this, too?"

For once I felt like defending Ray, but I stayed on course, intent on getting some answers.

"So," I said, "leave what alone?"

"Your mother's retirement for one, and you might want to show some gratitude for the education you were provided, as wasted as it was on you."

"Dad's pension paid for that."

"You don't know shit. After your old man vanished, the Coast Guard conducted an extensive search for him and discovered an inflatable life raft was missing from the boat."

I didn't know how any of this related to O'Malley, but any information about my father piqued my interest.

"Did they find the raft?"

"No, probably just blew off the tow somewhere along the way. But it led to a lot of speculation from investigating parties."

"So, there's a possibility dad was on that raft?"

"Don't even go there. His death paved the way for the barge company to enter into something like a workman's comp settlement for your mother's support and her kids until they were twenty-one, payable in the form of a lifetime annuity."

"What does this have to do with O'Malley?"

He slapped at his forearm. "Goddam no see ums." He lit a cigarette. "Gotta get a little fog protection going." He blew smoke out in short little puffs.

"O'Malley? You mean the home wrecker and mother of the bastard child? Yeah, she called, wanted money, but she was late to the party. Your mother wanted to help her out. If we had known something about her kid at the time of settlement—well, who knows?"

"Wait, who we talking about here? Sarah O'Malley, Riva's mother?" I felt on overload, not able to keep up.

"Sarah, the mother. Told her to move on. This well was dry. She knew what she was getting into with a married man. Besides, she never produced any paternal documents."

"Slow down. Bastard child? Paternal documents?"

"Jesus, for a college kid you're pretty slow on the uptake. Your old man fathered a child on the side. Surprise, ha? Well, your old man was full of 'em."

I felt gut punched.

"So, Sarah O'Malley just went away?" I could barely get the words out.

"She tried to play mind games with me, some Hare Krishna nonsense. She babbled something about karma, dharma, namaste, lovey-lovey whatever, told her to take her yoga back to India, cause it ain't selling here. Like I said, there wasn't enough to go around. You boys should be damn thankful we had your best interests in mind."

I felt my heart contract, my chest tighten.

"Did I mention your old man had a gambling problem? So he left your mother with that."

"I need to hear this from my mother." I got up and made a move for the trailer door.

"Sit down," Jack commanded. "You come all this way just to make your mother miserable? If you've got a point to make, make it with me."

"The point, the effing point, is that everything in this family is a goddam secret, and when things do finally come to the light of day, it's too late." I pounded a fist against the trailer siding. "Both Sarah

O'Malley and her daughter Riva, the bastard child, my sister, are dead."

Jack let my outburst settle for a couple of minutes. When he spoke again, I heard a softer voice than I thought possible from him. "Sorry about that, she seemed like a nice kid."

"So you talked to Riva?"

"She showed up at the house one day, a couple of years back, wanting to know about your old man, relatives, whatever. Figured it would come to no good, so I run her off." Jack stood up and collected his beer bottle. "I'm getting bit to shit out here, going inside."

I turned in circles, not knowing where to go or what to do from here. I walked out to the street and stood next to my car. I looked back at the trailer and saw mom fold back a curtain. She could read me and knew I needed her now. I needed her to lift the veil of family secrets.

The curtain dropped. I waited, but she didn't come out. The curtain opened again. Now mom and Jack were in the window, checking to see if I had moved on. I walked back into the yard, picked up the Saint Anthony statue and held it up for them to see. "Here's to all things lost," I shouted and then smashed it over the hood of Jack's pickup truck.

Upon landing back in the Twin Cities, I called Winona to share the mind-bending news that Riva O'Malley was my half-sister. She registered her surprise with a gasp and offered her heart-felt support for my loss. Then quickly added that I was needed at the mortuary—urgent.

CHAPTER 52

MISSISSIPPI

I found Winona sitting in the parlor, holding hands with my ex Jessica. Jessica's shoulders heaved with sobs. Winona handed her a tissue.

"Pete's dead," Jessica said, "I had nowhere else to turn."

"You did the right thing." I leaned in and gave her a hug. Jessica's and Pete's only other relative was their mother, who was afflicted with advanced Alzheimer's.

"We've been discussing arrangements," Winona said, "Jessica has requested that her brother be cremated and celebrated in a private ceremony."

"Actually, a picnic," Jessica said. "Pete loved picnics when we were kids, and I think it would be easier on Claire. Vince?" She reached up and took my hand. "Could you say some kind words on Pete's behalf? You know, he's had a hard go of it."

I considered my ex's request to pay tribute to Pete as something between tacit approval of my work as a eulogist and the only option on behalf of a guy who burned through his friends while feeding an addiction.

To get through this, I had to put aside my anger toward Jessica. She had deliberately thrown up roadblocks to keep me from visiting Claire. Sure, I still owed her child support payments, but I had taken quite a chunk out of that debt thanks to my eulogy work. She accepted the money, but considered anything to do with a mortuary to be ghoulish and didn't want Claire anywhere near it. To top off my frustration, I knew she and Claire would have run off to Wisconsin if Jessica's boyfriend hadn't bailed on her.

But I needed to put all of that aside and own up to the mess I'd created. Jessica, at the heart of it, was a kind woman. Now, I truly just wanted to help her any way I could.

Jessica, Claire, Winona, Truss and I set out for the picnic. No other guests were in attendance.

Harriet Island Regional Park was situated on the banks of the Mississippi River across from downtown St. Paul, a short drive from Truss Mortuary. The park, nestled between steep limestone bluffs and the river, held acres of green space punctuated by giant cottonwoods, and was the perfect urban oasis. The day held us in a seamless blue sky with a softly blowing wind. The park's historic pavilion, a bandstand, playground and a paddleboat on the river added to its character.

We found a shaded picnic table near the water's edge. Claire, with heaps of attention being directed at her, was full of questions. "Do you live in a teepee?" she asked Winona. "Are you a hundred?" she asked Truss. Her questions were all answered with the gentleness of people with genuine loving kindness for children.

I had been thinking hard about what I might say on Pete's behalf. He did have a rough go of it, and I felt guilty about always judging him. Jessica was his only lifeline to sanity and hope until two days ago, when he wandered onto Interstate 94 after sunset and was struck by a gasoline tanker truck.

I considered offering something humorous on Pete's account, but couldn't come up with anything other than, 'the last thing on Pete's mind was the grill of a Mack truck.' Probably true, but even I could see it was inappropriate. I also considered reading the itemized unpaid bar tab the O'Leary's Liquor Lounge's owner dropped off at the mortuary, hoping to be added to the 'memorials preferred to' list.

It was Claire's first encounter with death, and I let her presence set the tone for the ceremony. We simply shared some photos Jessica had brought of Uncle Pete, acknowledged the sadness we felt and the struggles he endured, and remembered how kind he could be.

The tinkling music from an ice cream vendor working the park lifted our heads and mood. It's as though the childhood melody was meant for Pete in celebration of past innocence.

"Ice cream! Can I have some?" Claire said.

"Of course, honey," Jessica said. I watched as they scampered off in the wake of the Pavlovian jingle.

Truss, Winona and I sat at the picnic table and settled into a relaxed conversation. For the first time, I noticed a ring on Truss' hand. "Is that a wedding ring?"

Truss seemed to give the question some space before he answered. "Good observation. I hadn't worn this ring in years, but today's the fiftieth anniversary of my marriage."

"What was her name?" Winona asked.

"Loretta. We lived above the mortuary. She brought a compassionate presence to the business, much like you do, my dear." He nodded at Winona with an appreciative smile. "I've always been the grim old man. Suppose that's what comes of four generations of undertaking." Truss' eyes moistened. "We had a daughter, Emily."

I looked at Winona. Did she know this? From the way she gripped my hand, I guessed not.

"You know, I have not spoken Emily's name out loud in many

years." Truss shifted his gaze to the river and its muddy brown current. "She drowned when she was nine. Beautiful spring day, sudden snowmelt, kids itching to get outside. Bunch of them went down to this very river to watch the ice flow. She fell in, and the swift, cold current took her away. Never recovered her body. A year later, my wife succumbed to cancer, although I believe her death was more from a broken heart."

Our collective heads bent in toward Truss, and instinctively we joined hands in a circle of support.

"So here we are," Winona said. "Children of deceased parents and parents of a deceased child."

"Yes, death binds us all in mysterious and inexplicable ways," Truss said.

"I imagine your daughter has played a part in the services you provide to the unclaimed and destitute," I said, thinking of my dead sister, Riva O'Malley.

Truss looked at me with a sense of appreciation. "I would hope, downstream, someone has found Emily and laid her to rest with dignity."

"How do you carry on with that kind of loss?" My voice held the weight of sorrow.

"The sun rises and sets as it always does." Truss looked at us. "Everyone's experience of time is different. The loss of a loved one can be an eternity or a season, depending on whether you have someone to share it with."

Claire appeared at Winona's side and pulled on her sleeve. "Let's go to the playground. Mom's on the swing. We want you to swing with us."

"I'm one swingin' gal. Let's do it," Winona said.

This left Truss and me alone.

"You've been on quite a ride since we first met," Truss said.

"I have no idea where any of this came from: you, Winona, the eulogy work, the Daltons. And Riva—I mean, hitching a ride in a hearse with my lost sister?"

"'Man attracts what he thinks about,' so said Ralph Waldo Emerson."

"No doubt, but I had a lot on my mind—my lost father, a daughter to support, a failing career."

"No single snowflake in an avalanche feels responsible."

"You pick that one off from the poet Stanislaw Lec?"

"No, saw it on a t-shirt."

Claire, leading Jessica and Winona back to the picnic table, arrived with a chocolate ice cream mustache. We broke up in laughter.

As we walked out of the park, Jessica fell in beside me. "Thank you," she said. "I've been such a bitch about your funeral work. It seemed so foreign and dark to me. Scary actually, something I wanted to keep Claire away from. But I can see now why people need it. And Winona's been so wonderful."

"I know. She is one of the good ones."

"She's also in love with you. Don't screw this one up."

CHAPTER 53
STEREOTYPES

After Pete's tribute picnic, I arrived home, bone tired. It felt like I hadn't slept in a week and immediately crashed. I awoke disoriented and spotted Ray at the kitchen table working on his computer. I had informed him of the fiasco in Florida by phone, but hadn't connected with him in person since my return.

"Where did those come from?" I pointed at a plate of cookies.

"Your ex dropped them off. Russian Tea Cakes, damn good."

Jessica knew they were one of my favorites—butter, flour, chopped roasted pecans, and rolled in powdered sugar. "Did she say why?"

"Left a 'thank you' card for helping with her brother's funeral." He handed me the card. His powder sugar prints we're all over it.

That Ray had read the card pissed me off, but I wasn't in the mood to joust with him. Along with Jessica's acknowledgement, Claire had drawn a stick figure tagged with *Love You Daddy*.

I spotted a stack of mail on the table addressed to me and picked through it. A fat envelope with a return address of Ganley's Bakery caught my attention.

I opened the envelope and found a note inside from Pam. *Vince, wanted to thank you for the sendoff you gave Zenk and Riva. They would have loved it. On a sad note, I stopped by Zenk's farm the other day, looking for any personal effects before the place goes up for auction.*

Both the mortgage bank and tax collectors have liens on the place. Found some things that look like they belonged to Riva. Didn't know where else to send them. Don't be a stranger, always got pie and coffee waiting, don't ya know. Pam.

I shook out the contents of the envelope on the table and froze.

"Son of a bitch!" Ray spread the post cards out on the table. We didn't need to compare them to our collection. They were identical except that they were addressed to Riva O'Malley.

"Look at this." I picked up a heart-shaped, hinged photo locket. I gently pried it open. My head shook in a fight with my vision as I tried to focus on the photo. My hand trembled as I passed it to Ray.

"You share the same eyes," I said, of my father's image. "The woman must be Riva's mother, Sarah O'Malley."

"Such a frigging disappointment." Ray looked at the river serpent on his forearm. "To think I tatted up for him."

"All dads disappoint their children, at least in small ways. It conditions them to the instability of life."

"Small disappointments I get," Ray said. "But dropping twenty years of deception on your family is beyond extreme. It's criminal."

"Yeah, we should have our day in court. At the pre-sentence hearing, we could blast him with our victim impact statement. Riva's too."

"Hoorah!" Ray shot his hand in the air, and we connected with a high five.

"But that ship has sunk." I moved in to temper Ray's vengeance. "We'll never see him atone for his selfishness."

"Hey, why don't you do a podcast on the old man? Test out some of your deep state mystery theories on his whereabouts, smoke him out."

"Who's going to listen? My eulogy podcast audience amounts to a few relatives and friends of the deceased."

"We'll bring Sage in on it. Seems like she was able to get the word out on Riva and stirred up some listeners."

"So you think Jesus freaks, druids and gawkers are going to tip us off to the old man?"

"Think bigger." Ray went to the refrigerator, opened a beer and pointed the bottle at me. "All the public radio stations share programming."

"So you're doing beer for breakfast now?"

"Cookies and beer, and it's almost noon, sleeping beauty."

I looked at the kitchen clock, unaware of how long I'd slept. "So how did you go from computer hacker to a broadcast distribution expert?"

"Game designer, asshole."

"Yeah, yeah, game designer. So the question is still the same."

"Radio is all Sage talks about: APR, NPR BBC, PRI."

"I didn't think you liked stereotypes?"

"You see, right there is exactly why you're not funny." Ray stood up from the table. "Just come up with something interesting and Sage will get it out there."

"I'll think about it."

"Where's our Riva buried?"

"Oakland Cemetery, but she won't be there long. She's going back to Baton Rouge."

Ray grabbed his car keys. "I always wanted a sister." He wiped the back of his hand against his moist eyes and left.

CHAPTER 54
DADCAST

I retreated to my bedroom, accessed the podcast app, adjusted the microphone and stared at the computer screen.

When I look back on my father through my memories, he always seemed so large, amplified, significant. Now he seemed so small, so deceptive. Theories as to how and why he abandoned his life and family bounced around in my head like pin balls. He likely staged his disappearance in foul weather to make it look like an accident. Perhaps he needed to escape his gambling debts, or maybe it was that he could no longer keep his stashed girlfriend and child concealed. Most probably he was alive and insane, sending strange postcards to torment his family. I didn't need answers as much as I needed to breathe.

I launched the podcast.

"Welcome to The Very Last Laugh. I'm Vince Locker, your podcast host. This is where we pay tribute to the dead or in the case of today's program, the presumed dead. I'm dedicating this to all of you who have been abandoned by someone who went out for the proverbial pack of cigarettes and never returned, despite the missing person posters tacked to telephone poles with your phone number dangling from strips of paper. For me, it was my dad, Earl Locker, and this podcast is my electronic missing dad poster.

"When I was growing up, they posted photos of missing kids on milk cartons. I always wanted to be one of those kids, to take after my dad, a missing kid of a missing dad. Weird, I know, but I've been obsessed with my old man's disappearance all my life to the point of, not long ago, hanging off a bridge in the middle of the night. I told myself it was all right to leave. Dad did it. His life was obviously messed up, and so was mine, so why not just jump? Wipe the slate clean.

"Crazy, right? Marinated in booze, drugs, shame and loss, I was ready to take the big leap, but a primordial instinct for survival resisted. My arms tightened around the bridge rail and my legs reflectively rooted and fought for balance. Overhead lights reflected on the dark roiling river below. I fought off a dizzying sense of vertigo and forced myself to look into the abyss. And I saw my old man's face.

"'Dad, I hate you!' I shouted, and heard my voice reverberate off the bridge work. 'I cried for you. Why didn't you say goodbye? You hurt me. It's now who I am. I chase that pain. It makes me feel closer to you, but I can't goddamn take it anymore. It's taken away my marriage, my daughter, my life.'

"I heard his reply on the wind as it raked through the girders, a mocking scream. I shifted my weight and hung a leg over the edge. Just one little push and I'd be on my way to float and dissolve into the expanse of pain-free nothingness.

"A river barge navigating the river painted me with its spotlight. My big night. The stage was now lit. In my addled state, I imagined an audience below, fingers pointed to the sky. 'Look everyone, there's a jumper, how exciting.' The audience laughed, then howled. A joke was in the air and I was the punchline, a self-absorbed fool trying to call his victimhood to the attention of an indifferent universe that fundamentally didn't give a damn.

"Then a hearse arrived. I swear, I am not making that up. A literal

Miller-Meteor classic hearse, right out of Ghostbusters. And that bizarre encounter gave me a new life.

"I am just now learning to breathe after holding my breath for twenty years, ever since dad left. Somehow, feeling responsible for his disappearance had not only constricted my oxygen but also cultivated a sense of clinging and selfishness. If only I had a dad, I'd be happy.

"Well, no.

"If you know anything about Earl Locker, let me know. He may be living large in the Caribbean or as a broken man in a rent-by-week room. He could also be dead, drowned as first reported or killed over gambling debts.

"Ultimately, it doesn't matter. I've arrived at closure. When I look at my daughter, my lungs now fill to capacity. In my work as a eulogist, I've come to understand that it's my responsibility to cope with loss. Pain is inevitable, but we get to choose what it means for us.

"Dad, I miss you, and I release you. Thanks for the memories."

The next day Sage called and said she'd managed to get snippets of my podcast distributed to radio stations around the country. I checked my email. The response from people with unresolved closure issues related to missing friends and relatives was overwhelming. I felt a twinge of disappointment, however, that no one alerted me with a clue as to my father's whereabouts. Not that I had time to dwell on it. I had received a subpoena to testify in the trial of Ross Dalton, charged with the murder of Riva O'Malley.

CHAPTER 55

TRIAL

Winona said she'd meet me at the Ramsey County Courthouse. My only previous visit to the twenty-story art deco skyscraper, built during the Great Depression, was to pay an overdue parking ticket. The awe-inspiring grand entrance featured a white marble floor with black marble columns that supported a gold leaf ceiling. I found Winona looking up at the entrance's centerpiece—a forty-foot, sixty-ton, white onyx statue of a noble, stoic warrior called the Indian God of Peace.

"Impressive," I said.

"Impressive would be if this rock paid homage to the victims of American Indian genocide," Winona said and wandered off.

The dedication plaque identified the statue as a memorial to Minnesotans who died in World War I, II, Korean and Vietnam Wars. At the moment, I was too anxious about the trial to add support to Winona's history of injustice. "The courtroom is on the fourth floor," I said, catching up to her with the subpoena notice in hand.

The charges against Dalton included the murder of Maureeva O'Malley and felony theft by swindle related to his fraudulent funeral home insurance practices. I had visions of the defense attorney leaning over the rail of the witness box, subjecting me to his coffee breath and nose hairs as he shredded my account of events into confetti.

We piled into a packed elevator and after a short, jerky ride, we were swept out into a corridor that led to the courtroom. The courtroom's wood-paneled walls emitted a soft golden glow that reminded me of an old church. The gallery congregates sat in well-worn oak pews; the judge presided from the elevated altar of justice; and the jury filled the choir stall.

"Where is everybody?" Winona asked.

The courtroom was empty. I looked again at the subpoena to verify I had the correct time and location of the trial. It checked out.

"Vince." The trial prosecutor walked into the courtroom. "Thought you might show up. Tried to leave you a voice message, but your mailbox was full."

I pulled out my phone with the cracked screen and looked at the missed calls. That pestering, nut case Toby had called me dozens of times in the last twenty-four hours and had overloaded my voice mail.

"What message?"

"We've been in plea bargain discussions with Dalton's defense attorney, and we're close to a deal."

"Just like Dalton, trying to weasel his way out of trouble," Winona scoffed.

"I want him tried!" I took an aggressive step toward the prosecutor. Winona hooked her arm under mine to throttle me back.

"I understand, but we're playing a weak hand on the murder charge. Most of the witness accounts will be canceled out, including yours. The Angel of Mercy supervisor, Tonette Morelli will be cast by the defense as an unreliable witness with hearsay evidence. Madelyn Dalton will deny your account of events on Zenk's farm. The Ramsey County Medical Examiner will serve up a rebuttal to Truss' forensic assessment. Our strongest position is to nail Dalton on the fraud scheme where we have witnesses who have been preyed upon, much like O'Malley."

"This is just wrong! You can't let Dalton get away with the murder of my sister."

★   ★   ★

Truss had hired tradespeople to handle updating the mortuary's building code issues. Winona and I pitched in with the grunt work. We were covered in dust from a trip out back to the dumpster when Truss held up two glasses of iced tea and told us to take a break. It was a sun-filled afternoon. We gathered up folding chairs and planted them in a band of shade alongside the mortuary.

"Appreciate the work you do. God knows construction clean-up is not within the job description." Truss smiled wryly.

"That the same job description that says, 'embalm and carry out'?" Winona asked.

"And don't forget the perks," I chimed in. "All the church basement funeral service food you can eat."

Truss shook his head. "Just got off the phone with Agent Kirchner, who got word of Ross Dalton's plea deal."

"I don't want to hear anything but death by firing squad." Winona extend her index finger and pulled the trigger.

"From the sentence handed out, Kirchner suspects the judge and the defense may have been toweling down together."

"Toweling down? You lost me," I said.

"It's an expression of favoritism, as in the defense attorney and the judge are old buddies from law school and play in a basketball league. Toweling their sweaty necks after the game, they chat about the evidence in the defense's case that's currently before the judge. If the conversation ever comes to light, the defense can be disbarred and the judge could be thrown off the bench. But quiet conversations are hard to prove."

"This doesn't sound good."

"The plea agreement provides for the dismissal of the murder charge and a guilty plea to felony theft by swindle, to carry an eighteen-month prison sentence, plus restitution and forfeiture of assets acquired through fraudulent activities."

I felt gut-punched and could barely catch my breath.

"Total bullshit!" Winona said.

"For once I agree with your uncountable, yet descriptive noun," Truss said, "but by admitting guilt, it effectively nullifies Dalton's claim to Riva's life insurance policy. It reverts to her estate."

"Her estate?"

"I'll get to that." Truss held up a finger. "Agent Kirchner further reported that through an extensive investigation into Maureeva O'Malley's background, it's been determined that her only known related survivors are Vincent and Raymond Locker, half-brothers."

I had never considered that possibility.

"The life insurance policy benefits become part of the deceased's estate and are included in the assets available to legally determined survivors through inheritance, in a process supervised by a probate court."

I was having trouble tracking the pathway from estate to survivor to benefits, to inheritance to probate, but Winona jumped right on it.

"Oh my God, that's two million dollars!" Winona threw her arms around me.

"There will be some legal fees and taxation to work through, but it is a very nice sum indeed," Truss said.

"I-I-I I'm blown away—stunned." I grabbed Winona's hand and let the tears spill. "Claire, oh my god, I'll be able to take care of her.

Thank you, thank you," I said to the heavens, trying to picture Riva.

"Hey, you all look like someone died," a voice boomed out. "What is this, a funeral home?"

"Toby, what do you want?"

"The Nationals!"

CHAPTER 56

NATIONALS

One month later, I was in 'Hotlanta'. A marketing term employed to hype Atlanta's sexy nightlife and entertainment scene. More appropriately, as I waited to go on stage, it represented the heat and nervous sweat that wicked through my shirt. Toby had nagged me like a dog on a bone to participate in the LaughCom National Contest. Exhausted by his pestering, I relented, with the understanding that the stand-up event would be a one and done. I felt certain in my commitment to Truss Mortuary. I had also let go of the ego-deflating belief that I was a sloppy second entrant, a runner-up in Louie's fixed regional contest.

Winona, who had never been out of Minnesota, accompanied me. We now lived together above the mortuary in updated accommodations. Both Ray and I wanted to honor our sister, Maureeva O'Malley, using a portion of the inheritance. For once we agreed on something and made a sizable donation to Truss Mortuary to support the respectful interment of indigents and the needy.

From the edge of the stage, I watched the comedians who preceded me. There were some insanely witty contestants, undeniable talent that would soon be in high demand on the stand-up scene. Whatever the results, I'd come to terms with whom I'd become, a comedic eulogist intertwining life and death. I was like a coin toss—the flip side of comedy is tragedy and both share the same medal.

The master of ceremony cleared the air between acts. "I want to give you fair warning about this next contestant. He'll knock you dead. Give it up for Vince Locker from St. Paul, Minnesota, who does comic stand-up tributes at funerals."

The saliva in my mouth evaporated. My tongue stuck to the roof of my mouth, and my butt cheeks were tighter than a rusted lug nut. The nervousness never goes away. I swallowed hard and launched the set. A frenzied, deranged death riff.

"Hi everyone and thank you. Yeah, I do funny funerals. Sounds like an oxymoron, like jumbo shrimp. Just plain wrong and desperate on my part, but the concept has really caught on.

"I've got dead people lined up who want to be taken out on a laugh. I have to tickle their feet to make sure they're not faking it."

A smattering of snorts, a start.

"Most people don't think they're going to die. Neither did I until I went to the doctor, filled out a medical history form and realized I had death in the family: great-grandfather, grandfather, father, even my dog. All losers.

"We all want to win, right? Life is the ultimate reality game show. At a funeral, you glance at the deceased—you're sad, but then a little cockiness creeps in. Another player kicked off the island and you're still a contestant. On the way out, you pump your fist in the air, singing 'Another One Bites The Dust' . . ."

Laughter.

"At some point, we all try to imagine how we're going to die. It's not what we expect and never fair.

"You've been a vegan all your life and get run over by a pig.

"Murdered over one little typo when you wrote 'Wish you were HER'. Oops, HERE!

"Laughed at while choking on a chicken bone, stammering cluck-cluck-cluck."

Crack-up laughs, keep it going, reel 'em in.

"And we're curious about who will show up at our funeral, and what they'll say. Of course, mom will be to there peering into your casket. 'You look bloated, my dear. If it'll make you feel comfortable, let it out.'"

Did I just do a fart joke?

"And in the milling conversation of mourners, someone testifies to the time of your death. 'He expired last Tuesday, at 3:01 a.m.' Expired? What, did someone stamp a 'best before date' on my forehead?"

"Then there are the snarky friends who talk about you with an air of detachment, as if they're in a fish market. 'He's gone belly up, yep, just plain ran out of wiggle room.'"

The punchlines were snapping like mousetraps and getting horse-laughs. Seven minutes into the set, I heard the applause from the back of the room roll up to the stage. People were standing and cheering. The electrifying response lit me up, and I bowed in humble appreciation.

"Thank you, thank you! Life is short, laugh at yourself. Share that twisted, off the wall, harebrained material that is uniquely you. And don't suppress that nervous breakdown—we're all a punchline. And when you arrive at that place where you can no longer laugh at yourself, allow others to have the very last laugh on you."

Dead End

Acknowledgements

Don Gorrie, Former Chief Investigator, Ramsey County Medical Examiner's Office; Dr. Tom Combs, author of the Drake Cody medical thriller series; Nokomis Writing Group; Kate St. Vincent Vogel, Loft Literary Center; Dave King, Story Analytics; Meghan Pardi, super beta reader.

Patrick Strait, author of 'Funny Thing About Minnesota', who perfectly captures the dysfunctional start of the Twin City comedy scene that evolved into a launching pad for nationally acclaimed talent.

Louie Anderson who reflects on the early days with Minnesota comedic comrades Scott Hansen, "Wild Bill" Bauer, Alex Cole, and Jeff Gerbino—"we were all trying to generate laughs, keep from freezing our asses off while, unwittingly, inspiring one of the most vital and vibrant comedy scenes in the country."

Louis Lee, Acme Comedy Club owner, who has persevered to keep Midwest comedy relevant and thriving.

A special appreciation for the enduring patience of my loving wife, Linda. And a sincere apology to the comedians whose jokes I've pinched along the way.